"All you had on you was your waterlogged phone." She pointed to the bag of rice in the corner. **"It can take days to dry one out, if it'll work at all. So, you don't know your name."**

"I do not."

"You seem pretty calm about it." Her comment sounded more interested than accusatory.

"Freaking out about it won't help." Hopefully staying calm would assist in returning his brain to its normal function.

"I know last night you were adamant about not calling the police—"

"No police." The answer was automatic, as if someone else had spoken the words, but as her frown deepened, he knew he meant it. "All I've got to go on right now is what my gut is telling me."

"I get that." But Darcy didn't look convinced. "Look, I have friends who are detectives. I also have some friends who are Feds. You could trust them."

"I can't trust anyone." The statement felt both instinctive and authentic. That wasn't a particularly pleasant commentary on anyone's life.

"You can trust me."

"How do you know? You don't know anything about me yet..."

Dear Reader,

It's hard to believe this is the seventh Honor Bound romance. When Darcy Ford first popped into my head for *Reunited with the P.I.*, I had the sneaking suspicion she'd end up with her own book, and here it is! Those who follow me on social media and subscribe to my newsletter know I'm not a plotter. I literally start with the characters and a general situation. This was a book that fought me a good deal of the way, but after I reminded myself to have some fun with it, it found its way.

I think of this book as a bit of a fairy tale. When we first see Darcy, she's lamenting her lack of a romantic match, like so many of her friends have found. Well, be careful what you wish for, because the next thing she knows, a hero to die for crashes into her life. To say her world is turned upside down by this unexpected arrival is an understatement. I often call my romantic suspense books roller-coaster rides, and this one definitely fits the bill. Trust me when I say I fell as hard for Riordan Malloy as Darcy does...and I hope you do, too!

Happy reading!

Anna J.

DEADLY VEGAS
ESCAPADE

Anna J. Stewart

HARLEQUIN®
ROMANTIC SUSPENSE™

Recycling programs
for this product may
not exist in your area.

ISBN-13: 978-1-335-59376-4

Deadly Vegas Escapade

Harlequin Enterprises ULC
22 Adelaide St. West, 41st Floor
Toronto, Ontario M5H 4E3, Canada
www.Harlequin.com

Printed in U.S.A.

USA TODAY and national bestselling romance author **Anna J. Stewart** is living the dream writing for Harlequin. She gets to fall in love with each and every book she writes and thrives on falling into new adventures. These days when she's not writing, you can find her in Northern California binge rewatching her favorite television shows and attempting (in vain) to wrangle her two monster cats, Rosie and Sherlock.

Books by Anna J. Stewart

Harlequin Romantic Suspense

Honor Bound

Reunited with the P.I.
More Than a Lawman
Gone in the Night
Guarding His Midnight Witness
The PI's Deadly Charade
Deadly Vegas Escapade

The Coltons of Roaring Springs

Colton on the Run

Visit the Author Profile page at
Harlequin.com for more titles.

For the amazing members of Northern California Romance Writers.

You all continue to inspire me every day.
Thank you for being my home.

Chapter 1

Riordan Malloy had run out of options and, if the headlights barreling up behind him were any indication, time.

Heart beating in a fast yet controlled rhythm, he pressed his foot harder on the gas and torpedoed the rented SUV into the darkness. The overgrown access road ran alongside the American River. Taking the curving, narrow road had been a last-minute impulse, one that nearly ripped the bumper off the front of the vehicle as he'd plowed through the chain-link fence a mile and a half back. He gripped the steering wheel, trying to recall the mental map he'd made for himself days before in case his stolen-military-weapons investigation went sideways.

The double assault of the high beams from behind

as well as the glow of his own headlights bouncing off the thick brush and forested debris had him squinting, but he kept his eyes narrowed on the phantom road he prayed would lead someplace safe. He touched a hand to the back of his head, winced at the growing lump he found. Served him right for letting his guard down. One big whack from behind had sent him falling over like a dead tree, only with a slightly softer carpeted landing. When he'd come to...

His stomach rolled. His hand fisted on the wheel. When he'd come to, one of his best friends was dead and he'd been holding the gun.

Tires ground over rocks, gravel and crisp February leaves. Branches scraped against the side of the truck, making Riordan cringe at the thought of the repair bill he'd receive from the rental company should he survive the night. He found himself ducking as an arch of trees loomed overhead and brushed the top of the cab as he plunged farther into the darkness.

Even with the windows closed, he could hear the rush of the river off to his right, but that didn't worry him as much as the growing rumble of the car whose occupants hadn't been fooled by his sudden turn. He clenched his jaw, mind racing as he glanced down at the cell phone silently vibrating and displaying an unknown number.

"Just keep going," he muttered to himself and hunched over the steering wheel to keep his eyes on the road. If he remembered correctly, there should be a path coming up that would eventually lead him to one of the overpasses near Sacramento State University. But as he continued to keep up his speed, doubt crept in. It had taken thirty-two years, but he'd finally come to terms with ignoring his better judgment. This is what happened when he veered from that lesson. When he refrained from anticipating the absolute worst-case scenario.

When, when, when, *when* was he going to learn that everyone always disappointed him in some sobering if not life-altering way?

There! An arc of light bounced into sight, disappearing as he took another turn in the road. Where there was light, there was potential safety and additional options. All he needed to do was drive straight—

The car following him sped up and, as Riordan glanced into the rearview mirror, crashed into the back of his car. He'd braced for it, but the collision still made his teeth rattle. His training had taught him everything he needed to get through this. But it was becoming more evident by the moment that his only way to safety was to get clear of the car. He could hide himself a lot easier than he could hide the SUV.

The car behind hit him again, this crash hard enough to make Riordan struggle to keep the wheels moving. He swerved, righted the steering and kept on going just as the attacking car took swing number three and this time hit him hard enough for panic to mount. As the wheels spun in the damp mud beside the bank of the river, he realized what the other car was trying to do. This far out, no lights anywhere and with only a stretch of apartments beyond the wide expanse of the river, would be the perfect place to pitch him into the water.

Better late than never, he thought, and prepped for it

to happen. He clicked the power windows to make certain they were up and sealed. Equal pressure was key to survival once a car hit water. This wouldn't be the first time he'd gone in, but it could most definitely be the last.

He saw the car speeding up to ram him again. But he also saw the road open up and widen in front of him. The mass of trees seemed to be on his side, as if stepping out of the way to give him more room to maneuver.

He'd thought the turnoff had been his last option, but he was wrong. The only way to put some distance between himself and his pursuers was to make them believe they'd killed him.

He tugged on his seat belt, ensuring it was locked in place, and pressed himself back into his seat as the headlights grew brighter in his rearview mirror. He stayed straight, kept his foot on the gas and, as the car drew closer, prayed his final action on this earth wasn't one of complete stupidity.

Waiting until the last possible second, pulse jackhammering so loudly in his ears it drowned out the river, Riordan ripped the wheel hard to the right and, with one last look in his mirror, plowed himself straight into a tree.

The sound of the impact, the crunching metal, the shatter of glass seemed almost dim compared to the explosion of the airbag. Powder coated the air. The metallic taste of blood filled his mouth. Shifting from seventy-plus miles per hour to a dead stop was definitely one way to get his bell rung and throw off the bad guys. And man, oh, man, was it ringing. Both the seat belt and airbag had done their job, but also their share of damage.

It hurt to breathe. His chest, shoulder and neck burned as if one huge bruise had been branded onto his bones and his head... He could barely move his head without pain crisscrossing his skull. He could see bright patches of red spattered on the white airbag that currently encompassed most of the front of the SUV. He lifted a hand to his forehead, drew away sticky, damp fingers and, as he unclipped the seat belt and shoved open the door, caught the smears on the window as he pulled the key out of the ignition.

He must not have been looking straight ahead at impact, and rather than hitting the airbag face-first, he'd pressed against the window. He dropped to all fours, his ears continuing to hum as his hands froze against the frigid ground. The ringing in his head blocked out most everything except the unsteady pulse picking up speed as one distinct sound made its way through his consciousness.

A car engine. He turned his head, blinked and wiped away the blood that was trickling down the side of his face. The red lights disappeared, but before he could breathe easy, white backup lights took their place.

As quickly as he could, he shoved himself up and dived back into the car, searching almost blindly for his phone. Pushing it into his back pocket, he made his way, dizzily stumbling and tripping, into the thick grove of trees on the other side of his totaled rental. He kept moving, struggling to stay quiet even as he heard voices yelling and bellowing behind him. Two, no, three men, at least one of whom had plowed into the foliage behind him.

He stopped, straightened, attempted to get his bearings, but his brain was foggy, his thoughts a jumble. February was a deadly time for the American River. The mountain runoff from the season's snow not only meant the water was cold, it could also very well sap what little strength he had left. But staying here wasn't an option.

Not if he wanted to live through the night.

Struggling to keep his balance, he took one shaky step down the embankment, then another, pulling branches and shrubs out by their roots. In the dim light of the waxing moon, he found a large log bobbing nearby against the shore. It was, he realized, his only hope.

He stepped one foot into the frigid water, felt his legs go almost instantly numb as he reached out and dragged the log close. Taking a deep breath he pushed off and surrendered himself to the river.

"So what was wrong with this one?"

Darcy Ford ducked under the trees along the side of her apartment building and headed up the nonexistent path toward the American River. Her fingers tightened around the cell phone tucked against her ear, her best friend Kyla's frustrated question making Darcy wonder, yet again, if she was being overly picky when it came to her dates.

"I wouldn't say anything was wrong with him exactly." The winter chill pulsed through the night, scraping over her skin and made her long for the summer months when the river was her second home. As a swim instructor and water rescue and recovery specialist, she knew the dangers of the river better than most. Nothing was more deceptive than water. It might look eternally peaceful on the surface, but beneath? Oh, beneath was more complicated and treacherous than anyone could ever imagine.

The river called to her, even in the dead of night when she should be curling up in bed with one of her adventure romances. "He's just wrong for me."

"Ephram's a great guy, Darcy." Kyla sounded almost defensive, which made sense, as Kyla was the one who had fixed Darcy and Ephram up in the first place. "He's got a good job, he's lived in the same place for more than ten years. He's good-looking, loves kids, wants to settle down—"

"He collects clown costumes." Even now, Darcy wasn't sure whether to scream or laugh. "Oh." Kyla cleared her throat, and Darcy could all but see her friend flinch. "Well. That's not entirely creepy."

Darcy heard a muted conversation in the background followed by Kyla conveying Darcy's tidbit of information to Jason Sutton, Kyla's fiancé. Kyla's recently achieved happiness was a big part of why Darcy found herself on the receiving end of multiple matchmaking attempts, but she was wiping out more than a newbie surfer.

"Okay, you win," Kyla said after another moment. "Jason agrees the clown thing is a deal breaker. Although in Ephram's defense, I'm sure he's not a serial killer. He wouldn't be working with me at the DA's office if that were the case."

Darcy rolled her eyes and pushed aside a branch. Overhead, one of the two working street lamps in the area cast enough of a glow across her usual walking path to keep the shadows at bay. "I'm not saying he's a serial killer." She hurried down the little path she'd carved out over the past few months. The solitude of the spot served as her refuge most nights. With the moon beaming down, she didn't need a flashlight, and while she knew walking this part of the American River wasn't the safest of places in the Sacramento Valley, she had mace in her pocket and a black belt in Krav Maga. Nothing, especially after a trying day, brought her more peace than being by the water. "I'm just saying, looking ahead, I can't imagine living with someone who hung up a big rubber nose and oversized plastic shoes in our shared closet. I'm sure there's a perfect someone out there for him. It's just not me."

"I'm beginning to wonder if there's anyone in the entire valley who'll pass inspection," Kyla said. "Or at the very least the first date."

"I'm a challenge, I know." Darcy laughed, because she knew Kyla was teasing. "That's one of the reasons you love me."

"I suppose." Kyla sighed dramatically. "You going to be okay? Want to take Ninja for a few days to cheer you up?"

The teasing had given way to concern, which made Darcy's belly do an unfamiliar dance. As much as she loved Kyla's Chiweenie pup, she wasn't in the mood to dog-sit. "I'm fine, Ky. I appreciate you wanting me to be at least partially as happy as you are, but I think maybe it's time we accept we're trying a little too hard. If I'm meant to find someone, it'll happen, so let's take a break from the fix-ups for a while, okay?"

"Oh. Hmm. Well."

Darcy's stomach stopped dancing and knotted. "What?"

"Nothing." Despite her talents as a prosecutor, Kyla wasn't the best of liars. "It's nothing. I can tell them to put their plan of action on the back burner for a bit."

"Them who? Kyla, what have you done?" Darcy nearly stumbled into the familiar bushes lining the edge of the river, which was running lower than normal. Typical given the lack of snow in the mountains these days. Mother Nature couldn't exactly make up her mind when it came to precipitation and runoff in California. The water was a good five feet below the bank, but it was running fast. So fast she could hear the roar of the water as it moved through the area.

"You and your social life might have been the topic of conversation at dinner the other night," Kyla said. "With…well, everyone."

"Define everyone." Darcy winced. "And please don't tell me Eden was part of this tête-à-tête." Good heavens, the last thing she needed was Eden St. Claire, former reporter and current cold-case investigator and blogger, getting involved in her challenging status of a love life.

"Simone might have had something to contribute. Allie too."

"Your boss at the DA's office and a psychiatrist. Great." Darcy toed out of her ballet-slipper flats and sank her bare feet into the almost nonexistent icy grass. Even with the stones and rocks and dirt, it felt like home. "At least Greta and Amber didn't add their two cents."

"Fair warning. Amber might have started a spread-sheet of potentials for you."

"Well, you can tell all of them I'm effectively on strike for the foreseeable future." She hoped she didn't sound ungrateful. That they all cared enough to want to see her paired off with someone meant a lot. She sup-posed. The truth was all of her friends had significant others now. They were starting families, expanding their circles while Darcy seemed to just be spinning alone in her own. And that was exactly how she felt at these gatherings her friends often invited her to. Alone.

But that wasn't the only thing niggling at her. Life had just felt so…boring lately. So predictable. Her rou-tine had become monotonous and depressing. What she wouldn't give for an adventure, some unexpected thing that would leave her breathless while reminding her that although her heart wasn't attached to anyone, it was indeed still beating. "I need to stop forcing things, Ky. I want to let things settle for a while and see what other options might open up."

"There is something to be said for going with the flow," Kyla agreed. "You free for coffee later this week?"

"I'm free for the next two weeks. I'm on vacation, remember?" And what a bang-up way it had started, with a dud of a date that left her with unending circus music playing in her head. She sank down and leaned back against one of the gnarled tree trunks. "Let me know where and when, and I'll gladly take a break from cleaning out my storage unit." After a few more minutes and assurances that she would not become one of the resigned spinsters from the novels she continued to lose herself in, she clicked off and set her phone on the ground beside her.

Tucking up her knees, she hugged her legs and looked out into the moon-kissed river. Bundled in her black poofy ski jacket that hadn't seen a slope in three years, she watched the chilly air escape her lips and drift into the night sky.

The soft rushing noise of the river was all the companionship she needed. So what if she wasn't married with kids? She was only twenty-six. There was plenty of time to find someone, and if she didn't, hey, she knew plenty of people who made the single parent thing work should she decide to go that route.

In the meantime, she was a successful woman with a good income, a stable life and friends galore. She'd made a livelihood out of what she loved most and was earning her stripes as an instructor and lecturer. She didn't have to be part of a couple to be a productive member of society. And while intellectually she knew all that to be true, it didn't stop the longing that wrapped around her heart, the desire to belong…to someone.

Humming one of her favorite animated fairy-tale movie theme songs seemed entirely too maudlin, but it was her fallback coping mechanism. Her phone lit up with a final text message from Kyla, followed in quick succession by texts from Greta Renault-McTavish and Dr. Amber Palmer, who made Darcy laugh by sending her a variety of clown images, which suggested there might be a bright side to the entire evening after all.

The sound of splashing had Darcy freezing in midresponse. A critter probably. There were plenty around the area. But there it was again. Slow, uneven, but definite splashing. Darcy jumped to her feet, heading instantly to the water's edge and after tapping her flashlight app aimed it into the water. A figure—dark, mostly submerged—struggled against the current and clung to a tree limb that threatened to sink with every move he made.

"Hello!" Darcy called and saw his chin inch up slightly. "Hang on! I'm coming to help!"

In the dim light of her phone, she saw a head lift out of the water. Blood poured down one side of his face. He let out a gasp, a gurgling sound that told her he'd been sucking in as much river water as air. Across the water's expanse and down quite a ways, a pair of headlights swerved as if turning, then taillights blinked into the night as it drove away down the utility road.

"Try to keep close to the edge! Close to the shore!" Darcy dropped her phone, stripped off her jacket and tossed it to the ground. She knew of an embankment just twenty yards beyond where she was. If she could get him there, she should be able to wedge him out of the cold water.

She sat on the ledge, carefully lowered herself down

until her toes brushed the water. She shook off the shivers. The swim instructor inside of her screaming how bad an idea this was even as she clung to the shore and let herself drop in. His body collided against hers. The cold water hit her like razors, cutting across her skin and making her teeth chatter. Moments like these were one of the reasons she had a stable job. The number of drownings and accidents she dealt with on a yearly basis was mind-boggling. Even now she admitted she was making some less than smart choices, but what option did she have? Help would take too long, and he needed to get out of the cold water.

Once submerged, she pivoted almost immediately, her instincts and training kicking in as she got to him, locked an arm around his chest and hauled him back so he was face up. He struggled, but she was stronger and, with a tightening of her arm, shifted around to stay close to the shore as the water continued to carry them. She shoved away the branch he'd been clinging to and watched it drift into the darkness. "I need you to grab hold of the bank in a few seconds, okay?" She moved her arm to jostle him to attention. "You hear me?"

"Yeah. Sorry. Can't…my head."

"I know." She could feel the dirt and mud digging between her fingers and under her nails as she fought against the current. "Do the best you can. It's just up ahead. I can't pull you out on my own. You're going to have to help."

He sank, nearly dragging her with him, but she kneed him in the back, losing her grip on the shore for a second. With her entire body straining, she struggled against the water and against him. "Count of five, you need to grab hold of whatever you can. I'll push you up. Okay?"

He choked and spit out water, but the ghost of a nod told her he'd heard her.

The break and dip in the bank loomed ahead, and for an instant, she was afraid they'd overshoot it, but he surprised her by reaching out and grabbing hold of a tree root.

Darcy took a deep breath, went under, came up beneath him and shoved him up with everything she had before she broke through the surface. Now it was her time to gulp air as her lungs burned. As she dragged herself onto the shore, she watched in relief as he rolled onto his back. He was alive. That was something at least.

"Hey." She slogged through the dirt and debris, feeling branches and sticks scraping and cutting her skin. Darcy dropped onto her knees beside him, turned his face so she could see him better. "Hey. Wake up."

She didn't wait more than a fraction of a second before she cupped her hands and began doing compressions against his diaphragm. Water dripped off her face and hair that hung like long, wet ropes around her shoulders. Her knees hurt from the rocks beneath, but she kept pushing until he spit water out of his mouth and, gagging, rolled onto his side and vomited up a good amount of the river.

"There you go. Okay. You're all right now." Darcy continued patting his back and waited until his breathing sounded more even before she helped him sit up. Wow, the man was big. And not just tall. His arms bulged beneath the soaked black T-shirt, to the point that his muscles seemed to have muscles beneath the fabric. The black cargo pants shone like leather, as they were soaked and clinging to every inch of him, but it was the still bleeding gash on his head that had her scrambling. "We need to get you to the emergency room. My phone's a bit away. I'll go—"

"No!" The man grabbed her arm when she moved, keeping her pinned to the spot. "No ambulance. Can't call anyone. Not safe." He winced, pressed fingers against his temple. "Just need some time…to think." He shook his head as if trying to dislodge water from his ears.

"Stop that." She caught his face in her hand. "You have a head injury. That's nothing to play with. I have friends, police officers, detectives actually—"

"No." His hold on her gentled, shifted to him slipping his fingers between hers. "No one can know where I am. No one. I'll be okay. Just…go. I'll be fine on my own." He released her. She stood and moved back as he attempted to roll onto his knees and push himself to his feet. Even in the darkness, she could see his knees wobble. The guy wasn't going to make it five feet.

As gently as she could, she pushed him back down. "Wait here." She ran back along the path. Good thing she knew this area as well as she did. She threw on her jacket, shoved her filthy, damp feet back into her shoes, grabbed her phone and used her flashlight app again to guide her way back. She found him sitting on the bank, his breathing ragged and labored, blinking confusedly at his own cracked phone.

"That's got to be toast." She clicked off her phone, slipped it into her pocket and bent down beside him. He looked wrecked and more than a little confused. Leaving him out here on his own was out of the question. "How about you come with me until you're feeling steadier?" Or until she could convince him to go to the hospital. "Can you tell me your name?"

"Name." He blinked, then groaned when she wedged herself under his arm and helped him stand up. He fell against her and she nearly buckled, but she braced her feet and, clenching her jaw, managed to get her balance. "My name. What's my name?"

"That's what I asked. I'm Darcy. Darcy Ford."

He grunted, seemed to be concentrating on putting one foot in front of the other.

"My apartment's nearby on the second floor. I hope you can manage the stairs since there's no way I can carry you." The man must eat tin cans for appetizers.

"I'll manage." She heard it now, the strength. The determination in his voice. "Just need a little time to reset."

No doubt that same determination had kept him alive in the river. It was pure luck she'd found him. She knew those currents as well as most people knew highways. Another few minutes, and he'd have been caught up in the fast-flowing water on his way to nowhere good.

"Just need to rest a bit," he repeated dazedly. "Then I'll be out of your hair. Pretty hair." He lifted a hand and caught a curl, an absent if not detached smile curving full lips. "What color is it? I can't tell."

"Red." The bane of her existence growing up. Her brothers and sisters had hit the brown-hair-brown-eye jackpot while Darcy had inherited her parents' recessive Celtic genes to the nth degree.

"Bet it glows in the sunlight."

Just her luck, getting hit on by a man with a head injury. Seemed about right for the night she was having. "You'll have to tell me for sure in the morning." Just her luck, she was going to spend the next couple of hours looking up how to treat a head wound on the internet. Step one, she would bet, would be go to a doctor. She bit her lip, focusing on keeping upright. She wasn't going to let him die, so if that meant calling an ambulance against his wishes, so be it. The last thing she'd ever be able to explain was a dead man in her apartment. And if the guy was in too bad of shape, he couldn't argue, could he? "You doing okay?"

"Looking forward to a rest." But he seemed to be moving better. Well enough that she took the stairs down the hill into the parking lot of her apartment building before they cut across the expanse of cars. She heard a few doors slam, raised voices, laughter. She shifted her hold on him, nudged him up straighter as they headed for the stairs.

"Hey, Darcy! You're finally ending your romantic dry spell, huh?"

Darcy started at the sound of her downstairs neighbor's voice. "Good evening, Mr. Vanderly!" Darcy cringed at her loud tone, then flashed him a quick smile even as she struggled under the soaked man's weight. "One too many margaritas. You know how that goes."

"I do indeed. You need help getting him inside?"

"No, I'm fine. Thanks." Given Mr. Vanderly was on the far side of eighty, she wasn't in any rush to have two injured males in her apartment. "Say hi to Snuffles for me."

"Darn cat's gonna eat me out of house and home." Mr. Vanderly tapped his cane on the ground and sighed. "Licked up half my pasta Alfredo tonight while I was looking for the remote control."

Given Snuffles was lactose intolerant, she anticipated a long night for both Mr. Vanderly and his feline companion.

"Have a good night! Almost there," Darcy whispered the last words when she felt her charge's body sag. "Just a few more steps." She had to let go of his arm and grip the railing on her way up the stairs. Even in her damp clothes, she was sweating by the time they got to her door. She dug her key out of her pocket and dragged him inside. "I swear, we're almost there. The place isn't much, I know, but…" She was huffing as she helped him down the hall, through the dining area and into her bedroom. He stopped, braced himself in the doorway, and she ducked free. "What's wrong?"

"Blood." He touched the back of his head, then his temple. "Get some towels."

He was worried about her sheets? Okay, that seemed…considerate. She clicked on the bedside lamp before retrieving a stack of towels from the bathroom. When she returned, she found him sitting on the edge of her bed, tugging off his shirt. His pants were unzipped and pushed down to his thighs. She froze for a moment, her brain going numb. Good heavens, the man was beautifully made. All those muscles and tanned skin and intricate ink. And blood. *The man's injured, Darcy. Get it together.*

"Um. Okay." She dumped the towels on the bed and dropped down in front of him to unlace his boots. Puddles of water soon formed on her carpet before she reached up and pulled his pants the rest of the way off. She deposited the armload of things into the bathroom, then returned in time to help tug his shirt over his head.

So. Darcy cleared her throat. He was a briefs man. Her cheeks warmed as he grabbed a towel, putting it under his head before he stretched out on her mattress.

"I really should call someone." The blood seeping from the wound on his head seemed to have slowed, but it hadn't stopped completely. "Please let me—" She hesitated when he opened his eyes, turned his head, and stared directly at her. *Blue*, she thought. Those blue eyes were the most amazing color, the color of sky she'd seen in travel magazines surrounding those faraway islands that tempted everyone from their ordinary lives. The blue of escape and promise.

"You can't call anyone. I'll be out of your way in the morning. Just need some sleep."

"But—"

"Don't call anyone, Darcy." He reached out and took her hand, squeezed as if in need. "It's not safe." His head lolled to the side. His hold on her went slack and he passed out, but not before murmuring, "I don't want them coming after you."

Chapter 2

It's not safe.

With her mystery man's warning echoing in her ears, Darcy pulled open the folding doors in her bathroom and—after going through his pockets in which she found only the cracked, dead cell phone—dumped his soaked, mud-caked clothes into the washer.

She stripped down herself, tossed her own clothes in as well and jumped into a hot shower. Once she'd scrubbed the river off her skin and out of her hair, she wrapped herself in the yellow terrycloth robe hanging on the back of the bathroom door and stood there letting her mind race, nibbling on her thumbnail.

Lots of things weren't safe. Hauling a half-conscious man out of the river and into her bed wasn't safe. Taking off her clothes without locking her bathroom door wasn't safe. She could just hear the litany of warnings her friends would have if they had a clue what was happening in her apartment.

As the washer ran, Darcy checked on him. She wasn't entirely sure what she was worried about. The guy clearly wasn't going to wake up anytime soon, and when he did, he wouldn't be steady on his feet. If it turned out he was dangerous, and her gut told her he wasn't, her apartment wasn't that hard to escape.

Who was this man, anyway? He never did give her his name, and his cell phone was deader than the seventies disco she had on repeat for her workout sessions. She blew out a frustrated breath. This train of thought was leading her right to one of the things she did best: worry. Nothing good ever came of that.

He hadn't moved. Not that she'd expected him to, but in the soft light from her bedside lamp, he looked almost harmless. His breathing was even and steady; the color in his face slowly coming back. She spun back to the bathroom and quickly retrieved a bunch of first aid supplies, which she carried over to the bed.

She caught her lower lip in her teeth, cringing as she sat on the edge of the bed. She touched careful fingertips to his arm and felt the cold chill of the river. Darcy reached down and dragged the folded blanket off her grandmother's antique cedar chest to place over his bare legs. She'd picked up enough triage training over her years as a member of the water rescue team to be able to do a quick once-over to see if he had any other serious injuries.

He was scraped up pretty badly, but she made quick

work of applying alcohol over those open wounds, which gave her time to appreciate the intricate ink on his arms and torso. It was excellent work, nothing half dashed or shabby by any means, telling her the images weren't for show. They meant something to him.

She couldn't be certain, not without closer inspection, but a lot of his ink appeared to cover up scars. Her imagination had her wondering if they were wounds, but that exploration felt a bit invasive. Maybe she'd ask him about it when he woke up.

Or maybe she wouldn't, seeing it meant she'd spent far too much time looking at his naked flesh.

After getting a washcloth and a bowl of water, she sat on the other side of the bed so she could concentrate on his face and head. She got rid of the dried blood caking his temple and cheek. He was striking, with a full dark beard accentuating handsome features that had her pulse jumping in a completely different way. He was the kind of man she read about in her books, the kind of man who rarely, if ever, gave her a second look. Rugged. Tough. Commanding.

If he wasn't a walking example of an alpha male, she didn't know what was, and she knew her alphas, if only because she'd been endlessly striking out with betas.

Not that there was anything wrong with betas. Darcy rolled her eyes. "Except maybe the ones who collect clown costumes. I'll bet you don't do that, do you." No, this guy struck her as the type of man who had a secret cache of weapons in a hidden closet or in some stronghold storage unit in a dodgy part of town. Doubt surged. What if he was a criminal? What if he was a wanted man and she was harboring him from law enforcement? That would explain his reticence for calling for help. "Okay, now you're just being ridiculous," she said to herself.

Her visitor's longish hair had some curl to it and, now that it started to dry, displayed streaks of dark gold among the brown. Her fingers trembled as she pushed the strands back to examine the gash on his forehead. She flinched in sympathy. Wiping the drying blood away started the wound flowing again, but nothing as bad as it had been. There was a bruise already forming, and from the way it looked, it would cover a good part of his forehead. The gash wasn't too deep, but head wounds bled like crazy.

She found butterfly-tape bandages in her medical kit and, after messing up the first one, got three more placed, then pressed her fingers against the pulse in his neck. His heartbeat throbbed strong and steady and she breathed a little easier.

After gathering up the trash and his cell phone, Darcy turned off the light and withdrew. In the living room, she made note of his pulse to use as a baseline. She then dug through her pantry cabinet and came out with half a bag of white rice, which she shoved his cell phone into.

Her own cell, which she'd left in the bathroom, had her rethinking her situation. Instinct still told her to call for help. Head injuries were nothing to play with. Whatever situation he was in, he certainly didn't deserve to die for it. She speculated more and walked back to the bathroom.

She could probably convince Ashley to come over and give him a quick checkup, just to be safe. She grasped her cell to her chest. The ER doctor was working the late shift at Folsom General, a good thirty minutes away, but her guest said not to reach out. If he was right and there were people after him, her own safety aside, she didn't want to put Ashley in any danger.

Darcy clenched her fist, resisting temptation. Bringing Ashley into this mess wasn't fair to her, especially since Ashley had had more than her fair share of experience with dangerous situations. Not that Ashley couldn't handle herself. She'd managed just fine after being taken hostage during a prison break last year.

But Ashley would never be able to keep Darcy's call a secret from Slade. Ashley's husband, Slade Palmer, was a former undercover FBI agent who could snuff out a falsehood at fifty paces. No. She glanced uneasily toward her bedroom door. Until her guest woke up and they had another conversation, until she knew more, she needed to keep him a secret.

Three hours. She'd give him three hours to wake up before going against his wishes. Darcy walked over to her sofa, snuggled up in the corner and clicked the TV on, letting the late-night infomercial attempt to convince her once again that this new countertop air fryer would be the solution to all her cooking needs. Ten minutes later she was sound asleep.

He awoke with a start and stared up at the unfamiliar ceiling with something akin to befuddlement. A ceiling fan circled slowly overhead, the movement merely pushing around warm air. Air that carried the hint of lavender thanks to the diffuser sitting on the table beside the bed.

He shoved himself up, instantly regretting the action as his stomach pitched. He'd be fine with being sick if it meant tempering the excruciating pounding in his skull, but the sensation passed. Mostly.

He touched tentative fingers against the throbbing on his forehead. Three thin bandages had been placed across the most sensitive area. Bandages he didn't remember putting there.

Come to think of it…and thinking wasn't particularly easy at the moment, he didn't remember much of anything.

He groaned, slid to the edge of the bed and rested his head in his hands as he waited for the pieces to fall into place. He scratched his fingers through his beard, frowning at the odd sensation tickling his fingertips. Where was he and what had happened?

He had a vague memory of being dragged out of the water. Of stumbling down a surprisingly steep hill and then… He shook his head and had to take some deep, deliberate breaths before he forced himself to his feet. He wasn't going to find any answers hiding in here.

He felt more stable than he expected. That was good. Except…

Except, at least when it came to details about himself, he remained an utter blank slate. He was also missing most of his clothes. Considering he'd woken up alone, he didn't think their absence had anything to do with a woman, although…

This was clearly a woman's bedroom. Neat and practical furnishings filled the space with more than a hint of feminine elegance. A long antique dresser that had clearly been refurbished in a dark Wedgwood blue with new, modern hardware sat across from the bed. The bed itself boasted a cushioned headboard of the same color, only accented with an antique gold trim and upholstered buttons. Framed photographs of beaches around the world hung on one wall.

Both nightstands were piled high with paperback novels, an e-reader and travel magazines, along with a file folder marked "DART Training Manual Upgrades." He lifted the folder's cover, saw the city notation and was able to find at least one piece of the puzzle. But Sacramento was the only tidbit of information his mind appeared to absorb.

In some ways, everything clicked. He knew what things were called. Heck, he even knew that DART stood for Drowning Accident Rescue Team. The only thing missing from his functioning brain at the moment was…himself.

Irritation and frustration twisted into a spinning circle of dread lodged in the center of his chest. He touched his forehead again. That must have been one serious whack if it had wiped out part of his memory. He needed answers, about a great many things it seemed, but first…

First, he really needed the bathroom, which he found through one of the two open doors behind him. When he finished, he popped open the washing machine lid, found his clothes inside tied up in a wet bundle held together by an enticing pair of pink panties.

His lips twitched. Clearly his sense of humor was still intact. One thing to be grateful for. After battling with the sopping fabric, he tossed everything but a heavy sweater into the dryer, then laid the sweater flat on the warming top.

On one of the shelves next to the combo unit sat a stack of folded up bathing suits in various colors and styles. Hanging and organized in the adjacent space were diving suits along with air tanks stored beneath on the floor. The water elements decorating the bathroom made him wonder if he'd somehow found himself a mermaid.

Mermaid or no, the sooner he got out of here and started filling in the blanks, the better. Obviously, whoever had given him shelter had cared enough to look after him and his clothes. *Trusting soul*, he thought as he tried to snatch at any thread of knowledge. Rather than stroll around in his underwear, he grabbed a towel out of the cabinet and slung it around his waist, then headed back into the bedroom.

The bedside clock read just after eight in the morning. He could see spotty patches of sunlight eking through the slatted curtains of the bedroom and a full morning blast waiting for him in the other room. He also found himself flinching at the hyperfrenetic tones of a TV cook fixing a brunch feast that made his stomach growl even as it pitched again.

He took the few steps into the living room and cast a quick glance around. The apartment was small, clearly only a one bedroom with a dedicated dining space that not only held a round glass table but also an empty pair of food bowls on the floor for what, as far as he could tell, was a nonexistent pet.

On the opposite wall, there was a thick wooden bookcase displaying novels, multiple photographs, and knickknacks. Rather than art, various posters—the type one might see in a travel agency—hung on the walls, while small statues of mermaids and glass creations of octopi added to the decor. The entire feel of the place had a calming effect on him, as if the ocean had been pulled inside and put on display.

But it was the woman pushing herself up on the sofa that truly captured his attention.

"You're awake." Her smile was soft, accentuating the round features of her face as she shoved thick, long red curls out of her eyes. She glanced at her watch, scrunched her nose. "I meant to check on you a few hours ago, but I guess I slept through the alarm I set. If you're up to walking around, you must be feeling better."

"Better than what?" It was the only question that came to mind as she stood, turned off the TV and moved past him into the kitchen. He frowned. "Who are… Darcy." The name sliced through this mind like a bolt of lightning. He remembered being in the water— the freezing, sharp water—and then he remembered being pulled out of it. By her. "You're Darcy."

"Guilty as charged. Take a seat before you fall over." She pointed to one of the tall barstools at the blue-and-green speckled marble breakfast bar.

He frowned. Trusting seemed to be an understatement. The woman was acting as if they'd known each other forever. What was wrong with her? Didn't she know how dangerous strangers could be? The impulse to lecture her on self-protection and making smart choices hovered behind lips he pressed shut.

He flexed his hands. Was he dangerous?

"There's aspirin in that small bottle just there on the turntable." Before he asked, she retrieved a bottle of water for him and set up the coffee machine. He downed three pills and half the water, eyeing her as if waiting for her to realize the situation she was in. "The coffee will take a few minutes, which gives you time to tell me who you are."

He cringed, wondered how hard he must have smashed his head to make his eyelids ache. "I don't suppose you found an ID or wallet in my clothes?"

She rested her hands on the counter in front of her. He didn't like the frown that marred her forehead. He didn't like the idea of her frowning at all. This was a woman who should spend all her time smiling and laughing. That riotous red hair of hers fit right into his supposition about a mermaid living here, and in those green eyes, he didn't see anything but kindness.

"All you had on you was your phone, which is beyond waterlogged." She pointed to the bag of rice in the corner. "Everything I read online says it can take days to dry one out, if it'll work at all. So, you don't know your name."

"I do not."

"You seem pretty calm about it." Her comment made her sound more interested than accusatory.

"Freaking out about it won't help." Hopefully staying calm would assist in returning his brain to normal.

She cleared her throat. "I know last night you were adamant about not calling the police—"

"No police." The answer was automatic, as if someone else had spoken the words, but as her frown increased, he knew he meant it. "All I've got to go on right now is what my gut is telling me." Screaming at him was more like it.

"I get that." But Darcy didn't look convinced. "Look, I have friends who are detectives. I also have some friends who are Feds. You could trust them."

"I can't trust anyone." The statement felt both correct and authentic, and a pang of regret chimed through him. That wasn't a particularly pleasant commentary on anyone's life.

"You can trust me."

"How do you know you can trust me?" He bypassed her comment. "You don't know anything about me, yet you don't seem scared at all." He frowned. Why wasn't she scared?

"The last thing you said before you passed out was that you didn't want me to call the police because you were afraid whoever did that to you—" she pointed to his scalp "—would come after me. With everything that must have happened last night, you were worried about me. That earned you some faith."

"And therefore I'm worthy of sleeping in your bed and drinking your coffee?"

She snapped her fingers. "Coffee, right." Pulling open an overhead cabinet door, she grabbed an extra-large mug and, after filling it, set it in front of him. "Do you know if you take cream or sugar?"

"I'll stick with black." He examined the image of the monarch butterfly under which read Butterfly Harbor, CA.

"A couple of girlfriends and I spent a weekend there last summer," she explained as if trying to fill the silent void. "Gorgeous beaches and the best blackberry pie I've ever eaten. Have you been there?" She poured her own mug and only added a splash of almond creamer.

"Nice try." He hid his frustration behind the mug. One sip told him he'd made a mistake and reached for both the cream carton and sugar bowl. "I think I've heard of it, though." It sounded familiar at least.

"Interesting." She leaned back and pinned him with a look. "So everything personal...name, profession, where you live "

"Gone. Which is what I need to be." He heard the buzzer on the dryer go off. "Thanks for the assist. I'll get dressed and out of your hair." Hair he'd be dreaming about for the next half a century. All that red spilling over her shoulders with hints of gold spun through, he could only imagine how glorious it was out in the sun. And his overwhelming desire to see it was just one more reason why he needed to go as soon as possible. He had to keep this woman—Darcy—relegated to his imagination.

"You leaving doesn't make any sense." Darcy trailed after him straight into the bathroom. "You don't know anything about yourself. You don't have a car. Where are you going to go? Your phone's not working and you won't let me call the police. What is it you think you're going to—oh! Okay."

He dropped the towel before reaching into the dryer for his jeans. When he glanced over his shoulder at her, her cheeks were the most adorable shade of pink. Her eyes went wide and she pointed behind her.

"I'll just let you—um. Yeah."

He might have laughed if he wasn't thinking about what she'd said. Where was he going to go? Other than away from here, away from her, he had no plan. He didn't know where he'd been, what had caused this or where he might need to go. The only thing he did know was that he needed to find out.

But that didn't stop him from tugging on his jeans, shirt, and socks and retrieving his still damp boots from beside her bed. He sat down to tug them on.

"You're just going to wander around outside and wait for your memory to come back?" Condescension didn't seem to be very familiar to her. "News flash, you do that long enough, someone else might call the cops on you. And what if whoever hurt you comes after you?"

"If I was worried about your safety last night, then I'm even more worried about it now." He wasn't going to let her get sucked into whatever had transpired. Clearly he'd almost gotten himself killed. He didn't want anything bad coming to an innocent bystander who had only been trying to help.

"You have a head injury," Darcy said. "You shouldn't be alone."

He tilted his head up, boot laces in hand. "Darcy, I get that you want to lend a hand, but there's nothing you can do." He was on his own. And his instincts were telling him he was used to that.

"What about helping you find out what happened last night? I know the river and waterways in this area better than most people. And since I dragged you out, that means you had to go in somewhere. And it would have to be somewhere close with the way the water was running last night. I can help you find that answer at least."

"Darcy—"

"Do you really think I'm going to just forget about you and not worry whether you pitch over with a brain bleed?"

He would have rolled his eyes if he didn't think the action would make his head ache more. "I don't have a brain bleed. A concussion, maybe."

"A concussion definitely. Ever had one before?"

"I yes?" He might have gotten away with it if the last word hadn't sounded like a question. "I appreciate everything you've done, but whatever I'm dealing with it can't involve you." He stood up, scrunched his toes into his boots when he felt himself sway even as she moved to stand in front of him.

"I'm already involved." That stubborn chin of hers inched up. "Give me a few minutes to get dressed."

"Am I not using the right words all of a sudden?" he asked. "Darcy, you aren't coming with—"

She poked two fingers hard against his shoulder and sent him falling back onto her bed. It took him a moment to realize what had happened even as he blinked up at the ceiling. He tilted his head as she stepped over him, hands on her hips. "You can barely stand up on your own let alone go out into the complete unknown. Either, I come with you, or I make some calls. Did I mention I have two FBI agents on speed dial?"

He leaned on an elbow and glared at her, unable to tell whether she was bluffing. "You do not."

"FBI Special Agent Slade Palmer. Well, former agent. It's…complicated." She waved a hand in the air as if erasing words. "But if you're picky as to whether they're currently employed by the bureau, I can call my friend Eamon. He's either in Sac, or he's in San Francisco for the week. Hard to keep track, as he goes back and forth a lot." She blinked and gave him a smile he felt sure she could use to sell ice to a penguin. "Slade's a better bet. Plus his wife is one of my very best—"

"All right!" Arguing with her was only going to eat up the day and give him a bigger headache. "Get dressed, and you can help me figure out what kind of accident I had last night. But that's it! No calls," he added when she spun around and disappeared into her closet.

She poked her head back out, face alight with excitement. "While you're sitting there—"

"I'm getting up." He lay on his back again and continued to stare up at the ceiling.

"Well, until you do, what do you want me to call you? I was thinking Arthur—"

"You were?" Baffled, he sat up and turned toward her voice. "Why?"

"Arthur Cur—you know, superhero water guy, looks

great in green Spandex. Never mind. How about Duckie? Too eighties?" She leaned back into her closet.

"I don't even know how to—"

"Bubbles? Flipper? Oh, Caspian!"

"Maybe I can make a break for it," he muttered.

"I've got it." She stepped out of the closet, her robe gaping just enough for him to get a glimpse of her toned thigh. "Clyde. For the river in Scotland. It's on my bucket list to visit. Yeah. Clyde works. At least until that noggin of yours starts working right." She nodded, pleased with herself and as if he had no say in the matter. "Nice to meet you, Clyde. I'll be ready in a jiff."

"Clyde." The name didn't come close to sounding right. For anything or anyone. But, for now, for this moment, he'd take it.

Chapter 3

Darcy could tick off on one hand the number of times she'd woken up to a man in her bed and still have fingers left unticked. Well, today didn't really count since she hadn't been in her bed last night, but still... Yep, she needed to get ahold of herself!

Dressed in jeans, a bright blue tunic sweater and her hiking boots, Darcy had braided her hair into a rope down her back before heading into the kitchen. She grabbed some quick on-the-go food—hard boiled eggs, packaged cheese and meat snacks, and four bottles of water—and stashed them in one of her backpacks.

"Can I ask you something?" Clyde's voice had her freezing midpack.

"Sure." Every nerve in her body seemed to be jumping to attention around him. Last night she hadn't had time to think what she was doing by bringing him home with her. Now that she had, her mind wouldn't stop spinning like one huge hamster wheel of unending energy. "Do you have a pet? I haven't seen anything scampering about, but there's…that."

Darcy leaned out of the kitchen and saw him sitting at her dining room table looking at the two empty bowls. "Oh, those are for Ninja. I dog-sit for my best friend sometimes. Rather than moving hers back and forth, I got my own."

"So, no pets."

"Nope. I've been thinking about getting a dog, but the idea of going down to the Front Street Animal Shelter scares me to death." At his puzzled expression, she added, "How do you choose one when there are so many who need a good home? I'll come home with a carload, and don't even get me started on kittens and cats." She was babbling. Her mother had always tried to break her of that habit growing up, but even attempting to restrict her verbal impulses tended to exacerbate the issue. Case in point… "A dog's better suited for my work given how much time I spend in and around the water. But, I couldn't stand the idea of leaving a pet alone during the day. So, in that sense, a cat would be better. That said, I've seen videos of surfing cats and…" She stopped, cringed and flashed him a grin. "That is way more than you asked for. Sorry. I'm ready to go if you're sure you're up to it. Here."

She handed him one of the protein bars she made on the weekends. "You'll probably feel steadier with something in your stomach. Wait." She snatched it back and frowned. "Do you know if you have any food allergies? What about nuts?" She almost laughed at her predicament. How weird had her life become in less than twenty-four hours?

"I'll take the risk." He accepted the bar as he stood up. "And if I go into anaphylactic shock you'll have the perfect excuse to drive me to the hospital. You like to travel. What?" He asked when she glanced away. "You've got pictures up from all over the world. I assumed—"

"I like the *idea* of travel." She did her best to keep her voice casual. "I excel at road trips. Seen most of the United States, so it's not like I haven't been anywhere. Just the idea of stepping foot on a plane gives me the wiggies."

"The what?"

"I wig out. Can't fly. Don't even like to look at planes…" She held up both hands in surrender. "I was supposed to go to Hawai'i with some friends a few years back. Managed to get all the way to the gate and had a full-on panic attack." Probably the most humiliating event of her life, and that was saying something.

"That's a shame. Aren't there therapies or treatments—?"

"Tried them all. Confrontation therapy. Hypnotherapy. Biofeedback. They all produced zippo results. Dreaming about all the places I want to go isn't so bad, and it's a lot cheaper." She'd been just about everywhere, thanks to her imagination and her journals.

She led him out the door, locked up behind them,

then shivered in sympathy as she hitched her backpack over one shoulder. "You don't have a jacket or coat."

"I survived the river in February. I'll be fine."

Yes, she imagined he would. She scooted around him so she could go ahead down the stairs. If he got dizzy or pitched over, she could at least pad his fall. Of course he'd probably take them both down… She was doing it again. Silently, but she was still babbling.

"I thought we'd start with where I found you last night, and maybe we can work back from there? Unless you have another idea?" She glanced over her shoulder, then tripped down the last two stairs. His hands shot out and caught her before she tumbled face-first onto the pavement. He tugged her back and she bounced into him, feeling the full strength of him against nearly every inch of her. Her cheeks went lava-hot red. "Thanks."

"No problem."

Oh, she was fairly certain that was a lie. But when he didn't release her, she tilted her chin up and looked into his mesmerizing eyes. "My family calls me a land menace. I can trip over a piece of fluff. Good thing I work in the water."

"I, for one, am grateful that you do."

As far as a thank-you, it was more than adequate. "Well, one thing I know about you," she said as his grip on her loosened. "You've a romantic bend about you. That's almost poetry you're spouting. Maybe you're an English professor or Shakespeare scholar?"

"I doubt it."

"Oh, I don't know." She grinned. "I feel a bit of romance about you."

Behind them, Mr. Vanderly's curtains shifted and reminded Darcy there were ears—however poorly they worked—everywhere in the complex. She led the way through the parking lot and over to the makeshift stairs up the hill to the river walkway.

"I don't remember these stairs last night."

"Because we came down over there, where there was more light." She hoisted her backpack higher up on her shoulders and walked slowly as she kept an eye on him. She had no doubt he was feeling worse than he was letting on. There was no way his head wasn't pounding like a summer thunderstorm. "I have the aspirin in case you need it."

"You were right about eating something." He shoved the empty plastic wrapper in his pocket and polished off the protein bar. "It's helped."

Darcy focused on the path ahead. He'd nearly drowned last night, had—at least as far as she could tell—a head wound serious enough to cause partial amnesia, and yet he was acting as if they were taking a Sunday stroll in the park. "So, here's where I was when I first heard you in the water." She stopped just shy of her secret spot and pointed. "The branch you were clinging to was pretty substantial. At some point, you must have caught just the right shift in the tide to drift over here. Come on."

She waved for him to follow her down the rocky slope toward the water's edge. She knew most people, especially around this area of the American River, tended to stay far away from its banks. It was a smart thing to do, to avoid it, given the levee system had only recently been shored up to tighter specifications. It wasn't a place for swimming, diving or jumping. Not by any stretch of the imagination. If Darcy wanted to go into the water, she knew of far safer spots, like down at Discovery Park and near the Sunrise overpass. Even she, with her years of water rescue and diving experience, wouldn't put a toe in these waters on a whim. Not if she expected to come out again. No. He'd either been forced in by someone or something, or it had been his only option. Neither of which boded well for his current circumstances.

"I was lucky you heard me." Clyde's voice washed over her from behind, as soothing as an ocean tide at midnight. "Wasn't I?"

"Very," she agreed, scanning the shore across the expanse of river. "Given the flow patterns this time of year, there's no chance you'd have come straight across. I'd guess that you went in somewhere…" she scanned the shoreline, and after touching his arm, pointed to the left "…around there. Where I saw the headlights."

"Headlights? What headlights?" The command and shock in his voice had her cringing.

"I didn't mention those?" She narrowed her eyes as if she could pull last night into focus. "I wasn't paying that much attention, actually. I only noticed them when I was coming down to get you. They moved in a kind of circle, then disappeared." Her stomach pitched. "You think those were the guys you were worried about finding me?"

"Maybe."

Well, that was…awesome. "So, what happened to you definitely wasn't an accident." While the observation wasn't a surprise, it did make her wonder yet again which side of the law he belonged to.

"I think that's a safe assumption."

"If you hit something hard enough to deploy the airbag, I'm betting the car's pretty damaged. Should make it easier to find." Speculating wasn't going to do any good. They needed to focus on what they did know. "Hypothermia hadn't set in, so I doubt you were in the water for more than a couple of minutes. The blood seeping out of your head wound had slowed, but was still steady, so that's another indicator. I don't suppose anything's coming back yet?"

"No." He crouched and braced his hand on an uprooted tree for balance as he examined the area. "I imagine it all looks completely different at night than it does now."

"Right." Darcy nodded. "There's nothing else to be learned here. Let's go get my car and we'll backtrack. The car you crashed has to be nearby somewhere."

He stood, brushed himself off and barely swayed. "You seem so convinced I crashed a car."

"I am." She traced a finger down the side of his reddened face. "These are airbag burns." She yanked her hand back as if she'd reached too far into the fire. Touching him was a bad idea. Mainly because every time she did, she didn't want to stop. That was a complication neither of them needed. "You were definitely in a car. Let's go find it."

* * *

He wasn't entirely sure what he expected Darcy to drive, but it certainly wasn't a sports SUV large enough to camp out in. He'd let out a sigh of relief as he sank back into the passenger seat, adjusted it and stretched out his legs. The throbbing in his head, which came and went, eased up significantly as she drove down and around University Avenue before turning onto American River Drive. This area of town seemed particularly quiet and serene, with its single-story homes and large front yards.

He kept looking for something, anything familiar, but as with his personal details, all he was coming up with was one big fat zero. What was he going to do if his memory never came back? "You could rent this car out on one of those tiny home sites."

"I know." She grinned, an action that loosened the tension that was building in his system. "My dad always taught us to choose vehicles we'd feel safe in. Sometimes I feel invincible behind the wheel of this thing. Then I encounter other drivers and realize that is not the case at all. Plus, I never know what I'll need to haul around in this thing. One time I ended up with a motorboat engine and enough diving equipment for an ocean voyage. Sorry." She cringed and narrowed her eyes on the road ahead. "I tend to have what my mother calls river mouth. It just keeps running and running."

"I don't mind." Hearing her talk drowned out the emptiness in his head and the mounting unease at the possibility they were going straight into even more unanswered questions. Besides, there was something calming and appealing about her voice. He still didn't like the idea of her tagging along, though. It was bad enough stepping into the unknown on his own but pulling someone else with him—an innocent Darcy—added a responsibility and a worry he honestly didn't want.

"Any idea who might have been after you last night?"

"Not a clue." If he didn't know his own name, he certainly didn't know who might have been trying to hurt or kill him. He looked out the window at the passing homes that seemed tidy and well kept, particularly the landscaping. While a lot of the front yards had switched to drought-resistant terrain, there were plenty with lush, albeit winter-bruised, lawns. "I saw the file on your nightstand. You work for DART."

"Yep." She nodded. "Have ever since graduating high school."

"But you're not working today?"

"Not for a couple of weeks. I'm on vacation. They don't offer payouts anymore for those of us who don't put in for it, so it's take it or lose it." She shrugged. "I also give swimming lessons at the Y downtown and do private lessons, but this time of year is always my slow season. Come summer, I'll barely be home."

"I don't expect there's much call for river rescue this time of year."

"You'd be surprised how careless people get around the water year-round." She took a right onto Watt Avenue, then, after crossing the overpass, took a sharp right again and swung around toward a marked dirt access road. "I've stopped being surprised, though. I also do evidence and accident recovery for the police and the DA's office."

"Is there a lot of that?"

"Sacramento's got a vast waterway, one of the largest systems in the country. Lots of ins and outs and back areas to cover. Plenty of space for accidents to happen. Water, I've learned, covers a multitude of sins. They're silent tombs in some instances. But nothing stays buried forever, especially not with water levels being what they are these days. Hang on. This doesn't look right." She pulled to a stop at the chained gate, parked and shoved open her door.

Part of him hated to move, but he wasn't about to let her out of his sight. He pushed open the door and joined her. He found her crouched and examining the chain.

"Lock's busted." She pulled the padlock free of the tangle of chain, unwound it and swung open the gate. "Some of these links are strained."

"Tire tracks." He stepped carefully through. "I'd say two, maybe three vehicles."

"And lots of broken glass." Darcy bent down as her feet crunched against something, and she came up with glass fragments cupped in her palm. She blew on them to dust them off and held them up. "Headlight glass. It refracts differently than a bottle or a tempered window."

"No telling how long that's been there."

"Well, we had a storm blow through two days ago, and this being toward the top of the tracks tells me whatever happened here occurred after the rain. I think we're on the right path, so to speak," she said and headed over to the truck. "Let's see where the tire trail takes us."

"We could just walk," he suggested.

"However far we go in, that's how far we have to come out." She assessed him with clear doubt on her face. "You really up for that?"

He took a step back in case she tried to push him over with two fingers again. Ego had him wanting to argue, but practicality won out. "Fine." Apparently he'd discovered his favorite word.

"Here." Once they were back in the SUV, she handed him her cell. "Aim the camera at the road and go full zoom. You'll see where the tracks stop before I will."

His eyebrows shot up. That wasn't a bad idea.

"If I'd thought about it, I'd have brought my camera equipment." She shook her head. "Must have been distracted."

"Can't imagine by what." She started the engine and they crept forward. He did as she suggested and, for the next couple of miles, listened to the sound of the river. Overgrown brush and trees had been tamed just enough to allow for maintenance vehicles to pass. He kept his eyes on the muddled tire tracks that at times swerved and seemed to vanish straight into… "Stop!"

She hit the brakes hard enough to propel them both forward. "What?" She looked both ways frantically. "What do you see?"

"One of the tracks ended." He pointed to the right and set the phone down. It was his turn to jump out of the car first and head for a large oak tree overhanging the slope of the river. He sensed her behind him, held his arm out to stop her from jumping ahead. "There's only one set of tires from here. The other vehicle must have crashed. Right here." He waited, hoping for some image or memory to come back to him.

The shrubs and brush surrounding them had clearly been traumatized. Branches and foliage lay broken and crushed while the giant oak displayed violent scars along the bottom portion of the trunk.

"More glass." Darcy moved around him, crouched and plucked up a chunk of headlight, then ran her fingers against the markings on the tree. "Paint scrapings, too. Looks black or maybe dark blue. This is recent. So where's the car?" She scratched off flakes of paint that drifted like ash into the air as he stood. "Where are you going?"

He stepped onto the narrow path leading into the trees parallel to the river rushing past. The sound was deafening, but the white noise triggered a niggling thought. He blinked against a flash of an image, the moon shining down, reflecting against the water as it flowed and tumbled over itself. Caught between the past and the present, he kept moving, his mind processing…something he couldn't put his finger on.

Hearing Darcy behind him had him whipping around, eyes narrowing.

"What?" she demanded. "It looks like you've remembered something."

"You were right…about the car." He shook his head, pivoted toward the river. "Makes sense this was the only path to get away."

"All right. Let's play this out. I'm right behind you."

He hesitated. She was. But she shouldn't be. That unease returned, this time at double the pressure. "I don't think you—"

"You shouldn't be on your own," she repeated again. "Besides. I'm on vacation. What else am I going to do with myself?"

"Stay safe." He didn't want her hurt. Especially not because of him.

"We'll stay safe together. Look, let's not rehash all this, okay? We're here. No one else is around. Let's find out what we can find out, and then we'll decide what the next step is." She turned him around and gave him a gentle shove. "Keep your eyes out for something you might have dropped, like a wallet or ID or something."

"Clyde not doing it for you anymore?"

"Clyde does it for me just fine."

The way she said it made his lips twitch. He liked that idea. A lot. He also liked how easily she blushed.

"I'd just like to find out something that's actually a fact," she said. "Blame it on all the mysteries I watch and the adventures I read."

"Don't tell me." He did as she wanted and continued navigating slowly through the shrubs and overgrown weeds. "You're a closet super sleuth."

"Hardly." Her tone dangled an unspoken sentiment he made a mental note of to address later. "Does anything else seem familiar?"

"No." It was more of a feeling—a panicked desperation to escape. He came to a stop when she did right at the shoreline. The river rushed past them only a few feet below.

"I dragged you out right over there." She pointed, and he saw the top of her apartment complex nestled among the thick line of trees. "It would have taken you only a few minutes to reach that spot from here."

"So, you were right."

She shrugged, tucked her hair behind her ear and cast her gaze about the ground. "I could easily be wrong. A few pieces of headlight glass and a dented tree don't prove anything. I'm not seeing anything else around to fill in the blanks."

Neither was he. They returned to her car, but as they passed the tree, she stopped, kicked her foot in the dirt and bent down.

"What did you find?" he asked her.

"This." She plucked up a fob, dangled it in the air. "Cars don't drive without keys. At least, not without some know-how."

"Cars also don't vanish on their own."

"Means someone cleaned up the scene in only a few hours." She gestured to the SUV. "Let's get back. I have a friend who works in the crime lab. I bet she can help us track—"

"No." He surprised both of them with his steely tone.

She rolled her eyes. "Whatever issues you have with the police you're going to have to deal with them. I'm telling you, you can trust my friends."

He set his jaw and stared at her. If he could explain his reluctance to go to law enforcement, he would, but with a giant void where his memories were stored, the only thing he could rely on was instinct. And right now, it was screaming at him to stay away from the authorities. "If you want to keep tagging along, that's my one condition. No cops. No labs. Nothing official. End of story."

She scrunched her mouth and narrowed her eyes. "You're either trying to get rid of me or doubled down on your stubbornness. Okay then. We'll go with plan B."

"And what's that?"

"Trickier," she muttered and moved close enough that he could smell the citrus fragrance of the soap and shampoo he'd seen in her bathroom. "But doable." She seemed to be studying him. "You're looking a bit green again. You need to drink some water, maybe eat more. Grab something out of the backpack when we're in the car."

When he climbed into her SUV, he found himself comparing Darcy to quicksand. The more he attempted to get away from her, the deeper he seemed to sink. But as he watched her circle around to the driver's side and throw him yet another one of her amused grins, he had to wonder why not being alone felt so good.

Chapter 4

Stomach clenched so tight that her muscles ached, Darcy took a right turn into the back lot of the Brass Eagle. *Tricky* didn't come close to describing the strategy she'd thought of or the jeopardy she was putting herself in. This was a risk, a big one, but they needed someplace to start, and if Clyde was adamant about not going to the authorities, what choice did she have?

"Interesting," Clyde said. "Your plan B is a bar."

"Plan B is above the bar." Darcy noted Jason Sutton's car parked next to them. "Vince and his brother Jason are PIs. Well, Vince is. Jason helps out, but Vince's side business is the bar, which doesn't open until noon."

"You not only know cops and FBI agents but also private investigators?"

"I know three of them, actually. Is that a problem?"

She had the odd urge to bat her lashes at him, but there was a difference between keeping things light and being obnoxious. "I also know the assistant DA, a nationally recognized crime blogger and an amnesiac with a penchant for silence and nuts."

Clyde's lips twitched. "And mermaids," he added. "Don't forget my growing appreciation for mermaids."

"Oh. Yeah, well." She felt her cheeks warm even as her heart skipped a beat. The man might not know a lick about who or what he was, but he definitely knew his way around a compliment. Given that gleam in his eye, he obviously liked pushing her off balance with comments like that. She cleared her throat and gathered her keys and phone.

"So this Vince guy—" he began.

"We're—I'm not here to see Vince." She checked the dashboard clock. "I'm going to talk to his brother Jason. He doesn't have a crime lab per se, but he's our best bet at finding out what car this key belongs to." He reached for the door handle, but she grabbed his arm. "No, you should wait here."

"You're not serious." For the first time, he looked offended. "Darcy, to reiterate, I appreciate your determination to help, but I'm not a wait-around kind of guy."

"How do you know?"

He inclined his head, arched his brow and had Darcy resisting the urge to squirm in her seat.

"Look, I get it," she protested. "But I can't go bringing you in there with me. Jason's engaged to my best friend. If he sees you—"

"Too late." Clyde gestured to her window, and when

Darcy turned to look, she spotted Jason Sutton dumping two huge bags of garbage into the trash bin behind the bar. As soon as the lid banged shut, he headed right for them. "If he sees me, what?"

"Crap." Darcy fumbled for her phone and keys and reached for the door handle. "Just...play along, okay?"

"Play along with what?"

"I don't know yet." Her mind was spinning as she dropped out of the SUV. "Jason, hi. Just the man we were looking for." She greeted him with a quick hug and kept her too wide smile in place as Clyde joined them. "Um, Jason, this is Clyde. He's..." Her mind went completely blank.

"I'm a new recruit at DART," Clyde said easily and offered his hand in greeting. "I'm also new in town, so Darcy volunteered to show me around."

Darcy stared, amazed and more than a little unsettled at how easily he slipped into the lie.

"Welcome to Sacramento, Clyde," Jason said with the barest hint of surprise. "You've got yourself a first-class tour guide. You don't have any clown costumes in your closet, do you?"

Darcy groaned.

"Excuse me?" Clyde clearly thought he'd misheard.

"Nothing," Darcy said and gently punched Jason in the shoulder before stepping back. "Inside joke about my pathetic social life."

"Even on vacation, you can't stay away from work, eh, Darcy?" Jason teased.

"You know me," Darcy said with a forced laugh and

waved her hand in the air. "Can't say no to a special assignment. You have a few minutes?"

"More than a few. Come on in."

Darcy glared at Clyde behind Jason's back. He grinned and shrugged. Darcy might not know anything about her mystery man, but she knew a "told you so" expression when she saw it. "Just so you know," she all but whispered as she caught up to him, "his sister-in-law is the assistant DA, so don't volunteer information that'll raise too many questions."

The humor faded from Clyde's blue eyes, and he nodded.

It occurred to Darcy as she followed the two men into the bar's spacious kitchen that Clyde and Jason were pretty close to polar opposites in the looks department. While Clyde looked as if he'd stepped off Hollywood action movie celluloid, Jason was on the tall and lanky side, with a close-cropped, neatly trimmed beard and mischievous eyes. His background was quite colorful and included an extensive stay in the state penal system for accessory to armed robbery, but since his release a few years ago, he'd been redeeming himself as a PI and computer security consultant. It was a stroke of luck for her and her friends, not to mention Clyde.

"You guys hungry?" Jason asked. "I was getting stuff ready for the lunch shift, but I can whip you up some breakfast." The spacious food prep space of the Brass Eagle was as neat, polished and pristine as the bar it belonged to. All of which made sense, because Jason's brother Vince was a former Marine who maintained his devotion to order and organization years after his honorable discharge from the service.

"Ah, no. We already ate," Darcy lied. "We were hoping you could help us with this project we're doing."

"For work?" Jason asked

"For fun," Clyde said before Darcy could come up with a believable story. "I was telling her about this online challenge group I belong to. It's a scavenger hunt kind of thing where we solve problems and complicated situations to move on to the next level."

"Ah." Jason nodded. "Finally getting to stretch those mystery-loving muscles of yours," he teased Darcy. "All those thrillers you read and watch are finally paying off." Jason's observation punched all Darcy's guilt buttons. "You stuck already?"

"Yeah, we are," Darcy admitted with a heavy sigh. "There's a car we need to find that we have the key to. But we only have the make."

"Is there cash involved?" Jason asked.

"Cash?" She blinked.

Jason frowned at her confusion. "As a prize for figuring out the puzzle."

"No," Clyde said. "It's one of those bragging-rights things. It's also about utilizing one's network to test your problem-solving ability. Darcy mentioned you have some talents that we can exploit."

Okay, Darcy thought. He was way too good at subterfuge for this to be his first go around.

"Say no more." Jason wrapped a metal tray covered with raw hamburger patties and stuck it into the industrial-sized fridge. "Let me just wash up, and we'll go up to the office. What's the model of the car?"

Darcy dug out the fob and handed it to him as they headed upstairs. The second-floor office door reminded Darcy of the film noirs she loved. Sam Spade and *The Maltese Falcon.* Only on this door, it said Sutton Brothers Investigations and listed Vince and Jason equally. "That's new," she said. Jason tossed her a smile over his shoulder. "Vince make you an official partner?"

"Uh, kind of in name only," Jason said. "I'm punching the clock here while I get through graduate school. The license thing is a bit tricky with my record but…" He shrugged, beamed at his name on the door. "What can I say? Helping take down one of the biggest drug distribution rings on the West Coast last Halloween came with a career boost." The pride in Jason's voice warmed Darcy's heart. His self-confidence was a long time coming and hard earned. Of course, her friend Kyla and the faith she had in him had done a bit of the boosting as well. Kyla had trusted him with her life and living up to the Sutton name he'd gone above and beyond to protect her. "Being his partner up here doesn't mean he doesn't still stick me with KP duty downstairs from time to time though."

"The pains of being a little brother," Darcy reminded him. "Will it take very long to trace the key?"

Jason's brows arched. "Is there a time limit, too?" He walked over to his desk in the corner of the room, tapped open his computer, and the screen buzzed to life.

"Bonus points," Clyde said with a warning glare at her.

Darcy sighed. She hated lying, especially because she was terrible at it. It was difficult to keep false things straight, and stress didn't help. She handed Jason the key and he sat down to type, while she shoved her hands into the back pockets of her jeans to keep from twisting her fingers together.

Clyde roamed the office, checked the windows overlooking J Street, paced the galley kitchen across the room and stopped in front of the TV, which was currently broadcasting the local news.

"High-end cars are funny things," Jason said as he grabbed a soft-sided pouch, unzipped it and pulled out a selection of small screwdrivers and metal picks. "You wouldn't think they'd skimp on the little things." He held up the fob before he worked one of the screwdrivers into the seam and popped it open. "But they do. Easy to get into these." He flipped the top up and exposed an engraved serial number on the inside. He typed the digits into his computer. "Your mystery car is a 2021 model. Navy blue."

"Does it have any owner information?" Darcy asked when Clyde seemed transfixed by the TV. "I don't suppose you can find who it's registered to?" She focused on keeping her smile and expression passive even as the excitement of finally finding some answers surged.

Jason arched a brow again but refrained from saying anything as he did an online search. "It's not registered here in California." He frowned. "Who exactly

are you looking to earn bragging rights on?" he called
to Clyde, still distracted.

"Just the other members of the online group," Darcy
improvised. Okay, maybe she was getting into the
groove of this lying thing. "What about nearby states?
Can we search there?"

"Can? Sure." Jason shrugged. "*Should* is another
story. It's not exactly…"

"Legal?" Darcy asked.

"It skirts the edges." He grinned. "Once upon a time,
I might have steered clear, but I've recently learned to
embrace that which makes me special." The glint in
his eye faded as his gaze grew concerned. "This seems
an odd request coming from you."

She shrugged. "The adventure of the unknown and
all." She silently begged him not to ask any more questions. Every lie she told felt like she was building a wall
between them as friends.

"You want to keep this West Coast?"

"Yeah." Darcy nodded. "Let's do Washington, Nevada and Oregon."

"All right."

She looked down at the innocuous fob. "Little thing
does a lot of stuff."

"There's also a GPS tracker in there in case the
fob gets lost. Let's get you some more bonus points,
though." He plucked out a microchip with a pair of
tweezers and set it into a chip reader. "The chips in
newer models can connect to the car's GPS."

"So, if the registration doesn't pan out, this might
lead us to the car itself. Awesome. Thanks, Jason."

"Hey, this is fun. And it's nice you thought to come to me for help. Even if it's under the table. Okay, here we go. No hits in Washington state or Oregon, but Nevada, ding ding ding." He tapped the screen. "The car is registered to a rental company based in Nevada. Looks like they mostly service corporate businesses and do the majority of their contracts out of the Las Vegas airport."

Vegas. Huh. That was interesting. "Anything else details-wise? Like whose name is on the rental agreement?"

"Near as I can tell," Jason said almost distractedly as he scanned the screen. "It hasn't been rented out. According to the company records, it should be sitting in the parking lot of their home office in Vegas." He arched a brow at Darcy. "Why do I think that's not correct?"

Darcy's face flushed. "Ah—"

Clyde clicked off the TV. "We need to go."

"We do?" Darcy blinked in surprise, then one look at his face had any argument she might have made vanishing. "Okay. If you come up with anything else, Jason, can you just text me?"

"Can do." Jason plucked the chip free of the reader, snapped it back into place and clicked the fob encasement closed once more. Darcy glanced behind her as Clyde opened the office door and stepped out. "Darcy? Everything okay?" Jason asked.

"Yeah, great. Fine." Darcy flashed him a smile.

"Okay." Jason's tone shifted into one of caution as he handed her the fob. "Darcy." He caught her arm when she went to move away. "What's going on? This isn't about some online scavenger game. Are you in trouble? Is he—?"

"He's a friend," Darcy assured him. "And he needs my help. Thanks for the information." She rose up and kissed Jason's cheek. "Tell Kyla I'll be in touch, okay?"

"I will. Oh, I'll tell Kyla all that and more." Jason called out to her as she followed Clyde downstairs and through the back door.

"What's going on? What happened?" Darcy hurried to catch up with Clyde.

"I'll tell you in the car. Get in." The clipped tone was so different than anything else he'd used with her before, and she hesitated, freezing in the middle of the parking lot. Was this the real Clyde? Terse, commanding. And just a little bit scary. But when he looked back at her, she also saw concern and a hint of fear on his face. He seemed to collect himself, then returned to her, touched a hand to her arm. "Second thoughts about sticking with me?"

Second. Third. Tenth. Something had happened in the last minute that shifted the fun and games straight into reality and…uncertainty. She stood there debating her options. Stay where she was safe with her friends or go with him into the adventure of the unknown.

"It's okay." Clyde moved closer. "I understand, Darcy." He caught her face in his hands and brushed his lips across her forehead, then, after seemingly debating with himself, pressed his mouth to hers.

It didn't last long, his kiss, if she could even call it that. But her life, for that moment, rocketed into the stratosphere. "I've got it from here on out," he murmured. "But I am going to have to borrow your car."

Unable to deny him, she dug her free hand into her pocket and passed him her keys. "Clyde," she whispered as he flashed her a grateful smile and hurried over to the car.

Something inside of her shifted. She waited for the fear, the dread and the worry to descend, but none of it came. Instead, she felt herself filled with an unexpected burst of excitement and hope.

Along with the absolute certainty that letting him go could very well be her biggest regret.

Clyde started the engine.

Darcy opened her mouth to call out and took a step forward as he put the car into reverse.

"Darcy!" Jason hollered from the open doorway as he slammed out of the bar. "Darcy, come back inside. Now!"

His tone jolted Darcy out of her trance. "Wait!" she called and dived forward to slap a hand on the back of her car. The SUV jerked to a stop. "Clyde, wait!"

She gave in and rushed to the passenger side, then looked back at Jason running toward her, cell phone in hand. "I'll be okay," she shouted to him. "I know what I'm doing!" Without a second look at the man behind the wheel, she jumped into the car and slammed the door shut. "Drive," she ordered as Clyde stared at her. "Before I change my mind."

"Where are we going?" Darcy asked.

"No idea." All he knew was that he needed to get

away and go someplace where he could think and figure things out. Work on bringing back memories that could answer every question he had. Maybe another bash on the skull would fix it. He was beginning to feel desperate enough to try. He hit the turn signal, looked at the street signs, swore and drove through another light. "What's with all the one-way streets in this city?"

"They're mainly in midtown," Darcy said in an overly calm voice. "Turn right, up here, head back to J Street, and that'll take us toward my place. Are you going to fill me in? Because I have maybe five minutes before my phone starts blowing up."

"My face is all over the local news. Artist sketch." He indicated the thin scar over his left eyebrow. "They got all the details. Including my name."

"Well, there's a silver lining. What is it?"

"Riordan. Riordan Malloy." He'd hoped, upon hearing himself say it, that it would somehow click everything else into place, but learning his name had done nothing more than add to his growing frustration.

Darcy reached over and covered one of his hands with hers. She squeezed and smiled when he glanced at her. "It's a nice name. It's no Clyde, of course—"

"I'm wanted for questioning."

"For what?" She snorted. "Arboreal hit and run?"

"Cute." He smirked. He took the turn she suggested, eased up on the gas so as not to attract attention, then cringed at her expectant look. "Apparently I'm a murder suspect."

"Murder." She blinked as if trying to process the information. "Oh. Okay. That's…unexpected."

Riordan chuffed out a breath. He wasn't so sure. Honestly, seeing his image flash across the screen along with the sketchy details hadn't come as a complete surprise. But the news provided enough of a jolt to know they couldn't stick around her PI friend's office. They had to get out of sight and fast. But how did they do that and find out what had happened to him? "I just need some time to decide what to do next."

"I promise you can trust my friends," Darcy said again. "I can call Cole and Jack. I know they—"

"Can't do that. Not now." He shook his head. "The man I'm suspected of killing was a staff sergeant with the Air Force." Jay Russo. The name meant absolutely nothing to him. "There's nothing your friends can do if it's a military investigation."

She frowned, sat back in her seat. "Hmm, I guess you're right. Turn left here. This'll take us straight home. We're going to figure this out."

No, *they* weren't. He'd been relieved back at the parking lot when she'd nearly stayed behind. It was bad enough he was stuck in this mess. Dragging Darcy down with him was only going to get her hurt, and he didn't want that. It left him with only one option.

He needed to get her someplace safe, then disappear. Somehow…someway…

"I was wrong." Darcy held up her ringing cell phone that displayed the name Kyla on the screen. "It only took three minutes." Instead of answering, she declined the call. "Jason didn't waste any time contacting her. She knows my license plate number, and she's got half the Sac metro police department on speed dial."

So, continuing to use her car was fast becoming a nonoption.

"Maybe you should have answered," he told her. "Buy us some time?"

"Not a good idea. I can't lie to her. I mean it," she said quickly when he winced. "She knows when I'm doing it. She's a great lawyer and I'm horrible at it."

"Not going to argue that last point."

"Ha ha. But maybe you're right. If she can't reach me, she's going to think even worse things about you."

"Worse than me being a murderer?"

"It's all relative, isn't it? Kidnapping versus murder. I mean, if you look at the two—"

"Let's not."

"Right. Babbling. Sorry." She took a deep breath. "I'll call her as soon as we get to my apartment. That'll give me a little time to come up with a believable story."

He tried to concentrate on the road, hoping it would be a perfect distraction. Like there was anything believable she could come up with to explain her helping him.

His mind shifted, and for an instant, he had a clear memory of a number. So clear the image had him slipping his foot off the break while at a stop sign. He caught himself before he collided with another vehicle.

"Hey!" Darcy reached over and grabbed the wheel. The flash of memory was gone. "What's going on? You okay? It's your head, isn't it? I knew you'd done too much too soon. Come on. Pull over there." She pointed to an empty street. "I'll take over."

"No." He needed to do this, needed to push through,

and he needed to stay behind the wheel, so his getaway was easier for both of them. "No, we're almost there. Sorry. There are these numbers—"

"What numbers?" she demanded. "Tell me." She got her phone out again, opened her notes app and waited while he recited them.

"Maybe it's a phone number?" she said, examining them. "I don't recognize this area code, though. Want me to try—"

"Not now." He certainly didn't want her making a potentially dangerous call from her own cell. All these tidbits of information were flying at him like glass shards in the air, but rather than landing with force, they skimmed by. He couldn't quite catch the fragments but longed to piece them together. Likely the only thing he possessed that could give him the answers he needed was sitting in a bag of uncooked rice on her kitchen counter.

"How do you feel about me watching the newscast?" Her fingers hovered over her cell.

He hated the idea. The possibility of her losing even a fraction of the faith she'd shown in him made him feel slightly ill. "Like it would be the responsible thing for you to do." He hated the idea of Darcy believing— even for one second—that he was a murderer.

Except…he very well could be.

"Watch it," he said, then cringed as she searched for the link and hit play.

"Authorities are urging all residents in the Sacramento area to be on the lookout for this man, a person of interest in the killing of an undercover federal agent.

Details of the crime have not yet been made available to us, but investigators are asking for the media and public's help in locating him. If you've seen him, please contact…"

Darcy scoffed and clicked off her phone.

"What? Didn't like my picture?"

"The number they listed? It's for Major Crimes. That's Jack and Cole's department." She started chewing on her thumbnail. "You were right. It's too late to call them for help without putting you right in the middle of it."

"You do realize it's entirely possible I'm guilty." He wasn't. He could feel it. But what he felt and what he could prove were two vastly different things.

"Uh-huh." She shrugged off the notion. "I'd say maybe fifty-fifty, which leaves it half right that you're innocent."

He paused. He couldn't be certain but he was fairly sure he'd never met anyone like Darcy Ford before. She just kept swimming, didn't she? It didn't matter what got thrown in front of her, she kept going.

"I don't need protecting," he told her. "I just need some time to try to get the pieces to fit."

"Then we'll get you some time. Hang on. I need to text Kyla and let her know I'm all right." She lifted her phone and, fingers flying, sent a text.

"Anyone could text her pretending to be you," he told her.

"I know. And so does Kyla." She waited for a response, feet tapping on the floorboard. "I told her to ask me a question only I'd know the answer to." The swooping beep echoed in the car. "And there it is." She shook her head, a healthy pink flooding her cheeks. "I swear I'm never going to live this one down."

"What did she ask?"

"My favorite clown." She typed with a bit more force this time. "For the record, I don't have one." She shuddered, then breathed a sigh of relief. "Okay, she's backing off. For now. But I have to text her again in an hour. You know, so she's sure you haven't dropped my body in a ditch somewhere."

"Ditch, right. Got it."

She shoved her hands in her hair and gave it a hard tug. "The last place she'd expect me to go at this point is my apartment." She pointed to the familiar building on their right. "Let's get in, I'll pack a bunch of things and get your phone and we'll go from there."

"Okay." She had her plan. He had his.

While he had no idea if he was a spiritual man, he felt safe in assuming his hopes that his cellphone could be salvaged were futile. He couldn't protect her against the danger, whatever it was, and he was not bringing her with him as long as his memory was a complete blank. He'd have to take it on faith that her police and lawyer friends would prevent her from being charged as an accomplice after the fact for giving him access to her vehicle.

His stomach hitched as he pulled into her assigned parking space. He looked around. Various cars in their spots; a few sedans and an SUV situated behind them. Hunched over the wheel, he looked up at her apartment window. "No sign of police. Anyone else have keys to your place?"

"Kyla and Ashley. Oh, and Greta Renault, but she's in Los Angeles this week for an art exhibit. You like art?"

He looked at her, marveling. "How do you do that? Think along multiple tracks at once?"

"It's a gift." Her flash of a smile thawed out his cold insides. "You coming?" She pointed at the building.

"I'll wait here."

Her eyes narrowed. "You don't wait, remember?" She leaned over, caught his chin in her hand and turned his face toward her.

How, with everything that was going on, could his impulse be to kiss her again? Because he knew what it was like to taste temptation and have it haunt him. Kissing Darcy had settled everything around him while kick-starting everything inside of him. It was as if he'd been a stalled engine waiting to be ignited, and Darcy Ford was the switch.

"Clyde. Riordan." She looked into his eyes, inclined her head just a touch. "Don't start lying to me. Not now."

"I'm not—"

"Good." She suddenly snatched the key out of the ignition. "Then you won't mind me taking this." She dived out of reach when his hands came up. "Come with me or stay here, your choice. But you're stuck with me. We're going to get to the bottom of this. Together. I need about fifteen minutes, tops. Clean underwear, jeans, better shoes. Warm clothes, just in case we get caught out…" Her self-mutterings faded as she retrieved her backpack and hurried to the stairs to take them two at a time.

He sat there, staring up at her window, shaking his head, even as his almost-kissed lips twitched. Darcy Ford was an unexpected force of nature, who had tornadoed her way into his empty life.

Watching her pull her house key from her pocket, he noticed movement in the window, which had him jolting up straight. Had he just seen…?

There it was again. Too clear to be his imagination.

Someone was in her apartment.

Chapter 5

Darcy could have sworn she heard her name as she closed her apartment door behind her. She hesitated, hand on the knob and frowned. She didn't hear it again, so she shrugged it off, tossed her keys, phone and bag onto the nearby table and headed along the short hallway to the kitchen.

"Darcy!"

As she spun toward Riordan's shouting, two gloved hands locked around her throat from behind. She gasped for breath as she was dragged back. Instinct and training kicked in. She threw her weight into the person, who stumbled, preventing them from cutting off her air.

Her front door burst open, banging against the wall with a solid thud. Even though her vision was blurred, the frame was filled completely with Riordan, a distraction she used to her advantage. She reached up, locked her hands around her attacker's wrists and squeezed. When his grip loosened, she clawed and ripped off one of his gloves.

Using the full force of her body weight, she hit hard and followed it immediately with an elbow to the chin.

As she backed away from the person's reach, a second figure moved toward her from the bedroom, but she barely had a chance to register anything about the figure before Riordan grabbed her arm and pushed her out of danger and then instantly landed a solid punch that sent attacker number two flying.

Riordan pivoted, following Darcy's attack with a right hook to the first person's jaw and a fist into his sternum. The man doubled over as Riordan landed one more upper cut that sent the guy sprawling. Limbs flailing, he knocked over a duffel bag that had been on her dining room table. The man and the bag hit the floor hard.

Attacker number two righted himself, crouched and paused as if evaluating his options.

He went for Riordan, who caught him with a roundhouse kick straight to the temple. The man flipped once in the air before hitting the ground face-first.

"You okay?" Riordan strode up to her and looked deeply into her eyes. "Darcy?"

"Yeah, I'm—look out!"

Her first attacker dived at Riordan and side-tackled him to the floor. They landed in one huge heap. Darcy darted to stay out of the way. She was too late, though. The intruder who was still grappling with Riordan took an extra beat to kick out and catch her behind the knees.

Her feet flew out from under her.

She hit the dec and groaned. She didn't just see stars. She saw planetary explosions.

Darcy rolled onto her side, trying to get her breath back, while around her, the harsh sound of fists meeting flesh struck her ears. Darcy saw both figures stumble to their feet and lunge out the door.

"No! Don't go after them!" she called at Riordan, who looked like a lion poised to strike his prey. "Just... we've got that." She waved a hand in the direction of the bag and pointed to the dropped glove. "And that. Let them go. Ah, man, that smarts." She rubbed a hand against the back of her head as the sound of tires screeching erupted. "Somewhere Curtis Malkah is screaming, 'I told you so,' and he has no idea why."

"What's that you're saying?" Riordan was looking at her with a confused expression.

"My Krav Maga instructor. He always said I was easily distracted. Guess he was right." She swiped a hand across her forehead. "I'm okay," she insisted when she saw the question poised on his lips. "Or at least, I will be." Eventually.

Her mind circled back to the men in her apartment. Black cargo pants, black T-shirt, short-cropped hair, tattooed forearms. Darcy hesitated, frowned at Riordan. "You guys must shop at the same stores." She didn't want to know the answer. She didn't want to think that her apartment had been, for want of a better term, violated. "How did you know what was happening?"

"I saw one of them through the curtains." There was that tone again. The intense one that made her shiver yet was perfectly in sync with his noble actions.

He knew how to fight. He knew how to defend himself and how to protect her. And after doing both, he didn't have a scratch or bruise on him that she could see.

"What's in that bag, anyway?" She advanced on the duffel, but Riordan caught her arm. "What?"

"It's a kill bag." He imparted the information so effortlessly it had to be second nature. Something so engrained it overrode his lack of memory where other aspects of his life were concerned.

"A—what? You made that up." Darcy's cell vibrated on the table. Irritated, assuming it was Kyla calling again, she stalked over, then bit her lip as she saw the screen name. "Ah, shoot."

"Who is it?"

"Mr. Vanderly from downstairs." She took a deep breath and tried to calm her racing pulse. When she answered, she may as well have been painted with sunshine and roses. "Hey, Mr. Vanderly. Sorry about all the noise."

"Land's sake, young lady. You just about gave me a heart attack! Snuffles here's howling up a storm." Mr. Vanderly's chiding tone brought tears to her eyes. "Thought I was back in San Fran during Loma Prieta with all that ceiling rattling. Can't believe you didn't come crashing through to land in my sink. Everything okay?"

"Fine. Everything's fine," she said for both his and

Riordan's benefit. "Just moving some furniture around." Darcy frowned. She hated that the lies were coming easier now. "I think we're done. Thanks for checking on me."

Riordan picked up the intruders' bag and set it on the table as she said goodbye and hung up. Her curiosity surged. Exactly what went into a kill bag? Chills raced up her arms at the silent question. And at the terrifying realization. "They were here to kill me?"

"Not immediately." Riordan popped open a solid plastic case and pulled out a vial of clear liquid. "They were going to ask you questions first. Scopolamine."

She stepped closer and punched down the horrified panic climbing into her throat. "You can't be serious—" She didn't finish that thought, since his look confirmed he absolutely was serious. "That's...vile."

"Its initial use was as a truth serum. Abused by military, dark ops, that kind of thing. It can make people do anything, even things they wouldn't normally do. In high doses, it can have hallucinogenic effects. It can also block a person's memory from the time it's administered to when they wake up."

She eyed him. "You seem to know a lot about it."

"Yes." Riordan frowned. "I do, don't I?"

"What on earth do I know that's worth someone injecting me with that?" Darcy asked.

"It's not what. It's who."

And the who was him. Had to be.

"Darcy, you don't seem to be the kind of person who'd have enemies."

He'd reached the same conclusion.

"The better question might be what do I know that they're this desperate to use you to find me?" he told her. The facade of fun and games that had cracked in the parking lot of the Brass Eagle now shattered completely, allowing doubt and logic to creep in. What on earth was he involved in? Had she made a massive mistake getting into the car with him at Jason's?

She stared at the mess in her apartment, the panic subsiding as a wave of fear surged. Mistake or no, she was in this, and whether Riordan Malloy wanted to admit it or not, he needed her. "We have to get out of here."

"I do." Riordan tossed the vial case into the bag and zipped it up. "What you need to do is call the police and get all this on record. You need to tell them what you know about me. They'll keep you safe."

"No." She shook her head. "No, if I do that I'll…" She almost said, *I'll never see you again.* That could have been utterly mortifying. But she didn't like the idea of him disappearing out of her life. Not yet, at least. "I'll never get any answers to this mystery of yours, and if there's one thing I can't stand, it's an unsolved mystery. Besides," she added, spying his arched brow. "You don't know this city. You don't have anyone else you can trust other than me. You need me."

"I'm a big boy." For the first time, his tone struck her as irritated. "Would you like me to explain in exact detail precisely what those men had planned for you because of me?" He hefted the bag as if it were full of tempting treats rather than a traveling torture chamber.

"Not really, no." She attempted to play it off blithely,

but the crack in her voice gave her away. "Ditching me now doesn't make any sense. You're a wanted fugitive. You can't go anywhere without taking the chance you'll be recognized and turned in, and I'm betting if that happens, you'll never find out what all you're involved in."

He slung the bag over his shoulder.

"And just to argue the point." She took a breath as her thought process kept churning. "If I did go to the cops, what makes you think that gives me some kind of protection? It's not like they're going to put me in WITSEC because I dragged you out of the river. They'll question me, then let me come back here. Alone." She leaned in, narrowed her gaze. "Is that what you really want to happen?"

"You're hurt." He carefully touched the bump on her head. The concern on his face battled with the panic she could see circling behind those blue eyes of his. He cared. Whatever else she didn't know about him, she could see whoever the true man was in front of her. He was concerned about her. That made him ten times more human than the animals who had been lurking in her apartment. "You need to get checked out and run as far away from me as you can."

"I've had worse injuries roughhousing with my brothers," she insisted. "I'm tired of having this same argument. Let's take this a step at a time and say you're stuck with me, at least until we determine exactly what this whole thing is about and how you fit in? If the bump on my head worries you that much, there's an ice bag in the drawer next to the fridge. Feel free to fill it up and I'll use it. I'm going to grab some things."

Before he could argue, she made her way into the bedroom and pulled out one of her go bags she kept stashed in the bathroom closet along with the restocked first-aid kit. She also stopped long enough to drag her gun box out, grab one of the two emergency cell phones she kept with her diving equipment, the lanyard keychain, her laptop, and lastly, she unplugged her cell phone charger, which she also stuffed in her bag.

Riordan Malloy came with all kinds of questions, but one she couldn't quite shake was that arguing with him acted almost like an aphrodisiac. She could all but feel his testosterone surging as he attempted to reason with her—something few people ever had success with. No, sir, once Darcy got an idea—or worse, a plan—in her head, there was very little that was going to stop her from carrying it out.

The adrenaline rush from the home invasion made her feel both steadier and edgier. So much so that she stepped over bloodstains on her living room floor with barely a note of concern. Something to deal with later.

She found Riordan filling up the ice bag. The intruders' duffle still sat on the counter. The bag of rice with his damaged cell phone inside nearby. Curious, she opened the bag of rice.

"Don't bother," he said. "I already checked. It's still dead."

"Oh." Disappointment crashed through her. "Well, it'll probably just take a while is all." Hope seemed futile, but she wasn't giving up. Not yet. She dug through her pantry and dumped all the nonperishable snacks she could fit into her backpack. "You ready?"

"No. I should lock you in a closet so you're safe."

"If they're coming after me in my home, I'm not safe here." She inched up her chin. "Grab those—" she indicated the duffle and her gun box "—and let's go."

She pulled her front door closed behind them, cringing at the thought of the repair bill she'd be getting from the apartment manager. And that would be on top of losing her security deposit.

Darcy caught up with Riordan at her car, which still had the door open on the driver's side. He pointed to an empty space behind them, then down at the ground. "What's wrong," she asked him.

"There was a dark SUV parked right there, and there are tire marks there now." He looked at her car. "If they found out where you live, then they probably know what car you drive."

"Awesome," Darcy grumbled and dropped her bags on the ground. "Now what are we going to…do?"

Mr. Vanderly's door opened, and there he was, poking his head out first, his wide bulging eyes falling on her.

"Wait here," she ordered Riordan and hurried over to her neighbor. "Mr. Vanderly, hi. I'm having a super crazy day, and now my car's giving me some issues. Is there any chance I can borrow one of yours?"

"Okay, pull in here." Darcy pointed to one of the empty spots near slip twenty-four at the Crest View Marina just off the Garden Highway in Sacramento.

Riordan could quickly count the few vessels occupying slips, but the emptiness of the location would serve them well.

The ride had been interesting in that it gave him a tour of the central part of town as she guided him toward the outskirts and into the maze of roads that banked the waterways. He kept waiting for recognition to strike, but if he had some emotional tie to the city, it hadn't manifested itself in his memory. At least, not yet. If anything, his brain seemed to recognize he was more desperate for answers and had locked them up even tighter.

Once the engine went silent, he paused for a moment of what he supposed would pass as reverence. Memory or not, he recognized the perfection of a classic car like the one they'd borrowed from Mr. Vanderly. Riordan turned to look out the back window, resigned to being impressed by her spur-of-the-moment planning.

"First a pristine sixty-four Impala to drive and now a boat." The long cruiser bobbed in the gently lapping waves, its polished wood cabin a beautiful accent against the off-white color of the hull. "The *Cop Out*." He read the name on the side. "You're just full of surprises, aren't you? Next thing, you'll be telling me there's a helicopter around here somewhere that you can fly."

"No way, no how. I leave the flying to my friend Eamon. Not that I've ever gotten in a plane or chopper with him. I'm purely a land and sea woman." She also turned in her seat to look out the back window. "I remember Cole saying the marina empties out from December through March. Of people, anyway. Most of the boats are stored here for long term. Like the *Cop Out*."

"Your friend doesn't use it much?" Longing struck him square in the chest. "Seems a shame. It's a beauty of a boat."

"Cole would be happy to hear it being appreciated. He and Eden lived here together after they got married, but then she got pregnant with Chloe Ann."

"Ah." That made sense. A baby would require far more space than a boat would provide.

"There's a grocery store just a few miles away," Darcy said. "Once we get settled on board and we lose daylight, I'll hit it up for supplies."

"I don't suppose calling for a delivery makes sense." He eyed her suddenly sheepish expression. "Or are you looking for an excuse to drive this car?"

"Maybe." Her smile reminded him of a slot machine paying off, all bells, lights and sirens jangling inside of him. "She is a beauty." She touched light fingers against the dash as if afraid of waking the Impala up from a nap.

"I can't believe this thing still runs," he said.

"Guess you have an appreciation for automobiles deep in your psyche." Darcy chuckled. "Mr. Vanderly had a classic car dealership for more than forty years. He kept a few of his favorites after he retired. He has an entire storage unit filled with them. Thankfully, he doesn't drive that much, but he rotates them in and out of his parking space every few months." Her lips twitched. "They're named after his girlfriends."

"You don't say? What's this one called?"

"Sammy." She shrugged. "He said he'd tell me the story when we bring it back. Sorry it's a lot more cramped than my SUV, but on the bright side, this baby is old-school and can't be tracked."

Riordan chastised himself. He shouldn't have said anything back at her parking lot about the other car. If they'd taken her SUV, he'd have been able to count on her cop friends to track them and give her the opportunity to walk away. Now he was going to have to come up with another plan. The only thing left he could figure was for her friends to track her cell. As long as she didn't give that up, he could see a way out for her.

"Is it my imagination?" He reached for the ice bag she'd dumped on the floor and pressed it against the back of her head. "Or are you enjoying this situation of mine more than you should?" He tried to hold the bag in place, but she shoved his hand away. "Hey, leave it there," he ordered. "You might not be bleeding, but you've got a nasty bump."

"And I thought I was the one playing doctor," she grumbled. "I need to make that call. It's been an hour already." She sat back and, after glaring at him, used one hand to hold the bag and the other to dial.

"It's not too late to change your mind," he said for the umpteenth time. "I'm sure it wouldn't take long for your friend Kyla or—"

"I thought we decided you were going to stop tilting at that particular windmill, Don Quixote. Kyla, hey. Yeah, it's me." She let out a sigh that added an odd layer of guilt to his pile of uncomfortable emotions. "I'm fine. I promise, okay?" She shifted her hold on the ice bag. "Kyla, stop. No, please, I need you to stop and listen to me, okay? Don't ask me any questions. If there hasn't been a call to 911 yet, I need you to send Jack and Cole to my apartment. Oh? Really? How long will Cole be gone?" Her eyebrows went up and her expression brightened. "Then Jack and Bowie maybe. There's been…an incident." She winced. "No, I told you, I'm okay."

She glanced at Riordan, and he sent her his best "I told you so" expression. "He's fine, too," she added. "In fact, if it wasn't for him, you'd probably be getting a call from the coroner's office."

"That should convince her everything's fine." Riordan looked out his window, trying to pull any threads of information he could out of his locked brain. Frustration gnarled at him. He needed to remember. He needed to get his faculties back so he could get her out of his mess and back to her normal life.

He'd returned the favor of her saving his life back at the apartment. They were even. It should have been more than enough for him to break away and move on. And yet…

"There was a break-in at my apartment," Darcy told Kyla in an abbreviated explanation. "There should be a glove on the kitchen counter from one of them. I just wanted to give you a heads-up before I disappeared for a little while." She held the phone away from her ear. "I'm in the same state, Ky. There's no need to screech. I promised I wouldn't take off without talking to you first, so that's what I'm doing. And you need to stop asking me questions I won't answer. Anything I tell you, you'd be obligated to report either to the police or Simone and the DA. I'm not putting you in that position." She was quiet for a moment, shaking her head.

A new wave of guilt washed over Riordan. It was bad enough Darcy was involved in this chaos. Now her friends were getting caught up in it, too. This area was fairly desolate, not many people around. He reached out and grasped the door handle. He could easily disappear into the—

Darcy dropped the ice bag and yanked the keys out of the ignition. When he glared at her, she simply arched a brow, tucked the phone into her chest. "I can hear the wheels grinding in your head." She pointed the key at his nose. "You're not ditching me. Yes, I'm still here," she said to Kyla.

Shock registered first, followed by an unexpected flash of irritation, couched by an odd wave of gratitude. He hadn't even been looking at her, and she'd known what he was thinking? He didn't understand why it meant something to him not to be on his own, but it did.

"No, Kyla. That's not the case at all. He's not... Kyla, I'm not a child who needs coddling. I trust my instincts. I can't explain it, but..." She looked at him, those green eyes of hers filled with determination. "I trust him."

In that moment, it dawned on him that this woman, this stranger, had more confidence and faith in him than he had in himself. Whatever she saw in him, he needed to see it, too. Otherwise, neither of them would get out of his situation alive.

By the time he surfaced from his self-realization, she'd hung up.

"What are you doing?" he asked as she dragged her purse into her lap, dug around for what turned out to be a toothpick. She popped her cell phone case off, then wiggled the toothpick into the SIM card slot and pulled it free.

"Better safe than sorry." She stuck the phone and card into the empty glove compartment. "In case she tries to track me, she won't be able to. Let's go."

She was out of the car in a flash, leaving Riordan to circle around and help with the bags.

"You know this isn't a game, right, Darcy?" It was worth one more shot. "This isn't one of your books with a nice, tidy happily-ever-after ending. There's no telling where my past is going to lead us." Or how much it was going to hurt her.

"Why does everyone assume I'm incapable of rational thought?" She shifted her backpack onto one shoulder and slammed the back door. "I told Kyla and now I'm telling you, for the last time, I know what I'm doing. I am exactly where I want to be. Understand?"

"I'm just saying you should walk away now."

She raised up her chin and looked directly into his eyes. "Is that what you really want me to do?"

Want? No. But maybe...

"The amount of time we're wasting arguing about me helping you could be better spent looking into who you are. What you are." Her expression, for the first time, unreadable. "Those men in my apartment. You're convinced they would have killed me once they got whatever answers they thought I have."

The question was asked so matter-of-factly he didn't even consider lying. "Yes."

She nodded. "They spent enough time in my apartment to learn a heck of a lot about me, including who my friends are. You saw the photographs all over the place, I'm sure."

"I did."

"I'm not putting anyone else in danger. If going along with this to help you isn't enough of a motivator, then I'll do it because I'm protecting them. Kyla and Jason, they're just starting their lives together. Allie and Simone are both pregnant, and the last thing Ashley needs is to get dragged into another…situation. If I go home, some, if not all of them are going to hover, and if those jerks think I know something—"

"All right." Riordan cut her off before she fully got going. Once again, she was proving her mind worked at twice the speed of his. He'd bet good money she'd been thinking this argument through ever since they left the Brass Eagle.

But she was right. The only thing he could do to stop whatever was going on was to uncover the truth. And it wasn't something he could do alone. "All right, you win. You've convinced me. But keep this in mind. There will come a time I'll have to leave you behind. No more games, no more fun arguments and witty banter. The time will come and I won't hesitate. Especially if it means keeping you safe."

She sighed and tilted her head back. "So dramatic."

"Men came to your apartment with weapons and a purpose." He punctuated every syllable of every word. "They did it in broad daylight, which meant their motivation was strong enough for them to risk being seen. There will come a time, Darcy. I need to know that you understand that. And I need you to promise me you'll do it—leave, whatever—when that happens."

"Sounds like a roundabout way of telling me you need me." Her attempt at humor, this time, fell flat. "If it means we can stop wasting time arguing about it, fine. I get it. So…" She cleared her throat and shrugged. "Moving on—"

"Not yet." He leaned in and slipped his arms around her, then ducked his head so that his mouth met hers. Her gasp of surprise felt—and tasted—delicious and confirmed what he'd first suspected in the parking lot when he thought he would be saying goodbye. This woman was like an intoxicating jolt of energy that bolted straight through his system and ignited every dormant cell he possessed.

She sagged as if his touch had sapped all of her strength, until she reached up and slid her arms up and around his neck. She held on as he slanted his mouth, pressed her lips open and dived in.

There was nothing to his life, to his mind, to his memory before Darcy. In this moment, as he kissed her, as she kissed him back with a desperation he willingly mirrored, the answers didn't matter. All he cared about was the woman in his arms.

The woman who, from the instant she'd pulled

him out of the frigid river, had stayed by his side, unwavering.

"Wow," she murmured when he lifted his mouth and brushed a gentle finger down the side of her face. She rocked back on her heels and gazed at him. "Okay, that could very well complicate a few things moving forward." She drew her hand down his arm until she threaded her fingers through his. "I have one question, in particular, we should probably focus on."

"What's that?" He liked the way her eyes darkened when she was thinking, as if tiny storm clouds were brewing out over the water.

"Whether you're married or not."

"Married." He echoed the word, frowning at the feel of it on his tongue. "No." He shook his head. "No, that doesn't sound remotely right."

"Hmm." She twisted his hand a bit, dropped her gaze to his fingers. "No ring. Or any sign that you've worn one previously. No tan lines or markings. What about your tattoos?" Her eyebrows arched. "Nothing triggered any memories to do with them?"

"No." He hoped his declaration would be enough to prevent a full body search. Because her being that close to him wouldn't uncomplicate what was already a very complicated situation. "It might be safer to start with an internet search on my case and the man I'm accused of killing."

"Spoilsport." But there was a jangle of nerves in her tone. "It was worth a shot. Come on." She produced a lanyard with keys and sorted through them as she walked. "Let's just hope Cole's still got his Wi-Fi working on this boat."

Chapter 6

Out of an overabundance of caution, Darcy waited until dark before she headed out for food. Using the key that Cole had given her for boat-sitting the *Cop Out* felt close to an abuse of trust, but being on the water was a good place for her to be. Plus, it meant she and Riordan were isolated enough, in theory, that they'd hear anyone approaching.

She thought once Cole was back from his law enforcement conference, and she and Riordan—it still seemed odd to know his real name—were on the other side of whatever was going on with him, she'd apologize to her friends. In spades. Cole and Eden's daughter was getting to the age when she could begin swimming lessons. Darcy would work something out with the detective and his wife to make up for her deception and intrusion.

She didn't possess quite the same reverence for Mr. Vanderly's Impala as Riordan, especially as it drove a lot heavier and clunkier than her SUV. But as she got onto the Garden Highway and headed toward one of the strip malls a few miles away, she had to admit there was something magical about the vehicle. Almost as if it had its own personality. It was like having somebody with her as she slipped into the night.

She'd left Riordan on the *Cop Out* with her laptop, a slightly hinky internet connection and the backpack full of snacks. Detective Cole Delaney being who he was, maintained a substantial bottled water supply onboard and kept the vessel tidy and clean so he could loan it out to his friends. Hearing from Kyla that the detective was out of town for a few days had definitely taken some of the pressure off. For now.

She'd checked her email obsessively over the past few hours, waiting for word from Kyla regarding the glove's prints. The message had finally arrived, along with a strongly worded missive that let Darcy know Kyla had been filled in on some of the bloodied particulars of Darcy's apartment. Even in writing, Darcy could hear her friend's concern, but the note also carried the faith Darcy had requested and the promise to be available when—not if—Darcy and Riordan needed help.

"It's good to have friends," Darcy sang to herself as she pushed a cart filled with convenience items back to the car. She'd hit the jackpot of stores and grabbed not only dinner, fresh produce and several healthier eating choices, but also found a significant selection of clothing for her fugitive companion. It wasn't until she caught herself humming that she realized his accusation that she thought this was some kind of game hit home.

Darcy stood up straight, taken aback by the sudden admission that she was treating this more like an adventure than a threat on someone's life. Okay, being kissed into oblivion by the man certainly hadn't helped to keep her head straight and her thoughts clear. Honestly, how could she think at all after that? The man had moves. Moves she'd pretty much given up hope of ever experiencing.

How a man like him—strong in stature and presence, and borderline deadly—could have been so gentle boggled the mind. But it was a boggling she was more than happy to embrace.

The hair on the back of her neck prickled. She scanned the parking lot that was almost full. She'd been so distracted by what she and Riordan had accomplished so far, not to mention what came next that she hadn't paid much attention when she'd arrived. He was right. This wasn't a game, and she had to get her head out of the clouds, especially the romantic ones.

She shivered, ran her hands up and down her sweater-covered arms and swallowed hard.

The phone in her back pocket buzzed. She pulled out the pay-as-you-go cell and scanned Riordan's message asking where she was. She'd lost track of time and had taken far longer than the hour she'd planned. A short text back promised she was on her way, and she quickly got behind the wheel. He'd been right. Again. Not that she was going to tell him that, she thought with a grin. She'd keep that epiphany to herself.

Driving out of the parking lot, she left the sound system off and kept her eyes on her mirrors. It was late enough for the darkness to cover her, but it also meant it was more difficult to notice if anyone was following her.

That unease she'd felt before, however, didn't abate. A cold sweat broke out on her face as she gunned the borrowed car through a yellow light, watching to see if anyone blasted along behind her. She let out a shaky breath when headlights faded into the distance.

"You're being paranoid." Still, she silently counted off the minutes until she neared the marina. As she reached the turnoff, she shielded her eyes against the glare of the car coming up behind her. Closer and closer...

Fear leapt inside of her. Was this what had happened to Riordan? Had he been run off the road? Left for dead only to find his escape in the river?

She gripped the steering wheel and increased her speed. The car behind her did the same. But it didn't close in, didn't move, as if it were threatening her. Though whoever it was clearly wasn't letting her out of their sight.

If she'd been in her car, she could have called Riordan on her dashboard media system. Instead, she could feel the outline of her phone in her back pocket digging into her as she tried to keep her heart rate steady.

She took the turnoff at the last second, purposely

neglecting to hit the signal before she veered onto the exit. It had seemed like a good idea, except the trailing car slid right in behind her. Panic welled up. She couldn't take the chance of leading anyone to Riordan. Not until they got some answers. She blasted past the *Cop Out* and drove to the end of the marina, skidding into an empty parking spot just as the car behind her screeched to a stop.

Darcy was out of the car and racing toward the unfamiliar vehicle when the driver's door popped open and an unexpected female figure leapt out.

"I'm surprised you didn't drive yourself off the end of the pier."

Darcy skidded to a halt, lifted her hands to shield her eyes against the glare of headlights as the face came into focus. "Eden?"

"You'd best be glad it's me and not some maniacal burglar out to even a score." Eden St. Claire stalked forward, long strawberry blond hair flying around her shoulders currently covered with a slick burgundy leather jacket. "Have you learned nothing in the past few years? Sticking your nose into murder cases only brings trouble. And who taught you how to lose a tail? Oh, that's right. No one, apparently."

Darcy found herself feeling both relieved and furious. Did all her friends think her utterly incapable of embracing the unexpected? "What are you doing out here?" Darcy demanded. "How did you know—"

"Cole installed a silent security alarm on the boat a few weeks ago," Eden said. "After Kyla called me to say you were disappearing, and you've turned off your phone, I put two and two together."

"Kyla did what?"

"Please," Eden scoffed. "Like Kyla was just going to accept you going off with a wanted killer—"

"Don't say that." Darcy cut her off even as a shadow loomed behind her investigative reporter friend.

"I'm sorry." Eden didn't sound remotely apologetic. "Suspected killer."

"Eden—"

"Your friend isn't wrong." Riordan's voice cut through the night like a lightning bolt.

Eden jumped and spun around. Darcy couldn't help but be impressed with Riordan's stealth. It took a lot to surprise Eden St. Claire. But there he stood, Darcy's gun grasped in one hand and held down at his side.

"Darcy?" His quiet, intense voice sent a different type of shiver racing along her spine. "You okay?"

"I'm fine." Darcy let out a breath and gave in to the impulse to bend over to brace her hands on her thighs. She took a moment. "Eden St. Claire, this is Riordan Malloy. Riordan, this is Eden 'can't mind her own business' St. Claire."

"Cute, considering you're using my husband's boat as a hideout." Eden smirked as she gestured toward his weapon. "You didn't shoot first, so that's working in your favor, Malloy. You'll lose your bonus points though if the safety's on."

Darcy couldn't stifle the surge of pride at the click of the safety being reengaged.

"Well, that answers that."

"Answers what?" Darcy asked Eden. Exhaustion was beginning to take over, and the impulse to just lock herself in a berth on the boat sounded beyond thrilling.

"He came out of hiding to check on you." Eden motioned for her to open the trunk and, as if in a show of faith, turned her back on Riordan. "He's protective and not in a self-serving way. Works in his favor. Come on. Jason filled me in on that missing car of yours." She waved him over the rest of the way. "Help unload and then we'll park closer to the *Cop Out*. You got dinner in there, Darcy? Chloe Ann's giving Allie and Max some toddler practice tonight, and my freezer's empty."

"I might have stocked up."

"Awesome." Eden hefted a bag out of the trunk and knocked it into Riordan's chest. "Boy, you're a big one, aren't you?" She looked up at him, narrowed her eyes. "Did you kill that Air Force sergeant?"

Darcy froze, all the questions flying through her mind coming to a dead stop.

"I don't know." Riordan's answer sent chills racing through Darcy.

She hurried to explain. "He's got—"

"Amnesia, yep. Kyla mentioned it," Eden said. "Thought that only happened in those books of yours," she told them. "After I talked with Jason, I stopped at the forensics lab and had a conversation with Tammy before I headed over this way. About the glove in your apartment," she said when Darcy started to ask for information. "We'll talk about it inside. By the way, when this is all over, I'm giving you a crash course in surveillance from both sides. Honestly, Darcy. I've been

trailing you since you left the marina two hours ago."
She shook her head as she walked to her car. "Makes
me feel as if I've failed as a parent."

"You're only six years older than me!" Darcy yelled
after her but received only a wave of dismissal in response. Eden climbed into her vehicle, hit Reverse and
stopped in front of the *Cop Out*.

"She seems nice," Riordan said, that hint of humor
returning to his voice.

"Yeah, so do Velociraptors, at first." Darcy shooed
him back to the boat. "I need to get the car... I'll just...
I'll be there in a second." She waited until he was on
his way before she slid behind the wheel and, resting
her forehead on it, let herself shake off the panic, and
wonder, honestly, for the first time what she'd gotten
herself into.

Back belowdeck, Riordan stood over the polished
table and stared down at the hard plastic case that had
stored Darcy's gun. Every minute Darcy had been gone
felt like an eternity. Not because he missed her, although he found that he did, but considering his current situation and that more than a few people knew
she was linked to him...

It felt like a minor miracle she'd returned to the
boat unharmed.

What had he been thinking, letting her go off on her
own? The speed with which she'd been traced to her
apartment meant they were dealing with professionals, albeit professionals who needed a serious refresher
course in self-defense. Getting her text apologizing for

taking so long had loosened some of the knots tightening in his gut, but it wasn't until he'd seen her headlights that he let go of the anxiety.

Until the second pair of lights appeared and triggered his nerves again.

His hand tightened around the semiautomatic. The Glock 22 had been stored properly without its clip and without a round in the chamber. It had taken him only seconds to load the weapon before he climbed the stairs at a practiced yet rapid pace. Second nature, he'd thought at the time. Instinctive and automatic.

The sense of calm had been a surprise. He didn't have any idea what he was going to come up on, but he'd moved effortlessly, carefully, as if his body knew exactly what it was doing despite having no frame of reference. He'd been in situations like this before.

He knew what to do.

"You know weapons." Eden, a tablet tucked under one arm, descended the steep stairs with ease.

She was taller than Darcy, not quite as curvy and displayed an alarming amount of confidence. Her eyes were sharp, assessing and, near as he could tell, incapable of hiding anything she was feeling. Or thinking. Skepticism blanketed her face and coated every word that came from her lips. No doubt in his mind she still considered him suspicious.

"You held that like a pro," she continued. "Finger on the side, not on the trigger. Barrel down until you identified a threat." She set her tablet on the table before heading into the spacious galley style kitchen to unload the groceries he'd brought inside.

"What kind of pro?" He didn't unload the gun when he set it back in the box. He didn't want to waste precious seconds next time. And there was going to be a next time.

"That is the million-dollar question. Still." Eden shrugged out of her jacket and hung it on a hook, then, making sure he was watching, she pulled her own weapon out of the back of her waistband, held it up, barrel facing away, and set it down. "Good habits tell a lot about a person."

"You came prepared." *To defend Darcy*, he thought and immediately shifted Eden further into the ally column. "You were worried about her."

"I saw pictures of her apartment after the fact." Ice rose in her gaze. "Yes, I was worried. And as I've had a little experience with the more violent side of unexpected events, I know how easy it is to get swept up in something like this. This is my husband's backup piece. Glad I didn't have to use it on you," she said with a slight smile. "Otherwise, I'd have some serious explaining to do when he gets back from his conference. You might want to relax before you sprain something, Malloy. Maybe breathe a little?"

Easier said than done. His lungs both ached and burned. It didn't feel as if he'd taken a full breath since he'd woken up in Darcy's bed. "I don't think that's possible."

"Mmm." Eden arched a brow and moved on to the next bag. "Rotisserie chicken and mac and cheese. Yum." She set the two containers down. "Knowing Darcy, there's some green stuff in here, too. Yep. Salad.

We'll just put that over here." She dropped the two bags of lettuce into the sink and grinned. "Oops."

His lips twitched. "My handling of Darcy's gun tell you anything else about me?"

"Like what?" She pulled plates out of one of the cabinets, retrieved flatware and motioned for him to clear off the table.

"Like whether I belong to the light or dark side of the Force."

"Anyone who can reference one of my favorite movie franchises can't be completely untrustworthy." Darcy made her way down the stairs with a handful of plastic bags and set them on the floor by the front berth. Without missing a beat, she joined them in the kitchen and rescued the lettuce bags from exile.

Eden snorted. "Since I can feel your anxiety from over there, this is from Jason." She handed him a manila envelope. "It's the rental and travel history on that car you asked him to trace." She eyed Darcy. "Good reason to turn your phone back on. So you can receive messages."

Darcy grimaced. "Excellent way to track us, too."

"Now why didn't I think of that?" Eden grinned. "According to Jason, the car you have the keys to hasn't left the rental agency lot in more than four weeks. Officially, obviously, considering its last signal bleeped last night at eleven fourteen right here in Sac. That around the time you crashed?"

Riordan glanced at Darcy, who confirmed with a nod.

"The timing fits," she said. "Can a crash disable GPS?"

"Depending on where it's located in the car," Eden replied. "But it can also be disabled with something as simple as aluminum foil being wrapped around it or, as a last resort, removing it."

"More likely, whoever retrieved the car is using a jammer. Easier than dismantling it." Riordan's observation was greeted by silence. He glanced up from the contract displaying a photocopy of his license along with his signature. "What?"

"You have selective amnesia then." Eden retrieved her tablet, tapped it on and handed it to him. "Maybe this will help jog something loose in your noggin. Darcy, tell me you got—"

"Beer." Darcy held up a bottle then clutched it against her chest as if having second thoughts. "What if he's in recovery?"

"I'm not." He glanced up from the screen. "This is my military record. No way I've moved this far up command with an addiction issue." He frowned when Eden braced her feet apart and held out her arms like someone learning to surf. "What are you doing? Some weird boat ritual?"

"In a way," Darcy answered for her friend, with a glint of amusement in her eyes.

"Pregnancy test." Eden moved from side to side. "Cole and I are working on baby number two. Considering how seasick I got with Chloe Ann from the get-go…" She sighed. "I think we're in the clear." She accepted the bottle Darcy held out. "Speaking of clear." She jerked her chin toward the tablet. "Anything coming back for you?"

Darcy circled around behind Riordan, rested her hands on his shoulders in a way that had him feeling oddly protected.

"Nothing beyond what I see in the mirror," he said.

"Army," Darcy observed as she looked through the file. "Nice dress uniform. Very snazzy. Almost doesn't look like you without the beard."

"Thought you'd appreciate that." Eden put food on the table. "Definitely better than a clown costume. I'll email that to you for future reference, Darcy. Meanwhile, the long story short is Riordan Malloy currently resides in Georgia, is second generation career military, served two tours in Afghanistan, has multiple commendations and citations." She shifted her gaze to him. "You're originally from Texas and are the only child of deceased parents."

"Oh, I'm sorry," Darcy murmured.

Riordan paused, waiting for something—any kind of emotion—to come storming back, but hearing the details of his life did nothing other than add to his questions.

"You've never been married," Eden said. "You don't have any kids, at least not that the Army knows about. And, as of two years ago…" She shrugged.

"As of two years ago what?" Darcy asked.

"Nothing." Eden's eyes hardened. "Nada. Zip. And when I pushed for more info, I was shut down."

"That's probably part of what's been redacted." The black lines didn't surprise him, but they did disappoint. He was so tired of the uncertainty, of the emptiness.

How was it he could look at the details of his life and feel no connection to them? To himself?

"This is all I could get out of one of my contacts with the secretary of the Army's office," Eden said. "Nothing I have here is going to set off any alarm bells, but there's more to your situation than he was willing to share. He also said to leave it alone, which I'm translating to mean you were probably working on something only very few people know about."

Riordan had to agree. He might not know Eden, but he knew his gut instinct, and he certainly wasn't inclined to argue with her or the information she'd gathered.

"I can make more inquiries elsewhere," Eden offered. "But if I keep digging—"

"Don't," Riordan insisted. "At least, not now. I don't want you getting involved in this. Not any more than you have already."

"You didn't read that file right, Malloy." Eden's gaze sharpened. "You're the one who takes orders, not me."

"That's not how he meant it, Eden," Darcy said.

"Yes, it was." Riordan set the tablet down. "Darcy, you're the one who said it wasn't safe to go to your friends and ask for help, especially after what happened at your apartment. You wanted to protect them, so that's what we're going to do." He turned his gaze on Eden. "You have a lot more at risk than Darcy does, Eden, not the least of which is your daughter. There's also your husband's career, not to mention your well-being. I'm not worth it."

He didn't have to see Darcy's face to know she

disagreed. He could feel her disapproval in how she squeezed his shoulders.

"That's so sweet." Eden brushed away an imaginary tear before she rolled her eyes. "But for the record, I don't find martyrdom remotely appealing. Just to cut to the chase, since you've gotten involved with Darcy—"

"We're not involved," Riordan snapped in a way that had Darcy snatching her hands back.

"All right." Eden's overactive brow arched again. "Rephrasing. You've got Darcy involved in whatever situation this is of yours, therefore you get all of us." She shifted her surprisingly sympathetic gaze to Darcy. "You're family. You've been there for us when we needed you, and besides, Chloe Ann would never forgive me if something happened to her favorite babysitter."

"That's me," Darcy said with more than a hint of bitterness in her voice. "Baby and pet-sitter extraordinaire. Now we can add 'military amnesiac' to my specialty list."

Riordan resisted the urge to flinch. Clearly there were issues Darcy needed to deal with.

"What about Vince?" Darcy asked. "Maybe he has useful contacts he could reach out to?"

Riordan gnashed his teeth together. "Apparently, people in this town have selective hearing."

"Not sure how much influence a Marine has with the Army," Eden said as if he hadn't spoken. "Even one as well respected as Vince, but it might be worth a—"

"No." Riordan shook his head. "I'm not certain about a lot of things right now, but we can all agree the fewer people asking questions about me, the better. For everyone's sake. If the Army is interested in tracking me down, I'm pretty sure they could. The fact they haven't released a statement or attempted to correct the news reports tells me they're biding their time." Or they'd written him off. Either way, it seemed he was on his own.

"What about the sergeant you're accused of killing?" Darcy asked. "What do we know about him?"

"Same rundown as I got on him," Eden pointed to Riordan. She claimed a seat and began to carve up the chicken. "Nothing stands out, apart from not a word being redacted in his file. Record's clean, steadily moved up the ranks, been at Travis Air Force Base for more than six years. Divorced, two kids. They and the ex moved to Kentucky three years ago. No red flags. Interesting tidbit," she continued as she served the chicken. "Major Crimes and Jack, in particular, have been notified their assistance is not necessary in the investigation. Side note, Darcy. Jack was not impressed with the security setup at your apartment, so he and Vince will be taking care of that once things have calmed down."

Darcy scrunched her mouth in clear disapproval as a wave of envy washed over Riordan. The one constant thought circling his brain was that he was someone who was used to being on his own. Solitary. A one-man band. As far as concepts, having friends, family, a support system and people to back you up no matter what, was one idea he had difficulty comprehending.

"The news hasn't reported much about Sergeant

Russo," Eden said. "Nothing about how or where he died. Only that Riordan is the primary suspect in his death."

"Sure got my sketch circulating in a hurry, though." Frustrating how every time he thought he'd found an answer, he also had more questions. "There's no mention of me being on active duty."

"No, there wasn't. Wait," Eden said as she dropped chicken onto a plate. "You aren't vegetarian or vegan are you?"

She really didn't buy the amnesia explanation, did she? "Really not on my list of things to worry about at the moment." His stomach rumbled, reminding him he'd neglected to eat anything of much substance all day. Heck, he was so hungry he could eat an entire flock of chickens. "Is it me or does it seem odd that my military history isn't being shared? I've got a good record as far as I can tell. How is it just a sketch and my name has been released and nothing official?"

"All good questions," Eden agreed. "And, no, you aren't an herbivore." She pointed to the way he dissected his half a chicken and took a bite. "I agree. The information being publicly shared seems purposeful and carefully edited. All the more reason for you to lie low—"

"I'm not lying anywhere for long," Riordan said. "I need to find out what I was working on before I went into the river. It must have been important enough for those two men to break into Darcy's apartment and wait for her." The thought of what might have happened ignited a fiery anger he doubted would ever be doused. He needed answers so she'd be safe. And that, if for no other reason, was motivation enough for him to keep going. "That reminds me, you said you got lab results on the glove we left behind at Darcy's place?"

"Right." Eden grimaced and pushed food around on her plate. "Odd, Darcy's intruder, well, one of them, is a dead man."

"Well, yeah, after the beating he took—" Darcy huffed.

"I don't think that's what she meant." A new pit of dread formed in the cavern of Riordan's belly. "Is it, Eden?"

"The prints in the glove belong to a Marcus Tate. Second lieutenant with eight years in the Army." Her gaze sharpened. "KIA eighteen months ago in Kabul. According to official records."

Riordan sat back in his chair, his mind spinning. What was going on?

"How is that even possible?" Darcy asked. "Obviously he's not dead."

"He's a ghost," Riordan clarified. "The other guy probably is, too. But the fact this Tate guy is military? That can't be a coincidence." Something twigged at the back of his mind. "Maybe I was working with them on something?" But that didn't sound quite right, either.

"Well, you're connected somehow," Eden agreed. "Local news is still broadcasting your sketch."

"They want all eyes looking for me." Probably to keep him in hiding. "I can't find out anything as long as I'm locked away on this boat. Plastering my face on every screen is a great way to keep me out of play."

"Yeah, but locked away permanently is what you're going to be if you don't find out what you're caught up in." Eden's grin was sly. "It would help if you could remember something other than how to breathe."

Riordan's lips twitched. Eden was definitely growing on him.

"What about the car you were driving?" Darcy asked. "The GPS might be dead, but Jason did track it to that rental company based in Vegas. I have the sheriff's department crime and accident alert app on my phone. I checked and didn't see any reports of an SUV being found in the past twenty-four hours."

"Must mean it's still out there." Eden scooped a large helping of mac and cheese onto her plate. "You okay with sharing the registration on that vehicle? I mean, outside our circle." At Darcy's confirmation, Eden nodded. "Good. I can help with that."

Chapter 7

"Give me the keys to the Impala."

"What?" Upon request, Darcy followed Eden out to her car, only slightly resenting the fact that she felt like a naughty student about to be scolded by the school principal. "Why?"

"Because you're trying to stay under the radar, and a car like that, despite it being severely behind the times technologically speaking, isn't going to stand up to what you're probably about to need." Eden pulled a fob out of her jacket pocket. "It also sticks out like a sore thumb. Take my SUV. You'll need to work around the car seat in the back and the Cheerios on the floor, but it'll do the job. I switched out my license plate and plugged a GPS jammer into the dash outlet."

"I'm sorry." Darcy blinked at the car key. "You did what?"

"You want to be invisible. This is the way you do it. The jammer will take care of your cell being traced as well, but you can still leave it intact in case you need to call because of an emergency. Speaking of cells, I've got a burner stashed in the glove compartment. Use it if you need it. The cash, too. I keep a couple thousand around for emergencies."

Oh, how Darcy wanted to ask what kind of emergencies warranted thousands of dollars being stashed in a glove compartment, but she had a feeling she might find out. "I don't know whether to be impressed or intimidated by your deceptive preparations."

"Yeah, well." Eden hesitated, then popped open the rear hatch and hauled out a small canvas bag. "I was on the fence about whether to give you this. Jason put it together for you after he got a look at Riordan's file." She unzipped the main compartment. "Laptop with some kind of magical powers Jason installed. It'll work off its own Wi-Fi and can't be traced. It also won't be identified on anyone else's system. There's also a portable jammer in here." She pulled a black device the size of a credit card out of a pouch. "One button on, one button off. Not as strong as the one in my car, but it'll at least give you some peace of mind where your cell is concerned. Speaking of cells." She pulled out a little plastic container with a small computer chip inside. "It's a tracking chip. Jason wasn't entirely sure about its range, but keep it close. Worse case, swallow it."

"Swallow it." She took the case, examined it. "I don't know. Does it come in flavors other than ick?"

"At some point, you're going to have to take this seriously, Darcy."

"Believe me." She shoved the plastic container into her front jeans pocket. "I'm only laughing on the outside." She was also beginning to feel like a British spy being outfitted by her tech team. "Does me taking all this give you peace of mind?"

Eden winced. "I won't have that until you're on the other side of this."

"The Impala belongs to my neighbor. Herbert Vanderly in 1C."

"I'll get it back to him tomorrow," Eden assured her as she zipped the bag back up and stashed it in the corner of the trunk. "You've got three days."

"Excuse me?"

"Three days before Cole gets back." Eden headed for the Impala. The door creaked when she opened it. The expression on her face left no room for argument. "Three days before he asks me what's going on and I tell him the truth. And I will tell him, Darcy. Not only because we don't lie to one another but because this situation with Malloy scares me."

Darcy wanted to make a joke out of the declaration, but her friend's admission only made her worry grow. Eden was one of the most unflappable people she'd ever known. If what was going on with Riordan had her freaked out...

"Guilty or not," Eden went on. "Protective or not,

Riordan Malloy is dangerous, and you have too many stars in your eyes to see you're not safe."

She couldn't help but be irritated. "Is this what you all talk about when I'm not around? How foolish and naive I am? Don't let Darcy out on her own. She might not find her way back. Or worse, I'll use breadcrumbs and end up wandering the forest forever."

"No one thinks you're a fool, Darcy," Eden said without missing a beat. "Least of all me. And I'd say you're trusting rather than naive." She took a deep breath, seemed to give herself a silent talking to and softened her tone. "I'm a bulldozer and have no inclination toward subtlety, I know, but it's because I care. There was a time only Allie and Simone were covered by my protective tendencies, but now, sorry, my expanded circle includes you." She stepped closer, rested her hands on Darcy's shoulders. "You are one of the cleverest women I know, but you wear your heart the way most people wear a shield. It's exposed, and it's eager to embrace that which should make you fear. I want you to be careful, and I want you to call me when the water rises over your head. Because I have no doubt it's going to, and none of us are about to let you drown. Understand?"

Touched, and because she knew Eden was far from being a sentimentalist, Darcy simply nodded. "Understood. Thank you. For the help. And the support."

Eden smiled and slid into the car. Once she'd started the engine, she rolled down the window. "While my gut says Riordan's one of us, and by that, I mean he's on the right side of things, that doesn't make him safe.

Not by any means. Not for a heart like yours. Remember, three days. After that, I'm calling in the troops." She arched a brow. "All of them."

Darcy stood with her back to the boat, watching as Eden drove out of the marina. The dead-of-night chill seemed particularly ominous accompanied by the slapping water against the hull and the ever so faint clang of a perimeter buoy in the distance. Part of her wanted to suggest to Riordan they take the boat and just head upriver, see where the current might lead them. But Riordan Malloy, memory or not, didn't strike her as the kind of man to walk away from a challenge.

She wrapped her arms around her torso, gave herself an encouraging squeeze. There wasn't any arguing she had feelings for Riordan, but she was logical and rational enough to realize a good portion of that attraction had to do with the excitement of the situation. Adrenaline plus boredom was a vicious combination, and she'd been bored for…well, for longer than she cared to admit. She sighed. At least she wasn't alone. One thing she definitely did not feel around him was lonely.

But if she wasn't careful, his presence, his very existence, could be like a drug she'd become addicted to.

She was shivering when she returned belowdeck, but the cold was forgotten at the sight of him hovering over her laptop examining the GPS map the new program made available to them. As for the laptop Eden and Jason had provided? She'd consider using that as her final option.

"You get a handle on that yet?" She retrieved the rest of the shopping bags she'd set by the forward berth.

"It's pretty straightforward," Riordan said almost absently. "How big a warning did Eden give you about me before she left?"

"Big enough to make me accept I'm not jumping in blindly," she admitted readily. "Not so big to make me think about walking away."

He shook his head. "From what I learned this evening, you have a lot of people who care about you, Darcy. Why you'd throw that away for—"

"A suspected murderer?" She forced a smile and shoved doubt aside. "Maybe I see someone worth fighting for. Fair warning, she took the Impala." She paused. "You don't look surprised."

"I'm not. That car isn't inconspicuous, nor is it a vehicle we can rely on for any potential situation. That Range Rover should get us through anything."

"Car seat included," she added. "Did you find your rental?"

"Tracing where it's been." He scrolled down to shrink the map on the screen. "Eden was right. There's not a blip of it since late last night, but the program she showed us mirrors the GPS record, meaning every time the car stops and starts, it registers the location in longitude and latitude."

"Took me ages as a kid to get those two straight." It didn't escape her notice that he seemed comfortable with the computer, adding one more thing to her vault of knowledge about him. Darcy stepped behind him, leaned in and peered over his shoulder. "So we can assume you picked up the car in Vegas from someone you must know since it's listed as still on-site."

"I must know someone there," Riordan mused. "Can't imagine any business would turn over a car like that to someone they didn't trust."

She reached out, traced a finger over the red line that did a bunch of circling in the same area before heading northwest. "You only made one stop on your way here from Vegas, and that was before you hit Davis. Travis Air Force Base. Two days ago." She planted her hands on her hips. "That would have been the day before I found you."

"Which means whatever happened that had me in that river, happened fast. Can't be a coincidence. How much you want to bet I paid a visit to Jay Russo?"

"Can't prove it one way or the other unless you feel like hacking into a military database." At his surprised expression, she continued. "These days, all visitor logs are digitized, right? You have to sign in as far as where you're going and who you're seeing. You show your face down there and it's game over."

"I've never wanted to hack something more in my entire life."

She knew the feeling. "So, this here is where you crashed by the river I take it." She pointed to one of the dots.

"There's nothing beyond it." Riordan pinched two fingers into the bridge of his nose. It was obvious he was running out of steam, which made sense considering they'd been going since daybreak. "Car's gone."

"Good. That means we've hit the proverbial wall and can get some sleep." She dug through the bags and pulled out a box of painkillers, shook them in the air to make sure he saw them. "I did some shopping for you. Just a few basic clothes, toiletries. Nothing fancy and nothing expensive. I didn't have a lot of cash on me, and I didn't want to use my credit card." She nibbled on her lower lip.

"You look as if that wasn't a good idea. Quite the contrary, those were all the right things to do." He got to his feet, accepted the items. "I appreciate it."

"I guessed on the sizes. Might have gone bigger than necessary, but…" She shrugged. "And there's also…" She dug around for the disposable razors, shaving cream and box of temporary hair dye. "So you can stop looking like you. It's this twist and apply brush thingy. Looks easy enough. I was going to get one for your beard, then realized that was dumb. You'd make more of a change by shaving."

"Yeah." He scrubbed a hand over his neatly maintained beard. "I was already planning on that."

"It's a shame." She reached up, touched her fingers to his face, tried to convince herself the spark she felt against her skin was nothing more than her imagination. "I like the beard."

He smiled. "Noted for future reference." His response surprised them both, but before Darcy could comment further, he stepped away. "What we both need right now is some sleep. I checked out the berths. You should take the main one at the stern." He pointed behind him. "The smaller one works fine for me. Eden turned on the water heater before she left."

"Oh. Right. Sure." It wasn't as if she'd expected to share a bed with him or anything. Her face heated like an overstressed furnace. "A shower definitely sounds great. In which case..." She stepped around him, retrieved her backpack and plastic bag of her own items and moved away. She was about to turn back, then hesitated, glanced at him.

"Go, Darcy." There was warning in his voice. But also longing.

"Yeah." She bit the inside of her cheek. "Good night, Riordan."

He was still standing there, watching her, as she slid the bedroom door closed.

At this point, other than his word, Riordan had very little to lay claim to. As anxious as he was to attempt to track down the car he'd totaled, without a solid lock on his identity—beyond the information he'd read in his file—or news of what he'd been working on before the crash, he admitted heading out unprepared would be beyond silly.

Besides, his head was clanging like an ocean buoy caught in a hurricane. His body was screaming at him to rest.

The kitchen clock read nearly midnight. No wonder he felt like a bag of wet cement. He'd been going full tilt since this morning when his feet hit the floor of Darcy's bedroom.

Darcy.

His gaze shifted to the sliding door separating them, an unexpected desire springing to life inside of him. It would be easy, so easy, to knock on that door and see what a third kiss could lead to. He balled his fists tight against temptation, then forced himself to gather his bags and retreat into the smaller berth before returning to the bathroom for a quick shower. He didn't have the energy to figure out the hair dye or to shave, and decided to tackle that in the morning. He quickly pulled on gray sweats and a T-shirt.

Back in his room, he retrieved the laptop along with the abandoned duffel bag and, after turning off most of the lights, closed himself off.

The narrow desk by the door served the laptop perfectly as he plugged in and sorted through the bags she'd given him. Not a lot of variety. She'd stuck to neutral colors, nothing that would stand out. The same could be said of the hair color which would darken his look significantly. She'd also found a pair of sunglasses that were large enough to cover the scar cutting through his left eyebrow.

"Woman's always thinking." Not for the first time, he counted himself fortunate their paths had crossed. But the sight of that kill bag sitting on the floor had his smile fading. She would have been hurt. She could be dead. Because of him.

He should leave. He should just take that key fob hanging on the hook by the stairs, get into the car and get as far away from her as possible. Although, if they stayed together, he had the chance of protecting her. Figuring out the truth about what had put him in the situation he currently found himself in was the only surefire way to keep her safe. Well, there was one other way, but staying out of Darcy Ford's bed could prove more difficult than evading the hired killers currently on their trail.

Anger built up like a fireball in his chest at the thought of someone bringing such ugliness into her private space. The drugs he'd found were accompanied by a disturbing array of blades and implements that could only be wielded by people without a soul. It all turned his stomach.

Terrible thoughts were filling his mind up faster than his memory was recovering. His memory.

Riordan repacked the bag, zipped it and stashed it out of sight. Next, he packed his new belongings into the collapsible navy blue duffle she'd purchased for him. He folded things with military precision without even thinking about it. While he couldn't remember it, he could feel his training taking over as he tidied up, organized and, after clicking off one of the two lights over the bed, finally lay down.

A small square glass window gave him a view of the starry night as once again that string of numbers floated through his mind over and over like a beacon he couldn't find or translate.

His eyes grew heavy as he evened out his breathing. With the solitary light burning and thoughts of Darcy Ford dancing through his brain, he dropped into a deep sleep.

Riordan gasped and sucked in air as if surfacing from the depths of the ocean. His limbs felt like anchors, dragging him down, stopping him from fully filling his lungs.

He peered into the darkness, waiting, listening, praying the niggling horror poking him in the back of his mind was only his imagination playing tricks on him.

"Riordan!"

The terror in Darcy's voice sliced through his subconscious like a dull knife. He stood, stumbled, braced himself against the wall as he found his way to the door and slid it open.

He stood there, frozen at the sight of Darcy tied to a chair, shadowy figures reaching into the bag he'd so meticulously repacked. The glint of blades against the stark overhead light had him shielding his face with one hand while the other reached out to her.

It took every ounce of energy to make one of his heavy legs move, but the rattle and clang of chain and shackle had him looking down. He kicked out, attempted to break free, only to feel himself pitching forward. On his way down, he reached out, keeping Darcy in sight as her terrified eyes locked on his.

"You did this," she whispered at him in a choked voice that tore his heart in two. "I was trying to help you. Why didn't you keep me safe?"

He startled against the sudden flash of light, lunged out with his arms as if he could swim across the floor and reach her. Only just as he did, Darcy vanished in a wave of smoke, replaced by the cloudy figure of a face he'd seen only in the news.

Jay Russo.

The man he was accused of killing.

Riordan wrenched himself awake, his labored breathing echoing in the room. He swiped at the sweat coating his brow.

Every muscle in his body ached, as if he was one giant knot of stress. He sat up, swung his legs over the side of the bed and willed his breathing to slow. It felt as if he'd only just closed his eyes, but it was creeping up on 5:00 a.m. He groaned, it was so early, but he'd slept enough to get to his feet to check the incessant beeping he assumed was coming from his laptop.

But the computer sat silent on the desk.

He slid his door open, wincing as the noise echoed through the boat.

Being as quiet as he could, he strained to locate the sound, walked slowly through the main cabin then stopped in the kitchen where the bag of rice sat on the counter. He pulled it toward him and dug inside. When he got the cell phone out, the home screen lit up. His heart nearly exploded out of his chest at the image displayed.

The overhead light in the cabin clicked on. "Is it working?" Darcy asked when he spun around to face her. How had he not heard her coming out of her room? But there she stood, eyeing him. She'd tied her long hair into a knot on the top of her head, but several loose gold-tipped red curls had sprung free. With her hip kicked out and a nervous expression on her face, it was obvious she was as anxious about the cell's re-activation as he was. "Well?"

Well what?

Snug yellow shorts covered her beautifully rounded hips and backside. The matching sleep tank had a kooky looking sea creature declaring You've Got to Be Squidding Me emblazoned in bright pink. Desire slammed through him.

Her bare shoulders and toned arms had his thoughts veering away from the mystery of his identity and swerving straight into inviting her into his bed. He'd be lying if he hadn't imagined feeling those legs and arms wrapped around him, trapping him in a cage he never wanted to be free of. Well what? It took him a moment to formulate an answer. She was a distraction. A beautiful one. An infuriating one. But a distraction, nonetheless.

She approached him one unintentional slinky step at a time. Once she was close enough that he could inhale that intoxicating fragrance rising off her sleep-warmed skin, she plucked the cell phone out of his grip.

He followed her gaze down to the lit screen.

"I was hoping your cell would give us a solution, a key to solving this, not leave us with more clues." As usual, when it came to Darcy's observations, Riordan couldn't argue. "I know who this man is." She pointed at the taller, younger biracial-looking man.

"Jay Russo." There wasn't just a military connection; they'd been friends. He could see that. Not only on his own face, but in the face of the man he was accused of killing. The picture may as well have been an indictment because, for the first time in days, his memory began to tingle.

"What about this guy? The one with the wedding band." Darcy indicated the man standing between them. Just as tall. Just as handsome, but with fair features and a more intoxicated look about him, thanks no doubt to the jumbo drink in his hand. "Any idea who he is?"

Riordan straightened his spine and shoulders.

"What're you doing?" Darcy's brows pinched together. "You look like you just shot to attention."

"Not intentionally." Riordan rubbed a hand against his chest. "Jay Russo was military. Maybe this guy is, too." The phone blinked out again. Darcy tapped on the screen, grumbled when the image flickered and went black once more. "Despite the Eiffel Tower in the background, that didn't look like Paris to me. That's the tower in Vegas."

"The party lights and crowds behind you give it away. Hang on." She disappeared into her berth, then reappeared with a charger and cord. "My phone's newer than yours, but it's the same brand. This should work." She plugged it in, then connected his phone. Instead of the phone blinking to life, it rebooted and, when the screen was accessible once more, asked for the PIN.

He heaved a frustrated sigh and tossed the phone on the counter.

"I'm sorry. I thought that would—"

"Not your fault." He scrubbed his hands down his face. "I would have done the same thing."

"At least now we have a second arrow pointing to Vegas. We know you and Jay were friends and that there's a third member of your group. Gives us someone to look for to get you some answers." She rubbed his arm. "And hopefully the proof that you're innocent. You look discouraged. It is something, Riordan."

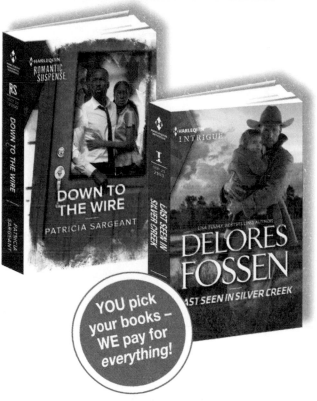

YOU pick your books –
WE pay for everything.
You get up to FOUR new books and a Mystery Gift…
absolutely FREE!
Total retail value: Over $20!

Dear Reader,

Your opinions are important to us. So if you'll participate in our fast and free "One Minute" Survey, YOU can pick up to four wonderful books that WE pay for when you try the Harlequin Reader Service!

As a leading publisher of women's fiction, we'd love to hear from you. That's why we promise to reward you for completing our survey.

IMPORTANT: Please complete the survey and return it. We'll send your Free Books and a Free Mystery Gift right away. And we pay for shipping and handling too! *We pay for EVERYTHING!*

Try **Harlequin® Romantic Suspense** and get 2 books featuring heart-racing page-turners with unexpected plot twists and irresistible chemistry that will keep you guessing to the very end.

Try **Harlequin Intrigue® Larger-Print** and get 2 books featuring action-packed stories that will keep you on the edge of your seat. Solve the crime and deliver justice at all costs.

Or TRY BOTH!

Thank you again for participating in our "One Minute" Survey. It really takes just a minute (or less) to complete the survey… and your free books and gift will be well worth it!

If you continue with your subscription, you can look forward to curated monthly shipments of brand-new books from your selected series, always at a discount off the cover price! Plus you can cancel any time. So don't miss out, return your One Minute Survey today to get your Free books.

Pam Powers

"One Minute" Survey

GET YOUR FREE BOOKS AND A FREE GIFT!

✓ Complete this Survey   ✓ Return this survey

◄ DETACH AND MAIL CARD TODAY! ►

1 Do you try to find time to read every day?
☐ YES   ☐ NO

2 Do you prefer stories with suspenseful storylines?
☐ YES   ☐ NO

3 Do you enjoy having books delivered to your home?
☐ YES   ☐ NO

4 Do you share your favorite books with friends?
☐ YES   ☐ NO

YES! I have completed the above "One Minute" Survey. Please send me my Free Books and a Free Mystery Gift (worth over $20 retail). I understand that I am under no obligation to buy anything, as explained on the back of this card.

☐ **Harlequin®**
Romantic
Suspense
240/340 CTI G2AD

☐ **Harlequin**
Intrigue®
Larger-Print
199/399 CTI G2AD

☐ **BOTH**
240/340 & 199/399
CTI G2AE

FIRST NAME   LAST NAME

ADDRESS

APT.#   CITY

STATE/PROV.   ZIP/POSTAL CODE

EMAIL ☐ Please check this box if you would like to receive newsletters and promotional emails from Harlequin Enterprises ULC and its affiliates. You can unsubscribe anytime.

HARLEQUIN® Reader Service —Here's how it works:

Accepting your 2 free books and free gift (gift valued at approximately $10.00 retail) places you under no obligation to buy anything. You may keep the books and gift and return the shipping statement marked "cancel." If you do not cancel, approximately one month later we'll send you more books from the series you have chosen, and bill you at our low, subscribers-only discount price. Harlequin® Romantic Suspense books consist of 4 books each month and cost just $5.99 each in the U.S. or $6.74 each in Canada, a savings of at least 8% off the cover price. Harlequin Intrigue® Larger-Print books consist of 6 books each month and cost just $6.99 each in the U.S. or $7.49 each in Canada, a savings of at least 10% off the cover price. It's quite a bargain! Shipping and handling is just 50¢ per book in the U.S. and $1.25 per book in Canada*. You may return any shipment at our expense and cancel at any time by contacting customer service — or you may continue to receive monthly shipments at our low, subscribers-only discount price plus shipping and handling.

▼ If offer card is missing write to: Harlequin Reader Service, P.O. Box 1341, Buffalo, NY 14240-8531 or visit www.ReaderService.com ▼

BUSINESS REPLY MAIL
FIRST-CLASS MAIL   PERMIT NO. 717   BUFFALO, NY

POSTAGE WILL BE PAID BY ADDRESSEE

HARLEQUIN READER SERVICE
PO BOX 1341
BUFFALO NY 14240-8571

NO POSTAGE
NECESSARY
IF MAILED
IN THE
UNITED STATES

But was it enough? His gut was telling him to keep moving. Vegas—and the possibility of finding someone outside this mess who knew him—seemed like the right, make that the only, play. "I guess I don't really have much of a choice, do I?"

"Sure you do," Darcy said with a shrug. "You could go against your instincts and turn yourself in to the police and hope it all works out."

Yeah, he had no faith that would happen.

"Or…" She waggled her brows at him before reaching around and clicking on the coffee machine. "We can head to Vegas, start at that car rental agency and find whoever this guy is and prove you innocent of murder. I know which option I'm leaning toward. And the sooner we get going, the better."

Before he could respond, she walked over to the staircase and, after climbing up, pulled a lever that unlocked the hatch. He followed, unable to take his gaze away from those enticing curves of hers.

"You locked us in?"

"I locked *you* in." She flashed a smile as she stepped back down, brushing against him as she faced him.

He stroked a finger down her cheek. "You don't trust me."

"More like I expected your Lancelot gene to kick into overdrive." The defiance in her eyes shimmered against the attraction. "If those guys hadn't turned up at my apartment, you'd have ditched me by now."

He wasn't about to tell her she was right. Nor did he plan to lie to her. Trust was a funny thing. It was fragile. Something he wasn't entirely sure how to embrace.

"If I haven't proven I'm an asset—"

"Don't go second-guessing yourself now," he chided. "Of course you're an asset." He struggled to keep his voice even against the desire coursing through his veins. "You're also a reason to stay hidden on this boat." *And let the world drop away.* What he wouldn't give to wrap himself around Darcy Ford and have everything else just disappear. "As appealing an idea as that is, I can't do that, Darcy. I can't let this thing go on without me trying to stop it."

"Who asked you to?" she said with more than a bit of attitude. "I'm the one who suggested Vegas, baby, remember?"

She had. But he wished she hadn't. "Maybe I should ask it of myself. If for no other reason than to keep you whole."

"Uh-huh, right." She rolled her eyes so hard the corners of his lips curled up. "Because men like you always trip over themselves for someone like—oh!"

He silenced her with a kiss. The kind of kiss he'd imagined more frequently than he cared to admit. The feel of her mouth under his, her warm honey-sweet lips opening for him sent waves of yearning crashing through him. He placed his hands on her hips, drew her softness against him and was thrilled at the urgency in which she kissed him back.

His tongue dueled with hers, dancing, enticing, drawing her closer to him. He could smell sunshine and summer against her winter cool skin as his empty mind filled with only her. And his desperate need to…

Keep her safe.

His pulse skipped before nearly skidding to a stop. He pushed her away, gently, just enough for him to catch the dazed, confused and all-too-appealing longing blanketing her face. He stepped back, extremely aware of how little it would take for her to send him off target again.

"Well." She slid her hands over his shoulders until her palms flattened on his chest. She rested them there, patting almost nervously as she pressed her kiss-swollen lips together. "So maybe I was a little bit wrong on that point."

"To clarify," he warned. "I am not like other men."

"No kidding." That laugh of hers made him smile. "Coming from anyone else, that would sound arrogant." She looked befuddled. "You are a man who definitely keeps me guessing. How about you fix us something to eat, then we'll take care of this, too." She plunged her hands into his too long hair, took close examination of his beard. "As much as I like having something to hold on to when you kiss me, we aren't leaving this boat until you don't resemble that sketch. Okay?"

He nodded, only to have her pop up on her toes and press her mouth against his.

"Now start cooking and let's get this show on the road."

Darcy waited until she was in her room again, back plastered against the door, before she caught her breath.

Kissing Riordan the first time had been exhilarating. The second time? Exciting.

Whoever had proclaimed the third time's the charm hadn't been joking. She was even happier when he'd actually thought about what he was doing with her. It had paid off in chill-inducing spades. If he invested that much attention to a kiss she could only imagine what he was capable of when—*if*—they got naked. No wonder every inch of her was buzzing.

If only she didn't also feel his strained reluctance, too. Not necessarily over her but because of their situation. They needed to get his memory back, get him on track again. He was an honorable man. She wasn't so far gone down the romantic diversion road that she could ignore that fact. He was a dying breed for sure, given her recent experiments at intimacy. A dishonorable man wouldn't have thought twice about taking her to bed, especially when she'd made her intentions clear.

No. He needed to be whole to take that leap. It wasn't enough for her to believe in his innocence; he needed to know it for certain himself. All of this gave her one important goal to work toward.

She grabbed her bag, found her jeans and got dressed, choosing a long-sleeve black turtleneck. She made the bed, straightened up the room, and once she was convinced the space looked untouched, she gathered up her things and pulled open the door.

"You're doing it again." Riordan flipped the visor down to stop the rising sun from hurting his eyes as he took the turnoff onto Route 88 East, heading to Nevada.

"Doing what?" Darcy asked from the passenger seat

after she'd plugged in his still recalcitrant cell phone. That blasted PIN of his was all that stood between him and much-needed info, but all the retrieval and reset options were reliant on him having a functioning memory.

"You're staring." Even as he said it, he ran his hand across his bare chin. If he'd thought he'd miss the feel of the beard, he was wrong. His palm tingled against the smooth skin, as if reacquainting itself with reality. This felt...right.

His head, on the other hand, felt anything but. He'd already downed two painkillers, but they had barely taken the edge off the increased pounding behind his eyes. He hoped the sunglasses Darcy picked up on her shopping trip would help.

"You left your hair long." She reached across the center console and tucked a strand behind his ear. "The lighter color looks good, though."

He didn't want to think about how he liked her touching him. Her gentle fingers acted as a kind of balm to his heart, which had been roughened by the past few days. She'd been the only good thing he had in his life; he wanted to hold her. To kiss her. To make love to her.

Almost as much as he wanted to keep her safe. Not only from outside forces but, if he was honest, from himself.

"We can't do much about your eyes or that scar when you have the glasses off. They nailed that part of the picture for sure." She pulled her hand back, settled into her seat with a sigh. "Fair warning, I drank way too much coffee before we left, so we'll have to factor in bathroom breaks."

"GPS estimates it'll take about nine and a half hours to Vegas." He glanced at the dashboard clock. Eden's Rover, while it didn't display as many of the bells and whistles as Darcy's SUV, felt more comfortable to him, almost familiar, especially when it came to figuring out what amenities it possessed.

"It'll probably be longer, considering we're taking the mountain route," Darcy said. "Skirting around South Lake Tahoe before heading toward the Ninety-Five means fewer chances of running into anyone and reduced odds of you being recognized. And I mean anyone," she added with a not-so-silent moan and roll of her eyes. "That stretch of road to Vegas is about as desolate as you can get, but with a beautiful view. So I guess that's something."

"It is." At least driving would focus his attention. They had a plan, enough of one to put his mind at ease. For a little while. He kept his eye on the rearview mirror, made note of any cars behind them. He hadn't thought to do it. It just happened. But by doing so, he bolstered the faith he had in himself. "You can turn on some music if you want." He gestured to the dashboard sound system. "Or a podcast maybe?"

"I'm good with quiet for now." Darcy looked out her window as the highway dipped in and around the Sierra Nevada mountain range. "I used to come up here all the time when I first moved to Sacramento. The snow in the mountains is ideal for skiing."

Okay, Riordan thought. Small talk it would be. "You like to ski?"

"Meh." She shrugged. "One of those things I always wanted to do, and then when I did, I didn't have to do it again. My dad got moved around a lot for his job, so we spent a good number of years in the South. Louisiana, Alabama, South Carolina. Two years in Florida. Not a lot of snow to be found in those parts."

"I suppose not." He racked his brain for a childhood memory to cling to, with or without snow, but the blankness had shifted into an odd white noise. "My file said I'm from Texas. I imagine it's the same."

"Do you think you'll return there? Once your memories come back to you?"

"Don't see why." He shifted in his seat. "My parents are gone, and according to Eden, I don't have any other family." He was alone in the world. Alone and on his own. Except he wasn't, was he? He hadn't been since Darcy hauled him onto dry land. "I've been thinking about that, actually. Considering no one from the Army has stepped up to claim or defend me—"

"We don't know what the circumstances might be."

"That's my point," he said. "According to my file, I'm still on active duty. If I was working undercover on something, it would make sense for my superiors to stay quiet for fear of blowing whatever cover I'd built up."

"Why do I hear an unspoken *or* in that statement?" Darcy asked.

Because she was perceptive. And because there was at least one other explanation he needed to consider.

Maybe more than one. None of which sat nearly as comfortably with him. "I may have gone off on my own and was looking into something I was warned off of. That could explain the silence and lack of communication."

"So could your dead phone," she said dryly. "You don't strike me as the kind of man who would disobey orders." She frowned, seemed to reconsider. "At least not without a darn good reason."

Not only did he want to believe that was correct; he wanted Darcy's appraisal to be accurate. He didn't like the idea of disappointing or disillusioning her in any way.

"Either would explain why Eden couldn't get many answers beyond your primary file," Darcy said. "Not sure speculating is doing us any good at this point."

"No." But there had to be a reason he ended up where he had, gone where he had. Started where he did.

"Therefore, we start over with what we do know." Darcy smiled softly at him. "And we know that you and Jay Russo were friends. Good friends."

"You think?"

"I know. You were having fun in that selfie You trust them. The way your arm's slung around Jay's shoulder and all of you are laughing."

"That might have been the alcohol," Riordan said, recalling the oversized drink in the hand of his unnamed friend. "Wish I could have read the name on the glass. Might give us a place to start."

"Yeah, because I'm sure men drinking those kinds of drinks are a rare occurrence in Vegas. Let's not feed our doubts, okay? We stick to the plan and head to the car rental place, see if anyone remembers you—"

"Me walking in there without the car I rented doesn't seem the best idea."

"*You* aren't going to walk in there at all," Darcy said now with an overly bright smile.

"Hold on—"

"You said it yourself. You can't go back there without the car."

"We don't even know what information we're hoping to find."

"Then we'd best decide so I can work on my script."

Her script. "Darcy, this isn't some improv audition for a movie role. We're dealing with a dangerous situation—"

"And you'll be waiting in the parking lot in case something goes wrong. Just…" She waved off his concern. "Would you not worry until there's something to worry about?"

"I don't like surprises." He rubbed his fingers hard across his forehead.

"Well, then you're in for a bumpy ride, because I'm full of them." She waved her cell phone in front of her. "I've already got the address pinned in my map app." There it was again, that restrained excitement in her voice. "I'd better text Eden… Ah, never mind." She sighed and set her phone down.

"What? Something wrong?"

"Reception's nil and it'll be a while before it's clear again. Just as well. I've had enough lectures and warnings to last me a lifetime."

"There are worse things than having people care about you, Darcy."

"No offense, but how would you know?"

"Fair enough." But while the memories still seemed unwilling to return, his feelings, his impulses, his instincts seemed to be kicking into overdrive. "You're a good person, open, trusting. Most of your friends seem to be involved in law enforcement and the like. They know what the dark side looks like. They know the damage that can be inflicted. They don't want to see you hurt. Besides, it's clear they're a big part of your life. I imagine if they weren't, you'd feel a large void."

"Can't argue that point." She stared down at her phone. "Is it wrong of me to wish they'd take as much care when it comes to setting me up with clown-favoring lawyers or accountants who bet on beetle fighting," she grumbled into her chest.

"I'm sorry, what? Beetle—"

"It's some online thing," she explained. "Where they set up beetles to fight each other in these weird cage matches—and that wasn't my point, by the way."

"Sure it wasn't." Talking about Darcy's love life felt like a really bad idea. One that should make him more uncomfortable than it did. From everything she'd told him, memory or not, he was head and shoulders above the other men she'd been dating. *You're not dating her!* The reminder came fast and swift from somewhere deep in his subconscious. "I'd venture your friends setting you up is coming from the best of intentions on their part. Look what happens when you give it a go yourself."

She smirked, and the irritation in her eyes dimmed. "At least with you, there's no creepy hobby or weird interest to deal with."

"That we know of," Riordan teased. "I could very well have a collection of hand-painted garden gnomes in my back yard or ventriloquist dummies hidden in the attic."

"For the record, the dummies would be a deal breaker." She shuddered and he laughed. "Talk about unappealing."

"What do you find appealing? Generally speaking."

"In a man?" She leaned her elbow on the edge of the window and rested her head in her hand. "If you'd asked me a few weeks ago, I'd have said breathing was my only qualification."

"You're joking," he accused, then looked at her. "Aren't you?"

"No doubt this explains my dismal dating record. I mean, a lot of them were okay guys. Take Roger Prince for example."

"If I must." He shouldn't have started this conversation. He didn't like the idea of Darcy dating. Or maybe he just didn't like the idea of her dating anyone other than him. He pushed that notion aside immediately. He had no right to those thoughts. "What was wrong with Roger?"

"Initially? Not a thing. He had a nice, stable job as a bank manager. Owns a house in the Fabulous Forties—that's where some of the oldest homes in Sacramento are. Tall, good-looking, has a great family, fabulous sense of humor. But on our fifth date, just when I'm starting to think it might be leading to something, he springs it on me." She rolled her head against the back of the seat. "Skydiving."

He wasn't sure so much disdain had ever been loaded into one word before. "And this is bad because—"

"Planes were built for transport, not to be launching pads."

"Actually—"

"I forgot who I was talking to for a minute." She gently smacked her palm against her forehead. "Of course you've jumped out of a plane, Mr. Army Man."

Riordan couldn't help but smile at the irritation in her voice. "Does it help I don't remember enjoying it?"

She shuddered. "Give me the ocean, a pair of flippers and a tank, and I'm good to go. Why someone would purposely step out of a plane and plummet—"

"It's not all plummeting. That's what the parachute is for." He paused to take a couple of deep breaths. All morning it had been as if he had a film reel was stuck playing in his head, catching and running at different speeds. Flashes of images, of memories, with details he couldn't quite grasp built on one another until his head ached. Some of those images featured Darcy front and center. Others? The deceased Jay Russo. The unnamed third man in the tower photo. But most everything else was in the shadows, as if waiting for someone to flip the light on.

"Turned out the skydiving was only the beginning," Darcy continued as Riordan worked on dividing his focus among the road, his rebooting brain and her. "You know what his real hobby was? BASE jumping.

Off buildings. His dream trip was to launch himself off that spire tower in Saudi Arabia. You know, the one they filmed that spy movie at?"

"I don't think that's legal."

"Who cares? Just the thought of it scares me to death. Why take such a risk? And my point—" Darcy arched a brow "—since you seem to have missed it, is that just when I think, *Okay, here's a guy with potential*, I get hit with a whammy. Every single time. A deal breaker. Which probably explains why I'm not losing my cool about you and your situation as much as people are expecting I should. This thing between us?" She waved a hand at him. "There's really not much left that can shock me at this point. It means I'm in uncharted territory, which, by the way, I plan to thoroughly embrace. You, Riordan Malloy, shall be the primary beneficiary of my disastrous dating experiences."

That should register with him as good news, shouldn't it? He'd be lying if he didn't admit Darcy embracing their—whatever this was between them— didn't feel like a bright spot in his life at the moment. But he was also a realist. The chances of anything good coming from him being suspected of murder were next to nil. All the more reason to keep things as grounded as possible. "What happened to Roger?"

"Huh?"

"The BASE jumper. I take it you didn't—"

"I can't put a foot on a plane. What do you think?" Her disbelief had him grinning. "He did, though. Ended up in the hospital for two months when his chute got tangled with another jumper's."

"That's unfortunate," Riordan agreed.

"He and his friends made the local news. Not because of what they did but how it went. And how he landed. The last social media post I saw him make, he was bragging about the fact he's broken nearly every bone in his body." She glared at him. "How is that even something to be proud of? I ask you!"

"I thought you said you wanted some excitement in your life," Riordan teased.

"There's excitement and then there's—I don't know—tempting fate?"

"People are complicated sometimes. You, on the other hand," he said carefully, "feel right at home in water, something I'm certain a number of people can't tolerate."

Her lip curled up like a famous frog puppet's when irritated. "So much for you being on my side."

"In this instance, I'm Switzerland. Sometimes you have to take the bad with the good in order to get what—or who—you want." He hesitated. "What do you want?"

The instant he asked, he realized he shouldn't have. He knew what he was hoping—that she'd say she wanted him, but that made no sense. His identity was in pieces. He was the last person who could fit her desires. Fit into her life.

And yet, he wanted to be her answer.

"You know what I want?" Her voice sounded almost dazed, as if she'd been pondering the answer for longer than she'd want to admit. "Someone stable. Someone…who's as happy to jump in the car and just drive for days but is equally satisfied spending the weekend binge-watching a bunch of sci-fi TV shows while gorging on popcorn."

"Someday you'll have to expand your style of travel. Limiting yourself to land vehicles—"

"I can assure you, there's nothing you will ever say or do that'll get me on a plane, so stop trying." There was both a warning and a hint of regret in her voice. "To further answer your question, I'm looking for exciting and a bit of spontaneity but also someone fun. And reliable. And, well, someone who likes me for me despite all my quirks and foibles."

Foibles. There was a Darcy word if he'd ever heard one. "It's not wrong to want what you want," he said. Finally, his ears stopped buzzing and his hands relaxed on the wheel. Whatever had been hurting his head had eased for the time being. "What's important is that you've given it some thought." It almost sounded as if he knew what he was talking about. Easy for him to say, wasn't it? When all he wanted was for his memories to come back and to pick up his life wherever he'd left off. "You'll get there, Darcy. It might take some time, but I'm sure you'll find what you need and want."

"I want what my friends have found." Her voice lowered as if she were talking more to herself than to him. "I want to take that breathless tumble that ends with knowing I'm never going to be the same again because of the person I've met. And when I'm faced with it, I want to embrace them and not find a reason to push them away or find some ridiculous—"

"Foible?"

"Yeah," she said, but her smile seemed strained. "I want to find someone who makes me want to push through all that other…stuff to get to what really matters. I want to stop being scared."

"I've yet to see you scared," Riordan observed. "You didn't hesitate to drag me out of the river, Darcy. You fought back when those men were in your apartment. You haven't stopped trying to help me despite me urging you not to. That's someone who embraces life."

The question was…did he?

"Vince and Jack would call all of that being careless," she told him.

"Vince and Jack aren't on the receiving end of your generosity and compassion."

She snorted.

"You've got a good circle of friends, Darcy. A truly supportive one from all I've heard and witnessed. There's someone in that circle for whatever you might need or want."

"Sure." Darcy shrugged. "But that doesn't make me feel any less of a fifth wheel."

"You're not a—"

"Sure I am. This time last year, me and Kyla and Ashley, we'd formed this unofficial club, right? We're all single and looking and setting each other up, and now there's just me left. Ashley got married faster than it takes to say hello, and now Kyla's engaged to Jason. That just leaves me and Eamon—"

"The FBI agent?" His tone came out tighter than he'd anticipated. "Are you and he—?"

"No, no, no." She shook her head and laughed. "He's

just a friend. There's nothing..." she trailed off, and when Riordan glanced at her, he saw she'd pressed her lips into a thin, invisible line. "Some people fall instantly into place in your life, you know? Like when I first met Vince and his wife, Simone. We were working together on a case. We ended up pulling a young woman's body out of the river. That experience formed a bond not a lot of people could understand. Then the group expanded, like I was attracting all these new electrons that stuck. And then there's..."

"And then there's what?" Riordan asked when she didn't finish the thought. She didn't have to. He knew what the rest of that statement was. *And then there's you* rang as loudly as if she'd uttered the words out loud.

"Nothing." She folded her arms in front of her, as if she'd accidentally opened up too much. She reached over and clicked on the radio. "What kinds of podcasts do you think you like?"

"No idea."

He let the conversation die, and while Darcy distracted herself with finding something to listen to, he fought off a bout of anxiety and uncertainty. Not because of his current situation as a wanted suspect but rather because of his own thoughts.

No. His thoughts were focused almost entirely on the woman riding beside him.

The woman who made him wonder if he'd ever smiled or laughed before he'd met her.

Whatever happened next, whatever awaited them in Las Vegas or even farther down the road, he knew one thing for certain: his life had forever been carved into two halves. Before he'd met Darcy Ford.

And after.

Chapter 8

"This has to be the fanciest car rental agency I've ever seen." Darcy brushed a nervous hand down the front of her sweater. SilverPeak's website had alluded to providing a high-end, ultra-exclusive experience. And, sure, the photographs looked as if the building was something out of the future with all that angular glass, but it was nothing compared to seeing it in person.

The cars awaiting customers in the pickup lot were top of the line, well out of her price range and ran from tiny flashy sports cars to what she suspected were bulletproof discretion vehicles that could withstand a tank assault.

The rental company was located more than a mile off the Vegas Strip. Riordan had parked across the street at a small strip mall that had seen better days.

Darcy couldn't help but think that SilverPeak Car Services looked more appropriate for visiting governmental higher ups, dignitaries or royalty as opposed to a walk-in-off-the-street redhead fronting for her amnesiac traveling companion. As exciting as she'd found her special assignment moments before, she was beginning to doubt her plan. "The entire building looks like it's made out of glass."

"Imagine being their window washer."

Darcy's lips curved up at Riordan's attempt at humor. He'd been taking swings at lightening the mood ever since she'd ended their getting-to-know-you conversation by taking a deep and loud dive into episodic supernatural television. Despite Riordan's assertion he wasn't familiar with the show about two demon-hunting brothers and their angelic sidekick, he appeared to find the podcast entertaining. Personally, she'd stopped listening more than half an episode in.

Three bathroom stops, two gas fill-ups and one major freeway backup later, they'd hit Vegas at just after four. Late enough for the sun to have turned on full blast, early enough that she was lamenting not eating more for lunch than a bag of cheese twists and a diet soda. But they had arrived. Finally.

It was as if the city were holding a deep preparatory breath before the nightly excitement took over.

Riding down the main thoroughfare, Darcy found it impossible not to feel that initial zing of excitement as they passed what seemed an unending line of skyscraping hotels and casinos, famous chef eateries and brand-name shopping venues. The crowds not only hustled and bustled; it was as if they were permanently set on Fast Forward, darting and mingling and making their way through one of the busiest cities in the country, hopping from one venue to the next.

Vegas was, if anything, the perfect city to disappear in. At least for a little while. As long as they avoided cameras that these days were…everywhere.

"Where's your cell? Wait, where is it?" She shoved open the door and scooted to the edge of her seat, ran her hands around to locate the missing phone.

"I stuck it back in the rice at our last stop," Riordan said. "I'm hoping another few hours in time-out might yield something more than a glitchy picture and give me time to remember my PIN. But I'm not sure this is the right move."

He swerved into a different topic so fast her head nearly spun. "We just drove over ten hours to check this place out. Don't tell me you've changed your mind." She did not need him feeding into her doubts right now.

"Not about going inside," he said. "I'm not sure you going in alone—"

"Don't you go jumping on the 'Darcy can't handle herself' bandwagon," she ordered. "I have a plan and it's going to work. According to their website, Silver-Peak only takes clients by referral, which means someone had to vouch for you. We find that out, and it could crack open something inside that memory of yours that gets us some info we can use."

"That isn't what I was thinking, necessarily," he added with a revealing wince. "I've got…concerns. And while this continues to reboot—" he poked a finger against the side of his head "—I don't have more to rely on than my instincts. That goes for both of us. If I know someone in there, someone knows me."

"If only you weren't a wanted murder suspect, we could just call up and ask," Darcy said. "Okay, look, we've already worked out the best story for me to give them, and it's not like we have a lot of other options." Even to her own ears, her voice sounded strained. "Unless you want to go waltzing in there, risk being recognized and ask about the car of theirs you've misplaced—totaled and misplaced." She corrected herself just to make her point. "I'm all you've got, and hopefully, I'll ask the right question and catch someone's attention. As noted, you'll be able to see me the entire time. I'll be fine."

He didn't look convinced. "Tell me again what you're going to say."

She rolled her eyes and, after hiking herself back into her seat, pulled the door shut again. "One of two things. Depending on the vibes I get, I'll either say I'm looking for my boyfriend, who took off the night before we were supposed to get married, or I'll play the angry ex card looking to hunt you down for the child support you owe me." She grinned. "Guess which one I'm hoping to use?"

"I really wish you weren't enjoying this so much."

"It's a car rental agency." Darcy was really trying to understand his concern. "The only criminal enterprise going on behind those doors is obscene rental rates. The more we sit here and worry over it, the more nervous I'm going to get. I thought you trusted me."

"I do trust you." His eyes flickered back to the building. "Hang on." He leaned over and popped open the glove compartment. "Call yourself. Then put yourself on speaker and pop in an earbud."

"You're serious." She balked, but at his stony-eyed look, she snatched the phone and did what he asked. She stashed her own cell in the front pocket of her purse and inserted the right earbud. "I'm betting there's some shady surveillance equipment store in this town if you want to stock up on bugging devices."

"We'll check into that when you get back." His smile was quick as he set the burner on the top of the dash.

"How about we find a place to stay first?" She shoved open the door once more and slung her bag over her shoulder. "But no place with a heart-shaped tub. That's just…weird." She slammed the door, but not fast enough to miss his shocked and somewhat amused expression.

The strip mall where he'd parked was half empty, with boarded up windows and For Lease signs. A hole-in-the-wall pizza joint boasted the best garlic bread in the city while a video game store with a half-lit neon sign looked as if it had barely survived the zombie wars. When Darcy reached the corner to cross at the light, she asked him, "Can you hear me all right?"

"Not too bad."

"My mother would be so proud." She picked up her pace. She was already nervous about this whole thing; she didn't need Riordan's added doubt boosting her jumpiness. Although, for the life of her, she honestly couldn't figure out what she had to be nervous about. She didn't have to lie about anything important, like her name or anything. She'd keep her questions and explanations simple and her "woe is me" attitude on full blast in order to find out. She was affable, likable and could make people smile. Someone in that rental agency knew Riordan.

She just needed to find a way to figure out who.

The high sheen on the metal doorframe sparkled against the streaming sunlight as the automatic doors whooshed open and she walked inside. There were a good half dozen customers seated in square chrome-detailed padded chairs while a dark-haired woman spoke with another at the counter.

"Good afternoon, ma'am." The man who stepped forward to greet her was a good three inches taller and a few years older than Darcy. But it was his eyes that caught her attention. Small. Dark. And intense. "My name is Shaun. How can I help you today?" He had a tablet tucked into the curve of one arm that was covered by a very well-tailored dark suit. Her planned stories flew right out of her head, she hadn't accounted for such a formal introduction or having an audience. "Are you checking in for an appointment?"

"Ah, no." Darcy cleared her throat. "I'm looking for my boyfriend. He said to meet him here, as he was planning to rent a car? We're heading to the Grand Canyon and want to be comfortable."

"A little off script but not bad," Riordan said in her ear.

"Of course," Shaun said with an obliging nod. "Your boyfriend's name?"

"Clyde. Clyde Winchester." Okay, maybe she had

been listening to that podcast after all. She could glom on to her original lie in private once it was clear there was no Clyde Winchester in their records.

"If you'd like to take a seat." He tapped information into his tablet, then glanced up and smiled. "I'll see what I can find out for you, Ms....?"

"Oh, just call me Darcy." She earned a muted irritated comment from her audio sidekick. "Thank you so much. I appreciate it."

"We were trying to stay under the radar, *Darcy*," Riordan said as she moved away. "Your name isn't exactly common."

"Unlike some people," she murmured under her breath, "I can only lie about so many things at once." She wandered the perimeter of the spacious lobby in what she hoped was a relaxed manner. The metallic gray wall across from the reception and service desk that led to a long hallway was elegantly arranged with an array of professionally framed photographs displaying numerous well-known personalities who were also clients, interspersed with large endorsements and advertisements from a number of pricey hotels.

Luxury rentals. Private security and transportation. Discrete services at rates so expensive they weren't listed anywhere in sight.

She meandered slowly down the hall, taking a mental picture of the signs and doors, keeping her ears open as she scanned the pictures, testimonials and ads.

"For the record, I'm even more convinced this was a bad idea. No one is going to tell you anything."

"We don't know that. Yet. Patience, please." She

hadn't seen anything of interest, actually. Not until her eye landed on a different wall. An arrow of panic shot through her and she stepped back, bent down to examine the staff photo more closely.

Two of the faces were chillingly familiar. "No way—"

"What?" Riordan's demand pierced her ear.

She stood back up, feigned disinterest even as she glanced up and found not one but three security cameras monitoring the waiting area. Either she was being paranoid, or all three were angled in her direction, tiny red lights blipping steadily. "Don't take this the wrong way…" she breathed when, out of the corner of her eye, she spotted Shaun approaching a big guy, even more intense-looking, wearing a similar dark suit, "…but I think maybe you were right. This might have been a bad idea."

Both men behind the counter cast spurious glances her way while speaking quietly to one another.

Darcy swallowed hard, forced herself to stay calm and not make any attention-grabbing moves. She was just a woman looking for her wayward boyfriend. That was all.

But that didn't stop her pulse from racing out of control when she saw Shaun nod and head in her direction. She pressed a finger against the earbud and whispered, "Call me." When she didn't get an immediate response, she clarified: "Hang up and call me back, Riordan. Now."

Her heart was pounding so hard it felt like it was trying to escape her body. She kept her attention on the wall, the faces blurring beneath her nervousness, counting the unending seconds until Riordan phoned her.

"Darcy." Shaun's tone held a decidedly forced cheer. "I'm sorry for keeping you waiting. There appears to be something wrong with our system at the moment. If you wouldn't mind stepping into one of our offices while we locate Mr. Winchester's—"

When Darcy's phone rang, it took every bit of control she possessed not to pounce on it. Instead, she waited a beat, then produced the phone from her bag. "This is him." She'd barely glanced at the screen but held up her phone as if for proof. "I'll just be a minute." She tapped Accept. "Clyde? Where are you? I'm here at SilverPeak waiting—"

"You've got about thirty seconds before I come get you." Despite his warning and tone, Darcy felt an immediate sense of relief hearing his voice.

"Oh." She bit her lip, turned her most embarrassed expression on Shaun and pressed a hand to her mouth. "Oh, no. I did it again, didn't? I got the name wrong. This isn't where you told me to be at all."

"You found something."

"Boy, did I," she said with a laugh. "Totally screwed up. I know. Impossible to believe, right?"

"Do you need help?"

"No, no, you wait where you are," she ordered. "I'll grab a Lyft and get to you as soon as I can." After she hung up, she said to Shaun, "That'll teach me to go by my memory. This isn't where I'm supposed to meet him at all." She shook her head. "I'm so sorry to waste your time."

"Not a waste," Shaun assured her and waved the other man over. "Why don't you let me get you a car? We'll be happy to reunite the two of you."

"Oh, heavens, there's no need for that." She raised her voice just enough to get the attention of the other customers as she made her way to the door. Shaun couldn't force her into doing anything with witnesses around. "You have these lovely people to take care of. No reason to worry about me. Thank you for your time. So sorry to have bothered you."

She could feel both men's eyes on her as she hurried out, focusing her attention on her cell phone as if calling for that car. She waited until she was at the corner traffic light before she looked back and found both Shaun and his coworker approaching a black SUV that had just arrived. She tried to tell herself she was being paranoid again, that neither Shaun nor the other man were interested in her, but the hairs prickling on the back of her neck and arms said otherwise.

When the light finally changed, she began to cross the street, only to realize halfway that Riordan and the Rover were gone. She eased her pace and clutched her phone against her chest.

There were a lot of things she was uncertain about, but he wouldn't have left her. Wouldn't have abandoned her. Even as the thought slipped through her mind, she caught sight of their own car in the distance, headed her way.

Her phone rang again. This time she put it on speaker. "I drove around the block," Riordan said when she answered. "Wait where you are and pretend I'm the Lyft you called."

"Okay." Fear and adrenaline made her voice shake. She stared at her phone as if tracking the car's arrival. She didn't think she fully breathed again until Riordan pulled up in front of her. She all but leaped into the car, sank back in the seat and let out a gut-deep breath.

"Okay, for the record, you were right. That was probably a big mistake, but—"

"It better be a pretty amazing *but*."

"I saw our ghosts." She tugged her belt across her chest as he took off down the street. "The two dead men from my apartment."

"They were there? Inside?" Riordan's voice snapped through the vehicle.

"No. But they're part of the staff photo for personal security." Her stomach was threatening to jump right out of her throat. "They work there."

"Are you okay?"

"Yeah, yeah, I'm fine." She shoved her hair out of her face, noticed her shaking hands and put them out of sight. One look at Riordan, however, had her frowning and forgetting about her own adrenaline crash. "What about you? Something's wrong. You look—I don't know—sick."

"It's nothing."

It was, Darcy realized as her stomach sank, the first time he'd lied to her. Or maybe it was only the first time she could tell. She ventured to guess he was afraid of worrying her, especially given her speedy retreat from the rental agency. She caught him glancing into the rearview mirror. And then again, she said, "What?"

"We've picked up a tail." The shift in his tone, the steel force of his words had her swinging around in her seat.

"Are you sure?"

"No." When the light turned green, he hit the gas, turned left and headed down the Strip. "Let's say we find out."

Darcy wasn't far off the mark saying he looked sick. He felt sick. His head had been pounding for the past few hours. He'd downed a painkiller once she'd left the car, but it had only taken the edge off. Even blinking was beginning to hurt.

The memories were flooding back. It was as if his life were being pushed through a very narrow pipe, propelled by urgency and pressure yet slowed by countless twists, turns and filters.

But he could feel his mind being filled one drop at a time, information trickling into place yet settling into a jumbled pool, threatening to drag him under the surface. It was not, he admitted as his hands tightened around the steering wheel, the time to be driving a car, let alone attempting to ditch whoever had decided to follow them.

There were names now flying through his mind. Names that sounded and felt familiar but still didn't connect to the faces he could see flashing in his mind's eye. The process of recovering his memory was, in a way, far more jarring than living with a blank slate the last few days.

"Where are we going?" Darcy's quiet question rattled his already frayed nerves. She was shaking. More than he was. There was no mistaking the fear he heard in her tremor of a voice.

"Not sure." It wasn't helping that he couldn't fully concentrate. He should pull over, let her drive, but the constant flow of traffic was working against them. He needed free rein to do the unexpected. Cramped in with all of these cars didn't give him many options. If any.

He needed a break. He needed to get out of this car. He needed some food and sleep and to give his body a chance to reconnect to his mind. Or to at least silence the evil little gremlin waging war inside his skull.

Until he got relief from any of that, there wasn't much he could cling to as a certainty.

Except for one thing.

He was not going to let Darcy repeat a stunt like her solo foray into the rental company.

Not because she couldn't handle herself; clearly she had extricated herself from the situation pretty well, all things considered. But he'd learned something very important about himself as he'd sat in that car listening to her talk not only to Shaun but to him in the only way she could.

Riordan did not like waiting any more than he liked being left behind.

Left behind...

It had been that thought that caused the nausea in

his stomach and made him want to fall into the oblivion of images swimming in his head.

"Which car is following us?" Darcy asked.

"The SUV farther back." He recited the plate by memory, something he hadn't even realized he'd absorbed. "It turned out of the rental agency parking lot just as we drove off." He glanced at her and she bit her lip. "My turn to ask, what?"

"The guy I was talking to inside, Shaun?" She looked back again. "He and the other one from the back office followed me outside and went over to talk to someone in a car that looks like that one. I can't say for certain it's the same one—"

"Let's assume it is." He pointed to her cell. "Pull up the map of the Strip on your phone. I want to know what's around here."

"All right. I'll look for a place to stay while we're at it." She tapped her phone. "What are you looking for?"

"Alleyways, side streets, parking structures, shopping centers."

"I'm seeing all of those." She glanced up at the traffic lights, then back to her phone. "How soon can you make a right? There's a parking structure about a mile and a half east."

He hit his turn signal but stayed in his lane. "We need to ditch the car. That's a good place."

"What? No, we can't do that! Eden—"

"Not permanently." Riordan kept one eye on the vehicle behind him. The SUV was a good two to three cars back. Not that they had much choice. "We can park it for a few days, make sure it's out of sight while

we hole up in a hotel and decide on our next move."
The car in the next lane shifted forward just enough
for him to see a path. "Hang on." He wrenched the
wheel to the side and practically floored it through the
multilane opening. His impulse earned a cacophony
of blaring horns as he made a sharp unexpected right
at the next corner.

He nearly clipped a parked car before pulling the
tires straight. His head swam.

Darcy twisted in her seat again, eyes wide. "No way
they can follow us out of that." Even now the horns continued to blare and brakes screeched. "You aren't win-
ning over friends in this city, Mr. Malloy."

"Not trying to." The only thing he cared about right
now was getting them—getting her—someplace safe.
He gripped the wheel lightly and made a series of turns
that brought them to a narrow back road behind one of
the main hotels on the Strip.

"Something's wrong," Darcy said. "With you. Your
head."

"I'm just tired," he assured her. "Everything just
sounds excessively loud now that we're in the city."

"Yeah." She leaned over and looked up. "The traffic copter overhead probably doesn't help."

Relief swept through him. A chopper was making all
that racket? Maybe his head wasn't so bad. He passed
a number of delivery bays and drove down the next
block, turned. Down the next. He took slow, deliberate
breaths, hoping to ease his churning stomach.

"Do you have a specific destination in mind?" There

was panic and more than a little sarcasm in the question. "That parking lot is in the other direction."

"Just following your advice and going with the flow." He hunched over the wheel to look down an alleyway and spotted an open space between two parked cars. It would be a tight fit into the narrow spot filled with trash bins and debris.

He hit the brakes, glanced behind him to make sure no one was close then backed up and turned in. "We're taking the long way around." But another look into his rearview mirror had him rethinking his plan. The now familiar SUV drove slowly down the road behind them. Biting back a curse, he hit the gas and clipped not one but two metal dumpsters in the process.

"Eden is going to kill me," Darcy muttered as she grabbed hold of the chicken bar over the door. "You don't get extra points for hitting them, you know!"

"This is why I prefer to fly." But he was good at spinning the cans into the other car's path. He'd barely gotten them out of the alley when another SUV slid in behind him. "Great. Now they're multiplying." Or he was seeing double. Neither was good.

"Can we lose him on the freeway?" Darcy asked. "There's an entrance about two and a half miles east. Turn left here."

Traffic had eased or, at least, thinned out which gave him more options to play with. He cast a quick look at the map app on her phone. Instantly, he could see the entire layout of Vegas in his head.

Chills erupted on his arms and the back of his neck, niggling at the instincts he'd forgotten to listen to. Doing as she suggested would only delay the inevitable. And make them even more visible in the open air space.

Air space...

He hunched over. Scanned the sky for the chopper.

"This is my fault," Darcy said. "They knew who I was the second I stepped inside that car place. I never had a chance at finding out anything that would help you, did I?"

"You discovered your would-be inquisitors work for that car company," he told her. "That's more than something." It wasn't her fault. It was his, for putting her in that situation in the first place. It was time to put distance between them. He could move faster on his own. Make riskier choices with potentially bigger payoffs on his own. "Darcy, I want you to listen to me."

"No."

"You don't even know what I'm going to say."

"Your Lancelot sword is showing." Even while one of her hands gripped the chicken bar over her door and the other clung white-knuckled around the edge of her seat, the defiance and determination in her eyes banked most of his doubts and worry. "Don't you dare think about leaving me behind."

It struck him that it should bother him more that she understood him so well. "There's a police station nearby. I can drop you—"

"You'd be dumping me, which I recognize because I've done more than my share of that. As I'm also familiar with the idea of Karma, you ditching me now would only be a short-term solution. If they suspected

I knew something before, they'll be convinced even more of it now. You really think they'll just ignore me and focus on you?"

No, Riordan had to admit, he didn't. "You should call your friend. The one in the FBI. Naymer?" Riordan suggested.

"Eamon?"

"Yeah. Call him now."

"Now he wants to call the FBI," she muttered. "Better late than never. Watch out. Red light. Red light!"

She stretched out her legs and raised up out of her seat as if slamming on her own set of brakes. He blasted through the light to the now familiar cacophony of horns and screeching tires. Their tail got caught in the confusion, giving Riordan some breathing room.

"Guess I'll need to add paying for traffic tickets to what I'm going to owe Eden. No!" Darcy held up a hand as she played with her phone. "You wanted me to call Eamon, I'm calling Eamon. Not giving you a chance to change your mind. Parking structure," she added and pointed to the left. "Two miles that way. Step on it. Eamon?" She swore.

"What's wrong?" The pain in his head was easing, but the world seemed to be tilting around him. He flexed his hands, checking for numbness, loss of strength.

"Went straight to voicemail. Don't worry," she assured him. "Eamon, hey, it's Darcy. Not sure if you heard, but I've made a new friend. His name is Riordan Malloy. He's military. Army. Intelligence according to his file. Anyway, he's the man wanted for questioning in the death of Jay Russo out of Travis Air Force Base.

We're currently in Vegas trying to find out who may have framed him, and we've run into some issues. If you could, I don't know, maybe work some of your FBI magic and come out here and lend a hand? And in case I'm sounding a little irrational, talk to Eden. Or Jason. They'll fill you in. Okay, thanks. Bye! Yeah, no, that didn't sound strange at all," she muttered after she'd hung up.

"Vegas is a pretty big place," Riordan said with all the patience he could muster as he frowned at the chopper that buzzed overhead like an irascible fly. "Tell me something. How is he supposed to find us if he does come out here?"

"With this." She hauled her purse into her lap and dug into it, produced the key fob from Riordan's rented SUV. "There's a GPS tracker inside, remember? Jason has the information. I don't think—hey!"

Riordan stole the key fob out of her hand and, after powering down his window, tossed it out of the car. It rattled when it hit the asphalt.

"Why'd you do that?"

"Why did I throw out the key fob I originally got at the car rental agency you were just in?" he repeated.

"But—oh." Her mouth stayed in that silent O for a good few seconds. "Guess I didn't think of that."

He should have. He scrubbed his hand across his forehead. He should have thought of that ages ago. His vision blurred and for a moment, and he lost his grip on the steering wheel.

"Riordan!"

"Yeah, sorry." He tried to shake it off and felt the

need for air. She unclipped her seat belt, making the warning alarm in the car blare. "It's okay. I've got it."

Darcy leaned forward and put her hand on the wheel. "No, you don't. Riordan, stop. Pull over."

"I will soon. We're almost there." He needed to get them to some kind of cover.

"Pull over, or I'll jump out of this car right now." Darcy was close enough he could feel her breath on his face. Hot breath. Determined breath. Even more determined eyes.

"No, you won't."

"Try me." One of her hands was still on the wheel. He could feel the tension in her fingers as she braced herself over the console with her other hand. "You need to stop, Riordan. Before you hurt both of us."

Being reckless with himself was one thing. "All right. What does that sign say?" He motioned with his chin. "Parking lot?"

"Next block up. I'm not joking. If you bypass it—"

"I won't. Promise," he added when her eyes narrowed. "I've got it, Darcy. Trust me." Here he was asking her to trust him when he wasn't sure he could trust himself. But he stayed true to his word and, after switching to the right lane, turned into the parking structure and headed up the ramp.

He skimmed the signs as they drove. Second floor, third. A reminder that the fifth rooftop floor was off limits except for clientele with helicopter access. They'd need a dedicated key card to get to the roof, which was probably just as well. The car would be less easy to hide exposed like that on the top floor.

"Here," Darcy ordered as if reading his mind. She pointed to a spot at the far end, directly across from the up ramp to level three. "Park right here."

Riordan wasn't about to argue. He was more than ready to relinquish operating their transportation. The second he stopped the car, he leaned his head back on the rest.

"Why didn't you tell me you were feeling sick?" Darcy demanded as she shoved open her door and ran around the front of the car.

"It's okay." He mustered every ounce of control he possessed. "It's passing." The nausea was still there, lurking, but his head throbbed less. She opened his door and, after he unhooked his belt, turned and dropped out of the car. The second his feet hit the cement, his stomach revolted. "Nope. Wrong." He dived toward the back of the car, made a sharp right, braced his hands on the corner wall, and emptied what contents were in his stomach.

"Here."

Darcy's soft voice was followed by her pushing a bottle of water into his hand. He rinsed his mouth, spit it out and downed the rest of the bottle. Only then did his knees feel strong enough to hold him.

"Better?" she asked.

"Yeah." He nodded and followed her back to their car. "That is the last time I eat gas station beef jerky."

"You should have told me."

"Why tell when I can clearly show?" If he didn't make a joke out of it, he was going to have to be embarrassed, and he didn't feel up to doing that at the moment.

"You need to see a doctor." She stopped and faced him, brushed her fingers against his temple. "Vomiting is a sign of a concussion. Or something worse."

"Well, I'm done with that now, so we can move on." He clicked open the trunk, returned to the cab to retrieve her gun they'd stashed in the console and shoved it into the back waistband of his jeans. "Grab your stuff. We need to get out of here."

"But—"

"We need to put more distance between us and that key fob." Finding that fob at the scene of his accident hadn't been a coincidence. He'd bet whatever money he had in the bank that whoever ran him off the rode had left it there in case he came back.

Darcy frowned, clearly considering what argument to make next.

"We'll see about going to a clinic once we're sure we're clear of those SUVs." He hoisted out his duffle bag that also contained her laptop. She stuffed a few extra bottles of water into her backpack before shoving a smaller canvas bag he hadn't seen before in as well. Hiking it onto her shoulders, she returned to the front seat, grabbed her purse and slipped the strap over her head.

Riordan didn't want to waste any time. For the moment he was feeling pretty good, and he wanted to take advantage of it.

"An exit. Over there." He pointed to the stairwell across the way and they walk-ran to the door. Just as

Darcy shoved at the bar and the door opened, Riordan felt an odd prickling at the back of his neck. "Darcy!" He yanked her backward just as a bullet plowed into the cement wall where her head had just been. She staggered away but stayed on her feet.

He scanned behind them for an alternate getaway but saw the black SUV idling at the edge of the ramp. "Go on but stay low!" He ordered and pushed the metal door open.

Another shot. This one hit just as they raced inside the stairwell. Darcy screamed. It was a sickening sound he never, for the rest of his life, wanted to hear again. Below them, a door slammed shut. Footsteps echoed up the metal stairs.

He moved in, pried her fingers loose from the railing she was clinging to. "We need to climb. Up. Next level. Then down, once we can. Darcy!"

He saw the terror in her eyes and wanted nothing else but to erase it then and there. "You're okay, Darcy. You're okay." She nodded, but not in quite the same trusting way as he was used to. "Go. Run. Up the stairs."

"But—"

"We go where we have a choice. Right now, down isn't one." As if the universe decided to prove his point, another shot rang up ahead of whoever was climbing those stairs. She yelped and ducked back to the stairs. "Go!" He followed at a slower pace. He was not near peak performance. His head was back to pounding in time with his rapid pulse. He grabbed the railing and hauled himself around to the top landing, where she was waiting.

"It's locked, remember? No access card." She seized the handle with both hands and tried to open the door.

"Stand back." He dropped his bag, pulled out the gun and aimed it at the keypad on the wall. He fired once, frying the circuits and sparks exploded around them. Darcy tried the door again. She shook her head.

The fear he saw on her face had him yanking what was left of the plate free and staring at the exposed wires. "No idea what I'm doing." Except it seemed he did. His fingers worked faster than he could think. Plucking and twisting colored wires together, singeing his fingers until he heard a distinctive click and catch. "Try it now."

Darcy pulled on the handle. The door flew open so fast she nearly toppled over. With lightning speed, she had her belongings in her hands and was sprinting through the door onto the fifth-story roof.

Riordan hustled behind her, gun in one hand. "Over there!" He pointed to a cement overhang housing trash bins on the other side of the chopper pad. He made a quick count of half a dozen cars parked on this level. None of them looked promising in the way of offering protection or containing anything they might be able to use.

The footsteps were coming closer. They could still hear them clanging on the metal stairs behind the closed door. There were more of them now. Riordan tossed his bag to the ground, and as Darcy raced for the security of the cement wall, he turned, gun raised and walked backward to focus on their pursuers.

The second the door popped open, he fired.

"Riordan!" Darcy yelled.

"I'm okay! Stay where you are!" He'd hit someone. He knew that as certainly as he knew how to breathe. They tried to come through again. He fired. Again. Three shots. Only seven bullets left in the clip.

He heard an engine rumbling from inside the lot. Tires screeched as if rounding tight curves.

"Riordan!" This time Darcy's voice wasn't filled with fear but with hope.

His internal debate was brief. He held off firing and, instead, ran to her and found her at the back wall, right next to a metal ladder. "Fire escape," she said. "We can—"

He nodded. "Go."

"What? No. Not alone." The terror was back. Her curly hair had caught the wind and blown across her face, nearly obscuring her laser-beam-like green eyes. "Not without you."

"I'll be right behind you. Go!" He returned to the wall and peeked around the corner as the stairway door banged open. He sucked in a shallow breath when he recognized the men as the two from Darcy's apartment. They were bruised, but there was no mistaking those faces. Rage undercut the pain in his head, and he saw red, but he hesitated a moment too long. Both men fired. Chunks of cement exploded around him. They weren't interested in interrogating him. They wanted him, wanted both of them, dead.

Riordan steeled himself, raised his gun. He had to give Darcy time to get down that scaffold. To get free. He leaned, aimed and fired two quick shots. The men leaped out of the way, separating and dropping from sight.

That car engine's roar grew louder. Stupid of him to think these two had come alone. Reinforcements were on the way. Time to get out of here.

The pounding in his head was as fierce as ever. His vision blurred, and he squeezed his eyes shut. Bad idea, as he felt himself sway and stumble forward. When he grabbed hold of the railing, a new panic surged. "Darcy!" She stopped where she was, a few rungs down the ladder, and looked up, eyes wide.

"What? What's wrong?"

The metal ladder creaked and strained. A bolt popped loose and dropped straight down the five stories. Darcy's gaze followed the bolt, and when it hit the ground, as if in slow motion, she raised her chin and met his gaze. "Riordan?" Dismay shadowed the terror. Memory or not, Riordan knew he was experiencing one of the worst moments of his life.

He shoved his gun into the back of his waistband, leaned over and stretched out his arm to her. "Come back up." She hugged the ladder now, almost flattening herself against the side of the building. Her oversized backpack was only adding to the weight, testing the metal structure. "Darcy, give me your—"

The hair on the back of his neck shot to attention. Before the chills could erupt on his arms, he straightened and slammed his elbow back. He made solid contact with flesh, heard the sound of bone breaking. He spun and followed that strike with another punch, sending one of the two men flying backward. When the second man moved in, gun aimed straight at his chest, Riordan realized his mistake. The slow sickening smile on the gunman's face only confirmed it.

A dark sedan, windows down, pulled to a screeching halt behind them.

An unmistakable bang sounded!

Riordan jumped.

The second man twisted and went down like a ton of bricks.

The first man, blood on his face from his busted nose, turned, weapon aimed.

Two more bangs!

He flew back, landed hard, wet darkness spreading against his black tee.

Riordan froze. Stared. Waited for the next shot to hit him point blank. But it never came.

Instead, the driver slid out from behind the wheel, tossed his sunglasses onto the seat and headed for him. "You okay?"

Riordan nodded and stared down at the bodies. "Who—?"

The man pressed a finger to his ear. "Yes, sir. Situation contained. I'm retrieving them now. Bixton is my name," he said to Riordan as he kicked the two men's weapons well out of reach and holstered his own gun.

Bixton was tall. Taller than Riordan, and that was saying something. He also had a good thirty pounds on him. Olive skin, dark hair and even darker eyes that didn't come close to registering as familiar. "Where's Ms. Ford?"

Darcy! He launched himself back to the roof line.

"Riordan!" Darcy's voice still held that thread of panic but also irritation that was all her. "Every time I move, another bolt drops."

Riordan reached out, but she was far enough away that only their fingertips brushed.

Bixton appeared next to him, seemed to take in the situation in an instant even as another bolt shimmied free. Beneath her, the entire ladder whined and rattled. "That was the third one that's come loose," she squeaked out as she drew her hand back and held on to the rung above her.

Riordan stepped back and started to kick his leg over.

"Don't." Bixton slapped a hand against his chest. "You'll only add to the weight and send it crashing down faster." He motioned to Riordan to return, removed his jacket and tossed it aside. "We don't have a lot of time. She's going to have to let go so we can grab her."

"Oh, no she isn't!" Darcy yelled. "Riordan?"

He looked at Bixton, at the determination and lack of doubt on the man's face. "If she falls, I'll—"

"If she falls, I'll come back from the dead and haunt both of you!" Darcy shouted up to them.

"Understood," Bixton confirmed. "One rung up. Then we can reach her. Yeah?"

Riordan would have nodded if his head wasn't already aching. The dizziness was back though. And he could feel the nausea kicking up again, but he swallowed the sour taste. "Darcy." He leaned over once more. "You need to move up just one more rung so we can reach you."

"One more rung. Right." She ducked her chin, pressed her forehead against the rung she was gripping then nodded. "Okay. One more. Or maybe…two." She lifted her right foot, planted it on the next rung and stepped up.

"No, Darcy, just—"

Two bolts burst free. Puffs of cement dust plumed as she pushed off and lifted her arms. Her foot didn't catch nearly the traction he'd hoped it would. Whatever height she'd intended to get dropped away, along with her.

Riordan and Bixton stretched down and locked one hand around each of her wrists. As her legs flailed, the entire structure crashed into a heap below. Darcy swung back and hit the side of the building, practically bouncing before they reached out with their other hands.

It hurt to breathe with the edge of the roof pressing into the base of his ribcage. The muscles in his arms and shoulders burned. "Look at me, Darcy! Don't look down!" Riordan ordered when she turned her head to peer over her shoulder. "Look at me."

She did so, and once she stopped kicking, they pulled her up, over the ledge and onto the roof. He didn't even wait to catch his breath before he hauled her into his arms. When he felt her cling to him, only then did he feel as if he could breathe again.

"Do me a favor," she said, panting, when he set her back and caught her face in his hands. She locked her fingers around his wrists. "Don't ever let me choose our escape route again." She started to walk away, but he stopped her. Turned her.

And kissed her.

Desperation tangled with need. The need to feel her touch, feel her lips, know that she was still alive and, most of all, know that she was his. Illogical. Rash. Impulsive. And absolutely necessary to regain what equilibrium he possessed.

When she pulled away from him he realized it wasn't to move out of reach but to give herself the room to touch his face in kind.

"I'm okay." Her gaze shifted to Bixton, then back to him. "Maybe later I can prove that to you, but right now…" she trailed off, her face losing what color was left when she saw the two dead bodies by the car. "That's…them." She grabbed his arm. "Those are the two men from my apartment!"

"They can't hurt you anymore," Riordan assured her.

"Yeah," she choked out. "I can see that."

"We need to get you both someplace safe," Bixton told them.

"What's that sound?" Darcy winced and covered her ears.

Dread pooled in Riordan's stomach. He looked at Bixton, who didn't seem concerned about the approaching helicopter. Questions remained. Suspicion surged. "Your boss?"

"Yes, sir."

There was something he recognized in the man's tone. In the way he called him sir. Those flashes of memory were coming faster now, driving the air out of Riordan's lungs.

"What? Who are you talking about?" Darcy shifted

closer, captured his hand in hers as the chopper descended and landed on the platform. "Did things just get better? Or worse?"

Riordan didn't have an answer, nor did one occur to him as the back door of the helicopter opened. The man who emerged buttoned his immaculate gray suit jacket as he ducked and hurried forward. He descended the platform stairs, shoved two hands through stylish dark blond hair that framed an all too familiar face.

"It's the third man," Darcy whispered. "The one from the picture on your phone."

"Bixton." The new man nodded at their rescuer and slapped a hand on Bixton's shoulder, but he passed him, his steady dark-eyed gaze firmly fixed on Riordan. "You never did like listening to me, Malloy. I told you to be careful, and yet here you are. Neck deep in trouble." He pointed to the bodies lying on the ground. "Some things never change."

"Who are you?" Darcy asked, her voice raised so as to be heard over the continuous whopping of the chopper blades.

"Foster." Riordan's response was as much a surprise to him as it was to Darcy, given her expression. The second he said the name, it was as if he'd set off a chain of explosions in his memory. "What took you so long, sir?"

Chapter 9

Darcy really didn't think dangling five stories above the ground could have been topped, trauma-wise, but that was before she stood staring down at two dead bodies. Two men who had just tried to end her life. How was she supposed to feel about this? What was she supposed to feel?

Even as she processed the last few minutes, she found herself attempting to decipher what she heard in Riordan's voice. Relief? Certainly. Disbelief? Definitely. Admiration? Possibly. But there was also confusion. To be expected. Riordan was in spite of it all grasping at the truth that continued to elude him. And that more than anything told her the good man she'd spent the past few days with still existed.

She touched two fingers to her tingling lips. If a kiss

like that was her reward for nearly plummeting to the street below, she might have to rethink her risk-taking tendencies. Dead bodies and all. A bubble of hysteria popped in her chest and she closed her mouth to stop it from escaping.

"Major Foster Krinard, Ms. Ford." Foster held out his hand and offered a smile that screamed charm. "Retired Army. I've read a lot about you. Pleasure to finally meet you in person."

"Thanks, Major." What else was there to say? His appearance, while potential good news for Riordan, only presented more questions for her. Like how did he know where to find them, and why was he even here in a parking lot just off the Vegas Strip.

The good looks she'd seen in the picture had not been an illusion. The blond hair, dark brown eyes, obviously spa-treated skin. But there wasn't any of the instant presence that had been caught by a cell phone. She saw a hardness now, concealed behind the friendly teasing greeting. This was a serious man on a serious mission.

As good as it was to meet him, Major Foster Krinard didn't seem eager to provide any additional details that might extricate them from the nightmare of Riordan's frame-up.

"Foster, please. I dropped the Major four years ago," Foster said. "Except for those who served under me, right, Bixton?"

"Yes, sir." Bixton straightened instantly as if he'd been brought to attention.

"I take it there's a story or two to be told about you

and Riordan, then?" Tales she'd have preferred to hear from Riordan. "Can we start with the last time you saw each other? Why was he meeting with Jay Russo?"

"We can discuss all of that, certainly," Foster said. "But first, we should get the two of you out of here as quickly as possible." He motioned to the stairs and the chopper that waited. "Please." Below the beating of the chopper blades, the echoes of sirens rang through the air. "We'll continue this conversation onboard."

"Ah, no." Darcy's grip tightened on Riordan. "I don't think so. Thanks though. How about we meet you somewhere—"

"I'm afraid I really must insist." Foster's tone shifted as he turned his gaze on Riordan. "Captain, the police are already on their way, and Bixton needs some time to deal with…" He gestured to the scene in front of them. "Unless the two of you would like to explain how this happened."

"Darcy," Riordan said without looking at her, "I think we should—"

"I'm not getting in that flying projectile." Darcy scrunched her toes in her sneakers and bid farewell to her stomach. Was it possible for a heart to flutter this fast? "You'd have to knock me out first."

"That could be arranged," Foster said with only a fraction of the charm he'd displayed earlier.

"That won't be necessary," Riordan said.

"Then work it out, Captain," Foster ordered. "And make it fast."

Riordan steered her away. "Don't manhandle me, Riordan. I can walk just fine." Her wobbly knees said otherwise. "I'm still Team Free Will even if you've switched sides."

"What's that supposed to mean? Darcy—" When he moved toward her, she stepped back and hitched her pack higher on her shoulders.

"When did it happen?"

He flinched. "When did what—?"

"You know exactly what I'm talking about." She jutted out her chin. "When did your memory come back?"

"It didn't. It hasn't," he corrected quickly. "Not...all of it." He looked as confused as she felt. But where his confusion ended, her hurt began. "Darcy, this isn't—"

"I promise, if you say this isn't what it looks like, I'm going to chuck you off this roof. We're supposed to be a team, remember? We're in this together. Or was that just—"

"You know it wasn't." All humor faded from his face.

"Do I? All of a sudden you're jumping at orders. Who is he?" she demanded.

"My former CO. From...years ago." He pressed his palm against the side of his head. "I don't know if I can explain all of this in a rush, Darcy. Like he said, we don't have time—"

She crossed her arms over her chest. "Got someplace to be?"

"Anyplace other than a jail cell. Foster's right. We can't be here when the police arrive. One of those bullets in one of those guys came from your gun, Darcy. I'm protecting you as much as I am myself."

"So, when all else fails you're going to scare me into

going with you." She arched her eyebrow and dismissed the fear threatening to surge. "Do you really think you can say anything that will change my mind about getting into *that*?" Her arm shot up and she pointed at the chopper.

"Something has to," he argued.

"I'd sooner take my chances with the cops." They both knew that was a lie. With Darcy's penchant for running her mouth, she'd probably end up confessing to kidnapping Hoffa once she was taken into custody.

Up until this second, she'd been able to decipher his expressions. It had always brought her some amount of peace, but now? Now she had no idea what he was thinking. And that, more than the idea of climbing into that machine, more than the sight of two dead men at their feet, frightened her the most.

"The way I see it—" Riordan spoke in a way that had her gnashing her teeth "—you have two choices. Wait here and explain all of this to the police and hope your FBI agent friend Ernest—"

"Eamon," she ground out and dropped her hand to her side.

"Whatever. Hope he pops up in time to stop you from being booked as an accessory after the fact or come with me and see this through."

"I didn't say I didn't want to see this through." But she was having doubts about him. About them. Far larger ones than when she'd stopped herself in the Brass Eagle's parking lot. "But maybe, Riordan, we don't jump in the first helicopter that shows up to help us?"

"Or maybe not jump into any helicopter at all?"

She crossed her arms again.

"I'm afraid we really must go. Now," Foster called to them.

"I promised I would get you out of this situation safely," Riordan said. "I know it's a hard thing to do after everything that's happened, but I need you to trust me."

"I did trust you," she told him. "Completely. Until about five minutes ago when Major Moody showed up along with your memory. I'm not sure who you are at the moment."

He winced, as if each word had punctured his heart. "Perhaps it's the real me you're finally seeing. I need to know what happened to Jay, Darcy. If you don't believe anything else, believe that. Come with me. I'll make sure Foster gets in contact with people who can help us. See this through with me and I will get you back home. Back to your life. If, after that, you don't want to see me again, I'll disappear. For good."

Emotion burned the back of her throat. The impulse to stomp her foot and throw a toddler-worthy fit felt overwhelming. That wasn't what she wanted at all. What she wanted...

What she wanted was him. She also wanted him to be proven innocent. And most of all, safe.

"Captain?" Foster approached. "Ms. Ford?"

"Darcy," she said grudgingly. "Where would we be going exactly?" she asked with slightly less fire than what currently burned in her belly.

"The Medallion," replied Foster.

One more tidbit of information to bowl her over.

"The new luxury hotel and casino at the other end of the Strip?" The building that had taken over four years to complete? The one that promised a top-of-the-line transportive experience from the moment you stepped inside? "The one with the million-dollar-a-night suite?" She eyed him. "How does a retired Army major have that kind of money?"

"Very easily when he's one of the most sought after private security experts in the world," Foster said matter of factly. "As the owner of Crowder Security, I'm afforded many business opportunities and benefits, not least of which is my choice of residences. I can assure you, once we are in the Medallion, the police will not be able to find you."

Yeah. Darcy smirked. And wasn't that convenient? There wasn't a lot the major said that she accepted as truth. But she had no doubt he wasn't letting her or Riordan walk away from this parking structure under their own steam. "Okay. Who am I to refuse a stay at a luxury hotel? I take it there's a pool?" Her question landed exactly the way she hoped it would. Foster's smile was back to being easy, friendly and, if she wasn't mistaken, more than a little condescending. *Good*, she thought. *Underestimate me. That'll work out great for all of us.*

"There are numerous pools, as well as many water features available to you during your stay."

The sirens were creeping ever closer, an audible reminder of the choice she had to make.

Darcy eyed the chopper and wondered if she could somehow leave her stomach behind. "There's just one more thing," she said and met Foster's gaze. "Riordan needs a doctor."

"Darcy!" Riordan began to say. "I—"

"He does. A good one. You want me on that thing, this is the price *you* pay," she told Foster. "He hit his head a few days ago. Woke up without being able to remember most everything about his life."

"Amnesia?" Foster's eyebrows arched. "You can't be serious?"

"I am," Darcy said. "I want him examined and, if necessary, taken to the hospital for tests."

"We have a full medical facility on-site at the Medallion," Foster said with a nod as he pulled out his cell. "I'll send for Dr. Bradford as soon as we arrive. Is there anything else you'll require?"

"Yes." She eyed both men. "A barf bag. A big one."

"Darcy, are you sure—?"

"Don't talk to me," Darcy snapped and dug her fingers even harder into Riordan's arm. "It's taking all of my energy not to be sick." The chopper dipped and turned and her closed eyes popped open. "What was that? Are we falling?"

Riordan wasn't remotely inclined to laugh. She looked and sounded positively miserable. And more than a little ticked off.

"Merely a change of direction." Foster settled into the leather seat across from where Riordan and Darcy had strapped themselves in. Plush high-back chairs faced one another to facilitate conversation.

The outside of the helicopter, painted in a bold combination of black, red and gold, gave no indication as to its interior luxury. Spacious and elegant, with compact amenities and tinted windows that not only kept the streaming sun and heat out of the passenger cabin, but also dimmed the view outside and below.

They'd left Bixton with their two dead attackers only moments before. How Foster's right-hand man planned to clean up the scene wasn't something Riordan particularly wanted to contemplate. Whatever tactic he used led to the same conclusion. His former CO, his friend, was existing in a world that, a decade ago, neither of them would have accepted. He remembered now in minute detail how he'd spent his last four years as an Army intelligence officer and that he'd put his life in Major Foster Krinard's hands on more than one occasion. He had to wonder if his brain had been scrambled to the point that he was unable to trust his judgment.

He didn't know what kind of magic Foster thought he could perform to pull Riordan out of the mess he was in.

"Here." Foster pried Darcy's hand free of the death grip she had on the armrest and pressed a half-filled glass into it. "Ginger ale. Mira swears it's a cure-all."

"Mira?" Darcy raised the glass, sniffed, frowned, sipped, and then took a long drink.

"My wife." Foster twisted the gold band on his finger. "Riordan hasn't told you about... Ah." Foster tapped his forehead, crossed his legs. "Your amnesia. Interesting. And here I've always believed Mira to be an impossible woman to forget. She's been away for a few days, so I haven't told her what's been going on. She would have worried," Foster added. "As much as she worries about any of her old friends."

Mira. There was something in Foster's voice that set Riordan's mind on a track he didn't necessarily want Darcy on. Just hearing the woman's name pulled the image of her face out of the shadows and stirred up feelings he wasn't in a position to evaluate just then.

"What happened to Jay?" Riordan asked. "Why did I need to speak with him so urgently? We tried to get to my case files, but—"

"Even you, with your myriad of talents, couldn't break through the Pentagon's cyber walls? That's who is handling the investigation. Bixton, however, was able to call in a few favors as far as Jay's murder is concerned. They took two nine-millimeter slugs out of him after his body was found in his home near Travis Air Force Base. No signs of a break-in, no report of gunshots—"

Riordan bristled. "How did the police get called in if no one heard anything?"

"Watson."

Riordan shook his head to show he was at a loss.

Foster clarified. "Jay's dog. The neighbors called in a noise complaint. Police arrived on scene, found the animal guarding the front door, barking his head off. They had to have animal control calm him down before they could get in, which is when they found Jay's body."

Watson. Riordan had the vague impression of Jay's pet, but…

"Watson is part of the reason the police believe Jay knew his killer. No way a stranger intent on doing harm would have gotten past that animal. Add to that Jay only having four off-base visitors check in to see him in the forty-eight hours prior to his death. Three have been questioned and dismissed as suspects. The other, a man, who witnesses claim had a very loud argument with him, was you." Foster glanced out the window as the skyline for New York-New York Hotel and Casino whizzed by. "Only one weapon found at the scene. Yours. Only one set of prints were found on the weapon. Yours. Your rental car was spotted by traffic cameras in the area. It's all stacked against you. They didn't come to this conclusion on a whim, Riordan."

"And I handed myself to them on a platter." Riordan grimaced and touched the back of his head. Flashes of the argument with Jay processed, but not the content. Not the details of the heated conversation. Only the residual feelings of anger and…disappointment.

"If you've been framed for Jay's death, whoever it is has done a bang-up job," Foster observed. "They've tied it and you up in one very nice, very neat bow."

"If?" Darcy finished her drink. "*If* he's been framed? Are you saying you think he did it?" Her grip on Riordan's arm eased enough for the blood to start flowing to his hand again.

Foster inclined his head. "The Riordan Malloy I know is a lot of things, but a murderer?"

Was he pausing because he was considering the question, or was it only for dramatic effect, Riordan wondered.

"No. I don't believe that's true. But what I believe and what the evidence says—"

"Never mind the evidence right now." Darcy frowned. "Can you help him or not?"

"Good question," Riordan jumped right in and asked, "Can you?"

"I can get you a little time to dig around, maybe push the investigation in a different direction," Foster said. "Everything I have is at your disposal. You can stay at the Medallion as long as you need to or until it's evident it's no longer appropriate."

"Appropriate?" Darcy repeated. "What does that mean?"

The chopper took a decidedly eastern turn. Riordan braced himself for another surge of panic on Darcy's part, but she had either gotten used to the turbulence or she didn't notice.

"Public scandals," Foster said, "especially ones that involve law enforcement, are not conducive to my business dealings, Darcy. My bosses and partners wouldn't take a polite view were I to find myself embroiled in a cover up even if it was in an effort to protect my closest friends."

"But you can hide the problem, or rather person, away until the situation resolves itself or you find a better way out of it," Darcy countered. Her eyes narrowed, then went wide. "So you can help your friend as long as your business isn't affected. Nice, Major." She leaned back, gazed out the window. "Guess it's good to have friends you can rely on, huh, Riordan?"

The observation came out slurred and her head lolled to the side.

"Darcy?" Riordan unhooked his seat belt and reached for her. Her eyes drifted closed and she passed out. The ginger ale glass tipped out of her hold and clunked to the floor. "Darcy?" He swung on Foster. "What did you do to her?"

"Removed her from the conversation." Foster reached up and flipped a switch. "Call ahead and have them prepare the Kousa Suite for guests, please." He clicked off the intercom, bent over and retrieved the glass, which he set aside. "Outrage isn't a good look on you, Riordan," he continued.

"I told her she could trust you." The accusation sounded disbelieving even to his own ears. "What did you give her?"

"Nothing harmful. She'll sleep the day and probably most of tomorrow away as well. You'll be glad for the time, Riordan. Believe me."

No, Riordan thought as disgust rose inside of him. *I don't think I will.* "She's not a threat to you."

"To me? No. Of course she isn't." Foster said with a derisive laugh. "But deep down, you know the less she hears about your current situation, the better."

His current situation. It was almost as if...

"I didn't kill Jay." Riordan wasn't sure if he was trying to convince himself or Foster, but it was evident by Foster's shrug that it didn't matter either way. "Foster, I didn't kill him." He'd been telling himself all this time he wanted, needed to uncover the truth, but now, faced with the prospect of doing just that, he wasn't so sure.

Foster looked at him, an odd expression blanketing his face. "I don't recall you being a particularly good liar, Riordan. This amnesia story of yours. You truly don't remember, do you?"

"I remember arguing with him. And I remember leaving the base." But what bits and pieces there were no longer made sense. "I don't remember going to his house." He certainly didn't remember killing one of his best friends. "I came to you here in Vegas last week because..." He couldn't quite put the words together. "I came to you, why?"

"For my advice and help."

"With what?" Riordan just needed someone to color in the blank lines around his past.

"Six months ago, an anonymous source came to you with information that multiple weapons had been going missing in small numbers over the course of several years. Without anyone to put on record, you started looking into it on your own. You were in the process of eliminating everyone who had visited the various bases over the time in question, tracing the inventory discrepancies, people who would or could have had access to the shipments, either before the weapons left or after they arrived." Foster's eyes barely flickered. "There were only a few names that appeared multiple times."

"Jay," Riordan whispered and sat back. "Jay was one of those names." He glanced at Darcy, felt his stomach clench at Foster's cruel arrogance. "That doesn't explain—"

"Army Intelligence doesn't take kindly to off-book inquiries, Riordan. You know this. You were determined to prove him innocent, but your superiors ordered you off the case. You were told to stand down, and you refused. So you took vacation time and came to me for help."

"And did you?" Riordan challenged. "Help me?"

"I gave you what information I could and convinced Jay to meet with you. Ah. We're coming in to land."

"None of this explains why you drugged Darcy."

"She has faith in you," Foster said as the chopper circled lower. "I thought it best to leave it in your hands whether that faith remains intact. That would require a private conversation, no?" Foster's smile was thin and veiled. "Now that your memory's returning, just how much do you really want her to know?"

Darcy had the oddest sensation of floating. Not flying. Floating. In and amongst the clouds, drifting up and avoiding the tall spires and arching windows of buildings and hotels dotting the landscape below. She stretched out her arms, turned and twisted as she felt not one iota of fear or dread but peace.

Until she dropped straight down, and the earth raced up to meet her.

The scream had lodged in her throat as she jolted awake, her mind unable to decipher where she was. When it was. She shoved her hair out of her face. Her mouth was as dry as the sand dunes of Nevada. Beside the gigantic California king, a small bedside table glowed. Her purse lay on the floor, her cell plugged into the outlet on the lamp. Her backpack sat on a chair in the corner.

Gold embossed wallpaper covered each side of the room, which included a dresser and a giant television. The stark white bedspread, which she'd been laid out on top of, was offset with a stark black cashmere blanket that had been placed over her. The pillows were marshmallow soft, and judging by the lack of tangled bedclothes, she'd barely moved for as long as she'd been here. The double doors into the bedroom were closed. Another door, the one leading to the bathroom, she assumed, stood open. All the knobs were bright gold while the trim was white with occasional splashes of red to break up the brilliancy.

She picked up her phone, blinked to clear her eyes and absorb the information on the screen. She'd lost a day. It was nearly noon. Her stomach rumbled as if it could tell time. Her messages, emails and voicemails had piled up. The half dozen from Kyla were what concerned her the most. All of them demanded to know if she was all right and to please call her back. But there was nothing from the only person she'd hoped to hear from by now.

Exhaustion clung to her like an itchy sweater. She wrote a text, letting Kyla know she was all right and that…

Darcy caught her lower lip in her teeth. The uncertainty circling refused to settle. She needed to ground herself. She needed to grab hold of something that was real. That she could rely on. That would refocus her.

Before she talked herself out of it, she dialed Kyla's number.

"Darcy! Where in the he—"

"I'm fine," Darcy said even as the tears clogged her throat. She hugged her knees into her chest. "No lectures, Ky, please. I'm okay." The sound of her friend's voice started the tears flowing. "I just wanted you to know I was all right."

"Well, you sound terrible, so I won't belabor it. What's going on? Where are you? When are you coming home?"

"I'm where I told you we'd be. Vegas." It was all she was comfortable saying at this point. "I'm coming home soon." She hoped. Her head was heavy. Foggy. She rarely needed any more than five or six hours of sleep a night, and here she was, waking up after almost eighteen! That wasn't…normal. "I don't suppose you've heard from Eamon lately, have you?"

"Eamon? No, he's been working an abduction case in Denver. Why?"

Darcy rested her head in her free hand. "I'd called him about something. Not important." Boy, was that a whopper. "Do me a favor, if you or Eden or Vince can get through to him—"

"Okay, now you have me worried. You want me to call our mutual FBI agent friend and ask him for help."

"Yes." She almost choked on the word. "And I need you to do it without asking me a lot of questions. I've left him a voicemail. He just has to listen to it, he'll know what I need him to do."

"All right." Kyla sounded far from convinced.

Darcy couldn't not ask, "What's the latest on the news about Riordan?"

Silence.

"Kyla?"

"Okay, it's totally weird, but as of last night, the story's just disappeared. No mention of Jay Russo's murder and no replay of Riordan being one of California's most wanted. Eden came by my office just a few minutes ago to ask if the DA's office had been brought in to consult or had anything to do with it, but we didn't. It's the oddest thing. For two days his face is everywhere, and today it's like—"

"It's like someone called for a story blackout?" Darcy suggested. "Yeah. I think I know who might have done that." She'd asked Foster what it was he thought he could do to help Riordan. Now she had her answer.

She glanced at the door, wondered who she'd find on the other side. "I need to take a shower and get something to eat. Vegas has not been kind so far."

"Don't tell me you guys went out drinking and partying last night," Kyla said with a good amount of disapproval in her voice. "That's not like you."

"No," Darcy said and scrubbed a hand down her face. "It's not. I just wanted to call and let you know I'm all right. When I'm not, you'll hear about it first, okay?"

"You'd better stick to that," Kyla warned. "Be careful, Darcy. Whatever it is you're doing—"

"I hear you," she said and swallowed another rush of tears. "Don't worry. I'll be careful. Bye." Darcy hung up, stared down at her phone. Then, after tapping open Eden's name, she typed a quick text and hit Send before she climbed out of bed for that shower.

Chapter 10

Riordan waited until he heard the shower running before he called down for room service. He was an old hand at it by now, having ordered twice since he'd carried Darcy into the elevator and to the top floor of private suites above the Strip.

He'd felt like a creepy fairy-tale prince depositing Darcy on the bed as if she were no more than a doll. The anger that had taken root inside of him hadn't abated in the hours since; it had grown in intensity. The only tangible thing he'd been able to do was ask that their suite have two bedrooms. Foster's disbelief had been present again then, much as when he had learned of Riordan's memory issues. But he'd agreed, with a bit of a bemused expression on his face when he called to make the adjustment.

Guilt, Riordan learned as Darcy slept, had a particular metallic taste to it. Like tainted blood on the tongue. He'd convinced Darcy to trust his friend. His former commanding officer. The man he'd fought beside in a war that haunted them both. Yet that friend had incapacitated Darcy without a second thought and, if their follow-up conversation was any indication, without a hint of remorse.

If he was friends with a callous man like that... Riordan began to pace again. What did his friendship with Foster Krinard say about his own character? And it was that question that heaped a truckload of doubt on top of the guilt.

He should have trusted his instincts that said bringing Darcy with him would be the wrong thing to do. Maybe he'd let himself believe in her adventure fairy tale. He'd convinced himself there was more between them than adrenaline and excitement and her need to fill her life with something other than predictable routine. Now he was faced with the reality of admitting he wanted her with him because... Because he wanted her. He cared about her. More than he'd ever cared about anyone before.

He'd believed it easily because he hadn't been ready to let her go and walk away. Only now...

Now he was beginning to see he didn't have a choice.

Darcy had to get as far from him as possible if she was going to stay alive.

Breakfast, or rather brunch, would be a peace offering of sorts. An icebreaker for his soon to be spoken apology that would set the stage for his plan. Since awakening, his mind had been much clearer. Almost whole, even though he accepted pieces of his life were never going to be the same.

Foster had disappeared behind obligation and hotel security duties, leaving Riordan to fend for himself, but not without restrictions. There was a security officer posted outside their suite, and the key card he'd been given, a card that granted him access to any of the amenities in the hotel, was being tracked.

Not that he had gone anywhere. He wasn't about to leave Darcy alone. Not in a place where he was at such a disadvantage. Though his presence couldn't keep her from being harmed. Foster had made that abundantly clear.

He'd relegated himself to occasional peeks next door in an effort to confirm that Darcy continued to sleep peacefully or, at the very least, was blissfully unaware of what was happening. The alternate thought that had him crawling in beside her and holding her as she slept was a nonstarter. How his arms ached to hold her.

The sophistication of his surroundings—the pricey furniture, the delicate fabrics, the attention to detail from the Asian-inspired floral screen paintings of Kausa dogwood to the antique lacquered chest placed just off the marble tiled entryway—did nothing to ease his concern. None of this felt comfortable. He couldn't help but think if he moved too quickly, turned too fast, he'd break something and rack up a fortune in damages.

The second room had been as spacious as the other, yet he'd slept fitfully. But at least he had slept, and when he'd woken, most of his life, his memories up until a few weeks ago, had slipped back into place.

The shower and change of clothes had done little to clear his overflowing mind. Being accused of Jay's murder still didn't make sense. He had a few more answers on that front, but most of his knowledge was based on hearsay from Foster Krinard. Rather than dwelling on what he couldn't recall, Riordan had taken the doctor's advice and focused on what he did remember and typed it all into a document on Darcy's laptop that he'd had in his bag.

Now, after almost a full day since they'd been sequestered in what amounted to a well-furnished prison cell, he'd run out of things to keep him occupied while he waited for Darcy to emerge from her shower. The only idea he had was to fix himself another cup of coffee.

Carrying it over to the plate glass window, he noticed the view made him feel as if he were a giant overseeing his kingdom of guilt, glitz and gluttony. He sipped and hoped--perhaps stronger than he'd ever hoped for anything before. That somehow the end to something might also be the beginning of something potentially wonderful.

Riordan knew when she'd exited the bedroom. Not because of the click of the door. But because he could feel her presence, her energy, pulsing from across the room.

He turned and found her standing there, barefoot, clad in an oversized royal red robe that she was clutching closed at her throat. Her hair hung in long wet curls, and her face was scrubbed fresh and clean and glowed beneath the soft lights. So many emotions were reflected in her eyes, but they flashed so fast he'd no sooner identified one than the next appeared.

"Did you see a doctor?"

"Yes." It wasn't the question he anticipated her asking first, but it felt good not to have to lie. "Dr. Emil Bradford. Hotel physician." He pointed to an envelope on the coffee table. "I asked for a copy of his diagnosis and report. Do you want—"

"What did he say? Are you all right?" She hadn't moved. Near as he could tell, she'd barely breathed.

"I'm okay. He confirmed the concussion, gave me prescription pain meds to manage the headaches, another for the nausea. They've already helped. A lot. Cleared the cobwebs away."

"Good. Anything else?"

Where to begin? Riordan nodded. "He suspects the concussion occurred before the car accident. That second whack only exacerbated the head injury."

"Before," she murmured. "Before when?"

"Earlier that night. At Jay's house." He may as well get it all out on the table. "It's coming back to me in waves. I was there the night he was killed. He was…" He struggled against the grief. "I don't know what happened, except he was alive when I got there. That I do know. I remember Watson. His dog." The Rottweiler/ Shepherd mix was a beauty to behold and friendly enough to have made a lasting impression on Riordan's fractured mind. "Then things fast-forward and I'm driving like mad, trying to put as much distance between me and the scene as I could." Why hadn't he stayed? What had happened that made him run like that? He moved, pointed to her laptop that was open on the desk near the window. "I tried to get it all written down, but it's coming out in fragments. Maybe you can help me piece it together."

The knock on the door had him setting down his mug displaying the giant gold M in a circle. He stepped around the black painted coffee table between the sofas. "That's your food. I ordered…well, I took a chance on what you'd like."

She didn't respond as he headed for the door. When the bellhop wheeled the cart inside, he wondered where she'd gotten to, only to see her emerge from the bedroom once more and hand a significant bit of cash to their server.

"Thank you," she murmured with a smile. A smile that dimmed when Riordan closed the door.

"Thanks for covering that," Riordan said. "I'm still out of cash."

"I'm surprised Major Giggles didn't take care of that for you." She curled herself into the corner of the sofa he'd slept on sporadically, lifted one of the silver domes off the plate. She sighed, her brows in a V. "Eggs Benedict. Evil."

"Like I said."

"You hit a home run. It's my favorite." She leaned back and pulled what looked like an external hard drive out of her pocket. She pushed a button on the bottom corner. A high-pitched whine emitted before going silent. She set it on the table beside the sofa.

He moved closer. "What's that?"

"Something Jason gave me via Eden." She picked up her fork. "It's a signal jammer. I was really hoping I wouldn't have to use it, but—" she shrugged "—needs must."

"Did she give you anything else to help us?"

"I'm the one who gets to ask the questions right now, Riordan. And now that we're alone, I feel like I can."

"The suite isn't bugged," he said as she stabbed a crispy potato and dunked it into the thick, buttery sauce. "I checked." Twice.

"And Major Maverick wouldn't have predicted that. Do you really think your security expert of a pal put us up in his hotel so we could hide and evaluate our situation? Or was it so he could keep tabs on us?" There was that look again. Suspicion. Disappointment. Anger. "He drugged me, Riordan. I hardly think he'd blink twice at surveillance."

"No, you're right." She'd been right about a lot of things.

"Did he happen to tell you why he drugged me? Did you ask?"

"Yes, I asked." While it was fair of her to be suspicious, the question grated against his pride. "He said it was because he didn't know how much I wanted you to know."

"Interesting."

He sat down across from her, watched as she checked under the other three domes. She plucked up a strip of bacon and squashed the whole piece into her mouth.

She was intriguing to him even while she chewed. How was that possible? "I didn't know—"

"About him drugging me? That's the one thing I do know, Riordan. If I thought for one second you had a hand in that, I'd not only be gone, I'd have told the police where you are and put the cuffs on you myself." Her frown increased and she reached for a glass of orange juice. "End of story."

"As long as we're on the same page on that front, at least."

"Not that it needs to be said at this point, but I don't trust your *friend*."

He stared down into his coffee.

"So we should assume he knows—"

"Everything," Riordan said, cutting her off. "At least that's what he claims. He told me he's aware of what I was working on and why I came out here to the West Coast. He also said I was conducting an off-the-books investigation without my supervisor's approval and against orders."

"Uh-huh, now I know he's a liar." She cut into the stack of crisp English muffin, ham and oozy poached egg. "Bologna."

"Which part?"

"That you disobeyed an order. I don't buy that for a second."

She stuffed a bite into her mouth, chewed. After she swallowed, she got up, fixed herself a mug of coffee and returned to her seat. She cut another bite of eggs and aimed her fork at him. "Total bologna."

Riordan had had a lot of surprises in the past few

days, but this one caught him completely off guard. And lightened his mood. "Why do you say that?"

"You're so military your blood cells probably wear teeny tiny tailored uniforms."

His lips twitched.

"You shot to attention when you saw your former Army buddy," she continued. "You're not built to disobey. Question? Maybe." She shrugged. "But disobey? Nope. Not buying it for a second. If you were told to stay away from the investigation, you'd have stayed away or found a less invasive way to find the answers you needed. You certainly wouldn't have driven across the country to throw it in their faces. He duped you as effectively as he drugged me. He also made it so I'll never drink ginger ale again." And just like that, as she continued to eat, the Darcy he'd come to rely on these past few days, the Darcy who had walked away from her life to help save his, the Darcy he'd fallen tail over teakettle for was back. "And another thing..."

"Here we go."

"As far as I'm concerned, everything he says is suspect. I don't buy this act of his. He's smarmy. Yep. That's what he is, smarmy, and you know what else?" She looked around the room. "I bet he knows a lot more about what really happened to Jay than he's saying. His face was all over those photos at that car rental agency, can you believe it? He owns it."

"Yeah," Riordan murmured as he drew a hand down his face. "I know." It was one of the things that was bothering him the most. Coming to Vegas might have exposed the truth about Jay Russo's murder, but it had also put him and Darcy firmly in the lion's mouth. "But—"

"Don't go defending him." This time she poked both her knife and fork at him. "I don't care that the hotel he protects is probably one of the most gorgeous places I've ever seen or that his food is making me want to weep it's so good. He's a liar. He lied to you, and he's done nothing but lie to me ever since…what? What are you doing?" Her flatware clanged onto the plate as Riordan got to his feet and walked around the cart. She took a drink of orange juice as he approached. "What's going on?"

He bent down and kissed her. He couldn't have stopped himself if he'd wanted to. And he didn't want to. If he had to choose only one activity for the rest of his life, it would be to kiss Darcy Ford.

"I'm eating," she murmured against his lips. "And it's really good." She curled a hand around his head and kept him close. "You taste even better." She pressed her mouth to his again. "What was that for?"

"For believing in me." He kissed her again, longer this time. Deeper. And took an inordinate amount of pleasure in watching her eyes glaze over when she looked at him again. "For the record, I don't trust him, either." Riordan retrieved his coffee and sat beside her and, now that his appetite had returned, he picked one of the slices of perfectly cooked bacon and ate. "There are a few places I didn't check for listening devices."

"Oh? Like where?"

"The bathrooms. Your bedroom." He trailed a finger along her bare knee. "Your bed."

She smirked, shoveled in another mouthful of food. "Did the doctor clear you for that kind of thing?"

"He might have suggested I restrict myself to non-vigorous activity."

"Hmm." Her mouth twisted. "Planning on making me do all the work, then?"

He chuckled. No one made him laugh like Darcy did.

"Sorry to disappoint you, but I've got some mad to work off before we succumb to our desires," she told him.

"We could kill two birds with one stone." He lifted a hand to her face, stroked her cheek, skimmed beneath the collar of her robe.

"Or I could end up killing us both." She turned her head, and when he touched her lips with his finger-tips, she flicked out her tongue to tease him. "There is something I need to do."

"Yeah?"

"Swim." She pushed herself up and over the arm of the sofa. "I need water and a lot of it."

"You want to go swimming. With everything that's going on?"

"You wanted to have sex," she countered. "One wastes just as much time as the other."

Masculine pride surged. "Now hang on—"

"You know what I mean." She rolled her eyes. "I usually do my best thinking in the water. It clears my head. And I would definitely like a clear head when I take you to bed."

Intrigued, Riordan sat back.

"I'd also like to keep Major Scary Boots off guard. We can't sit around plotting and planning what we're going to do next, especially once I turn off that jammer. If we leave it on much longer he's going to get suspicious. He thinks he's giving us a place to hide. Let's play along and enjoy what this spot has to offer. Nothing says we can't use that to our advantage until he's played his next card."

"His next card is dinner. Tonight. Our presence has been requested."

"Of course it has." She shook her head. "Your friend is reminding me more and more of a spy movie villain. All that's missing are the circling sharks and ejector seats."

"Don't give him ideas," Riordan teased. "Go put on your suit. I'll check with our escort about what pool we can use."

"There's one for you, too, in the bathroom," she added. "How about you come with me? I could use a lap partner. When we get back, I'll read through that stuff you wrote up, and we'll go from there. Okay? Okay." She darted into her bedroom before he could even think to argue.

Beneath the surface of the dark lagoon-inspired pool, Darcy felt her fear, disappointment and anxiety melt away. Her arms wavered in the cool water, legs kicking gently as she gazed up at the flickering lights casting shadows into the blue depths.

The private swimming area was an oasis of solitude reserved, according to hotel signage, for the most exclusive high-level guests. Or, in Darcy and Riordan's case, mock prisoners.

Water wasn't just her sanctuary; it was where her heart and soul thrived. The river. The ocean. A pool. Even one created to mimic the deep rainforest areas with lush, thick greenery and flora nestled in the outcropping of rocks that outlined the large open space of water.

Feeling her lungs begin to tingle, she kicked harder, pressed her arms down and, head back, broke the surface with a gentle gasp.

"I was beginning to think you'd stay down there forever." Riordan's deep voice left her tingling for an entirely different reason. She swiped the water from her eyes, slicked back her hair and smiled. She swam over to where he lounged against the side of the pool.

She ducked under the surface, placed her hands on his thighs and pushed up and into the circle of his arms. "I thought you were going to swim laps with me."

"I'd have to be a fool to think I could ever beat you in a swim race." He brushed a hand against her cheek, an action she was fast becoming accustomed to. The appreciation she'd felt at seeing him that first night, lying half naked on her bed, was nothing to the admiration she felt building at seeing him in her element. There wasn't an inch of him that wasn't taut and toned, tempting her to discover if he—if either of them—possessed any kind of pleasure threshold.

"I didn't say we'd race."

He chuckled. "I read between the lines. That first morning, I thought I'd found myself a mermaid." He leaned forward, pressed his lips to hers. "I was right. You're glorious."

She pushed off the stair he was sitting on, caught his hand and pulled him with her. "That's an adjective a girl could get used to hearing."

He moved with her, almost effortlessly.

The entire lagoon was theirs. At one end, a thin fall of water trickled down over man-made stones, the ripples making their way through the rest of the water. The rocks and plants didn't stop at the surface, but trailed down beneath, providing a burst of color against perfectly placed lights illuminating the darkness.

She led him across the width of the pool, laughing as uncertainty creased his brow. "You're in my element now," she murmured and released his hand long enough to push herself forward into his embrace. "Here, we can both trust." She surrendered to him, wrapped herself around him, encircled his hips with her legs. "Here we can both forget," she said as she entwined her arms around his neck.

She kissed him. Softly at first, a test of what was to come. She waited until his arms came around her, skimmed down her bare back and dipped beneath the fabric of the green one piece suit. Nowhere did she feel more powerful than the water. Her inhibitions, her fears, her insecurities evaporated into the mist rising off the surface of the water. She pressed open his mouth, tilted her head and dived in, wanting, needing to taste more of him. To taste all of him.

His timidity in the water vanished at her touch. His legs continued to kick, keeping them both above the gently lapping ripples, as his tongue and hers met and teased.

She tightened her legs, felt the hard strength of him pressing against her core. The fabric that separated them felt like layers upon layers. Layers she wanted gone as she pressed herself to him, flattening her breasts into his bare chest.

"You were right," he gasped when he tore his mouth free. His eyes glinted with humor. His lashes were spiked with water, his hair a stunning mane she sank her hands into it and held on. "You are going to kill us both." A laugh escaped her lips, and he caught it with another kiss. He propelled them back toward the stairs.

"Not feeling adventurous today?" she teased, then gasped when he gave a sudden kick, swam forward and her back touched the middle step. "Oh!" She let go of him, reaching over her head to grab hold of the ledge as his mouth trailed down the side of her neck. "Okay, so maybe…yeah." She felt herself reveling in his touch. "Okay, this could work, too."

There wasn't a part of her body that didn't feel caressed. Either by Riordan or the water. The way his gentle hands moved, sliding under the surface, skimming up her sides, down her back and over her hips, it was as if the water had come alive and taken possession of him.

"Open your eyes, Darcy." He swam forward, braced one hand on the step behind her as his other hand skimmed along her shoulder, drawing the strap down until her breast was uncovered. She moaned, pressed her thighs together as the pressure built. A pressure that intensified as he lowered his head and pressed a kiss against her exposed flesh.

"You've done this before," she said. Thought was difficult if not impossible.

"Not like this I haven't," he assured her. "You taste divine." His tongue circled her nipple, and when she gasped, he caught the puckered nub between his teeth. The pressure, the pleasure, was blissful. She drew her legs up, pulled him closer. She held tighter to the ledge. "I want you, Darcy."

"Hmm," she groaned and tilted her chin up. "I'm getting that message loud and clear." She could feel her breath catching, feel that desire for release intensifying and he hadn't even gotten her naked yet. "Only one problem." She wasn't sure if that last sound was a groan or a sob as he pressed forward and opened her thighs. "I didn't exactly anticipate this happening down here."

"Really?" His other hand moved beneath her suit and found her core. "Down here?"

She sucked in a breath as he pressed a finger just inside of her.

"Is this where you meant?" He pressed his lips against the side of her throat. "Or did you mean…" He moved his finger only slightly. "Here?"

The climax shot through her in an instant. Whatever sound she made next was lost because he'd covered her mouth with his with such expert care and ferocity that she nearly cried. The rocketing surge had him moving with her, moving with the water, in time to the motions of his wicked tongue. He'd stolen the breath from her lungs, every drop of energy from her body, and as she slowly came back down from heights she hadn't known before, her legs suddenly felt like anchors threatening to drag her beneath the surface. But he kept her close, held her as he drew the strap of her suit back into place.

"Now." He caught her face in his palm and she looked at him. Looked into him. Those eyes of his that she would gladly drown in given the briefest of chances. "Let's say we take this upstairs? Find a large comfy bed so I'm more in *my* element."

"I don't know." She fake-heaved a heavy sigh even as she was already halfway to the room in her head. "I'm pretty good right now." She grinned when he raised an eyebrow. "Something else you think we should…oh!" She burst out laughing when he ducked down, into the water and pressed his head—

"I'm sorry to interrupt."

Darcy yelped and nearly kicked Riordan as she disentangled herself and spun around.

Riordan surfaced, sputtering. "What in the—Mira."

Darcy froze. The woman standing at the edge of the pool was stunning. Tall, slender, with Mediterranean features offset by the stark white linen slacks and dark red button-down silk blouse she wore, Mira Krinard slowly pushed her long, espresso colored hair back over one shoulder. "Foster told me you were in trouble," she said in a concerned tone. "Clearly he was exaggerating."

"He wasn't, actually. We're just—"

"Taking a break. Yes. I can see that." Darcy's feminine radar sounded a stark warning. Even if she hadn't seen the frosty glint in Mira's dark eyes, she'd have suspected there was something between the woman and Riordan. "And in my pool."

"Foster told us you were out of town." Riordan swiped a hand down his face. He moved as if he were going to haul himself out of the pool, then Darcy's well-placed foot stopped him. Instead, he submerged himself back into the pool and drew his arms up to hold on to the ledge. "He didn't think you'd mind."

Mira's lips flicked into something resembling a smile as she slid elegant, slim fingers into her trouser pockets. "I'm not normally one for sharing." Her sharp gaze stared daggers at Darcy before she shifted her attention back to Riordan. "I returned early. I thought perhaps I could lend a hand helping you sort things out. As usual, I see my husband neglected to mention the smaller details of your arrival."

"No need to worry," Darcy said and splashed a hand out of the pool. "Oops, sorry." Mira looked down at the droplets beading on her white designer stiletto pumps. "Darcy Ford." One of the smaller details. "Great pool you have." Seemed like a good time to throw in a few misconceptions and play up her supposed ditzy girlfriend role.

"Thank you." Mira's lips curved. "Well, I'll save my concern for dinner conversation, shall I, Riordan? I believe Foster said you'd be coming?"

Darcy snorted. Riordan dropped a hand and, under the water, pressed it into the small of her back, reigniting that doused flame of desire. "We're looking forward to it," Riordan told her.

Mira's gaze flickered from Riordan to Darcy, back

to Riordan. Darcy wasn't particularly surprised by the disappointment and distrust on Mira's face. But the flicker of anger was something unexpected. "I'll see you then."

She turned and walked back to the solitary door, her heels clacking like gunshots as she moved. Darcy waited until the door closed before she looked at Riordan. "How's that memory of yours holding up?"

"What are you—?"

"Please." Darcy scoffed. "It was written all over her face. You've slept together."

"No, actually." Riordan frowned as Darcy pushed off the wall and swam away. "We haven't. Not that the opportunity hasn't been there."

"I'll bet it has." There was no mistaking that possessive glare in Mira's eye. "Before or after she married your friend?"

"Both." The fact he admitted it earned him bonus points. "Foster met Mira years ago when he was still active military. She was a pilot in the Turkish military. Helped the three of us out of some tight spots. Don't," he warned when she laughed under her breath. "She made it clear she wanted a different life, and, okay, maybe she gave each of us a test run before she settled on Foster. She's got everything she wants and needs now as his wife and as his personal pilot. That is, when she's not traveling for her own business."

"Uh-huh." Darcy rolled her eyes.

"I may not know everything about myself at the moment, but I do know I don't sleep with my friends' wives."

"I was teasing, Riordan." It was impossible to mistake the irritation in his voice. "Badly, obviously, and I'm sorry for it. She doesn't like competition. And she doesn't like surprises." Funny. Darcy currently qualified as both. She wasn't used to being disliked on sight because of her connection to a man, but this entire escapade with Riordan Malloy was full of twists and turns. "Does Foster know? About his wife's proclivities to attempt to seduce his friends?"

"He knows. They have...an arrangement from what I understand. She has her affairs. He has his. She doesn't have anything to do with us, Darcy."

"I know. And I really was teasing." Although it was nice to know Riordan's honorable tendencies were the real deal and not limited to his sworn duty as a military officer. "We all have a past, Riordan. Getting upset with you for something that happened before I even met you is the very definition of *futility*. But if you think she's set you aside and given up, I'd think again."

"Yeah?" He glanced to the door and earned a splash in the face when he looked back at Darcy. "Kidding!" He grabbed for her, but she swam out of reach.

"Time for you to get out of this lagoon paradise," she ordered and kicked more water in his face. "I want to get some actual laps in before we head back upstairs. Go away."

"Fine. I'll leave the pool," he said as she began to swim in earnest. "But I'm not going away."

Not yet, she thought. But even after a few short days, she felt safe in betting that Riordan Malloy was already halfway out of her life.

* * *

"The longer this adventure of mine goes on, the more I feel like I'm a character caught up in a spy novel." With her damp hair twisted on top of her head, wearing the hotel's comfy, velvety red robe again, Darcy stood at the foot of her bed and looked at the shimmering green gown that had been set out for her.

The color matched the vibrant green swimsuit she'd peeled out of before her shower. It was as if a fairy godmother had waved her wand and magically deposited it while she'd been swimming laps in the pretty lagoon.

Darcy wasn't sure what bothered her more. The dress's unexpected appearance, that it had made said appearance while neither she nor Riordan were in the suite, or the fact that it looked to be a perfect fit. Add in a selection of I-dare-you-to-walk-in-these shoes in varying sizes and a simple gold clutch, and the entire ensemble definitely gave off movie magic vibes.

She touched tentative fingers to the fabric, felt her long-neglected glamour girl groan in silence, then lifted it up and held it against her body. She turned to the full-length mirror and stared at her reflection. Taken aback, she pressed her hand against her stomach. The dress was so far out of her norm that the two didn't exist in the same universe, and yet…

Riordan rapped his knuckles on the doorframe, poked his head in as she spun around. "Wow." His wide-eyed approval warmed her cheeks. "Okay, whatever comment I was going to make about not liking being dressed by somebody else just flew completely out of my head."

"Seeing as Foster doesn't strike me as the fashion-conscious type, I'm going to guess Mira is responsible." The thought generated another level of worry, but this one, she refused to entertain.

"Mira would be my guess. She's dabbled in fashion for years." Riordan's outward signs of their intimate pool activity were almost gone, save for the damp sheen in his hair. He smelled like spring. Fresh and filled with promise.

He stepped into her bedroom, inclined his head. "You might want to wait a while to put that on."

"Oh." Disappointment crashed through her. "Why?"

"Because the longer you're wearing it, the longer I'm going to have to think about getting you out of it."

Darcy paused. Coming from any other man, that line might have sounded rehearsed, but she'd come to understand Riordan was not one to throw compliments around without meaning them. He was an honest man who spoke his mind and, in this instance, filled her heart.

She turned back to the mirror, embarrassed by the tears that burned the backs of her eyes. He couldn't know how she'd longed to hear words like that spoken to her. Words she'd only read in her books, spoken to characters she longed to be like.

How typical that she'd be looking for a reason not to believe him. How many years had she spent enduring the teasing and bullying, hearing the homely girl comments as she passed down the hallway first in grade school, then in the early months of high school? Rarely had she ever felt beautiful with her tempestuous, unmanageable hair, her pale, freckled skin and added pounds that latched on with what seemed like a mere thought.

She'd gone along with all of it, but only until she'd found her place in the water. In the water, she was the best, and she'd proven it when she was fourteen. As the youngest member of the swim team, she'd earned her high school its very first championship medal. She'd silenced those bullies then. The naysayers who, even after her wins, never seemed to see the real Darcy Ford.

Sometimes she wept for the little girl whose nose had been permanently planted in books, her head filled with dreams of a fairy-tale hero sweeping her off her feet and into a world of unpredictable surprises. The little girl who had never been completely forgotten or pushed aside. That little girl danced to life inside of her now, and as a full-grown woman, Darcy embraced her.

Riordan moved in behind Darcy, reached around and tucked a finger under her chin to tilt her face up to look in the mirror. "Stunning," he murmured and caught her gaze.

She blinked a solitary tear, swiped it away and opened her mouth to explain, but he plucked the dress from her trembling hand, set it on the nearby dresser and came back to her.

He caught her face in his hands, pressed his forehead to hers. "You are, without a doubt, Darcy Ford, the greatest distraction of my life." He kissed the tip of her nose, then her forehead, and then finally her lips. "I've never met anyone like you. You are what every man should dream of."

"Don't," she whispered, shutting her eyes against the wave of desire that threatened to overtake her. "Don't... don't say things I know aren't true."

"Don't tell me what to believe."

The next kiss, the one simple kiss that followed his declaration filled her with such hope, such promise that she didn't think her feet would ever touch the ground again. "We should stop," he urged her. "Tell me we shouldn't do this." He kissed her again and they moved toward the bed. When her legs brushed the mattress, she fell, all of her wants and desires exploding to life at once. "I want you too much"

She reached up, fisted her hands in his hair and looked so deeply into his eyes she could all but see herself shimmering in them. "You aren't alone." She breathed him in. "Let's not stop. Ever."

She kissed him now. Kissed him with every bit of passion she'd kept bottled up, waiting for him. All this time, all these years, she thought she knew what the ultimate temptation would feel like, look like. Taste like. But as she opened her senses, her heart and her body to him, she admitted she'd had no idea.

There was nothing that could have prepared her for the overwhelming reality of Riordan Malloy. Greed pulsed inside of her. Greed and urgency at wanting the hot bare skin of him against her. Her lips fused to his, her mouth open to take in whatever he had to give her. Her fingers clawed at the hem of his T-shirt, dragging it up. Her fingers all but sizzled against his torso, the flat muscles of his stomach and chest. She released him only long enough for him to tug the fabric over his head, but before she could claim him once more, he unknotted the tie of her robe and slipped his hands inside.

The robe fell back off her shoulders and dropped to the floor. The cool air of the hotel room drifted over her skin, puckered her breasts even as his hands cupped her, lifted her. Inhibitions that had plagued her for decades faded into nothingness as the sexual power of need surged through her.

"Beautiful," he breathed as he skimmed his palms down her arms, held onto her fingertips and stepped back to admire the full form of her, his eyes lingering on the juncture between her legs. Raining kisses along her neck and shoulder, he teased her open with his fingers. She gasped, clinging to his shoulders as she felt the need in her rise once more. That incredible, wondrous pleasure she'd only felt with him.

"No," she murmured against his lips when he tried to claim her mouth again. "Not yet. Not until…" She smiled. A slow tempting smile as she flattened her hands against his waist and slipped them inside the band of his sweat pants. She moved out of his grasp, tossed the pants away, but when he clearly expected her to return to him so he could kiss her again, she hesitated, knelt and cupped the hard, jutting length of him in her palm.

The low sound he released felt like a bolt of confidence capturing her heart. He groaned as she stroked him, held him and placed a soft kiss against the tip of him.

"Enough." He bent and lifted her up. And as she

laughed, the teasing faded beneath the focused passion she saw reflected in his eyes. "I want to be inside you. Touch you, kiss you, know you inside and out." Riordan mouthed the words into her ear and she relished each syllable. He reached down and ripped the comforter back from the bed. "I want to feel you shudder around me. And then." He bit the tip of her ear.

"And then?" she breathed, in wonder.

"And then we'll do it all again." He eased her down, and she panicked for an instant when he disappeared from view, only to smile when she saw he'd retrieved a condom from his sweat pants.

"One thing," she said when he placed a knee on the bed after he'd covered himself.

"What?"

"Let's make it fast. All of it." She pressed a hand against his chest, thrilled at the staccato pounding of his heart against her palm. "We can try slow another time. Don't think." She touched his face, stared deep into his eyes as eagerly as she hooked a leg around his and drew him down on top of her. "Just love me, Riordan." If he heard the implied declaration, so be it. She couldn't feel the way she did at this moment, with this man, without loving him. It was, she accepted, a necessity to balance the sense of absolute abandon coursing through her.

The weight of him felt perfect. How his hips nestled into hers. It was as if he'd been made for her. She felt him press against her, firmly. Slowly his length penetrated, withdrew, slipped in a bit further as she opened for him. Her back arched and she drew her knees up to take him deeper.

"Perfect." He said softly as he began to move. "Absolutely perfect."

She writhed beneath him, lifting her hips to meet each thrust, and even then, it didn't feel like enough. Gripping his shoulders, she pushed up, pressed her mouth to his and swallowed his moans as he drove her, drove them, to the peak of ecstasy. Every cell in her body screamed for release, and when she climaxed in his arms, he thrust one final time and followed her over the edge.

The tumble.

When she could think once more, she knew it had happened. That blissful tumble she'd longed for and dreamed of? She'd taken it.

Riordan had given her everything she'd ever dreamed of.

"Riordan?" His response was muffled into a pillow, but he didn't jump out of bed, he didn't leave her. He simply rolled onto his back, smiled at her and drew her to him. "Oh." She snuggled into his side, hooked a leg with one of his.

"Question," he asked a moment later.

"After that, you've earned the right to ask me anything you'd like." She moved her head, pressed her lips against his shoulder. "What?"

"Just curious about something you said earlier. That being mad when we made love might kill us both."

"Mm-hmm." She was crashing now. The energy was draining out of her.

"That wasn't mad, was it?"

"Nope." She smiled. "Not even close."

"Heaven help me, then." He tucked his chin to his chest and stroked her cheek. Kissed her. "I've never wanted to argue with you more. Now… How about we try this again." He reached out, caught her hips and slid her over him. "Only this time, you get the condom, and let's go much, much slower."

Chapter 11

Hours later, Riordan stood at Darcy's bedroom window and looked out at the setting sun. He'd never felt more resentful in his life. Not because he'd been framed for murdering one of his best friends. Not because his life had just gone off the rails into a minefield of chaos and uncertainty. And not because he was unsure what the future held in store for him.

No. He resented that he'd felt compelled to leave the one place he wanted to be.

He hadn't wanted to move out of Darcy's embrace, let alone her bed. However, the rapid knitting together of thoughts in his head had driven him out of Darcy's bed and the first decent sleep he'd had in days. Save for a few slivers and fragments that had yet to settle, he was whole again.

He was, memories and all, Riordan Malloy again.

The universe had a cruel sense of humor putting Darcy into his path at this time in his life. He knew now what his mind had been protecting him from. The betrayals even more excruciating the second time around.

He had been set up. But not by unknown forces or random criminals. He'd been done in possibly by the two people he trusted most in the world. He didn't want to believe it; still hoped for some other explanation, but…

If Foster and Jay had been in this together, he felt sure Jay wouldn't have realized how far he'd gone until it was too late. There had been remorse, but only a flash of it before he was dead. Perhaps Jay had gotten the better deal, not having to live long with the knowledge of what had been.

Riordan's hands fisted at his sides. He had to give Foster the chance to prove he wasn't responsible for everything that had happened.

Maybe it was Darcy's view of the world that had him wishing his life-long lesson that everyone always lets him down could be challenged. That he could be wrong.

Even though he knew he wasn't.

It had been the first lesson he'd learned at the hands of his disinterested, distant parents. The Army had been a respite, providing the possibility of an alternate reality for him, one of camaraderie and community, and he'd given in to that. He'd never come close to having what Darcy had with her circle of friends and allies, but he'd come close with Foster and Jay.

Or so he had believed.

He wondered if he somehow deserved this harsh reminder, or was he doomed to repeat the same mistakes over and over. Jay and Foster must have been in this together. They had to be. That Foster had been able to get Jay to stop avoiding Riordan's calls should have been the first clue. The ease with which Riordan had gained access to the base, even the argument with Jay felt...manipulated somehow now. He'd seen it in his friend's eyes when Riordan had accused him of being responsible for the weapons thefts. No denial. Only... resignation.

In that split second, years of trust evaporated like toxic smoke. Foster was the only person who could have managed those high-grade weapons in those large quantities. He had the connections, the money. The planes. He could have obtained them through Jay, sold them and gotten them out of the country without a whisper of blame. If his friends' actions had hurt only him, it would have been one thing. But they'd betrayed their country, their oath to it. The country they'd sworn to defend. And they'd gotten away with it.

For years.

How was he supposed to ever trust anyone again? And yet...

Riordan glanced over his shoulder as Darcy stirred, reached out for him in her sleep. "And yet there's you," he whispered.

As if his words pulled her awake, she sat up, that stunning thick curly red mane of hers spilling around her shoulders and halfway down her back. Naked, her skin lit only by the glow of the lamps, Darcy was what he'd declared her to be hours before.

Utter and complete perfection.

She untangled herself from the sheets and came to him, sliding her arms around him, hands pressed firmly against his chest. "I missed you." She pressed a kiss to his arm. "What's wrong? What's bothering you?"

He shook his head "Nothing." *Everything.*

"Riordan." It was a tone that made him smile. A tone that both commanded him and humbled him. Even when he'd been without a memory, she'd known him better than anyone ever had. There were no walls between them. No barriers. Until now.

"I'm...whole again. My life. My memories. I know what and who I am."

"You sound as if that's a bad thing." She sighed and moved closer, and he wrapped an arm around her. "Memories didn't make you the Riordan Malloy I fell in love with," she whispered without looking at him. "You did that."

He squeezed his eyes shut, absorbing the words and holding them close. "Darcy."

"I don't expect you to say it back." Despite her light tone, he heard a tightness in her throat. A tightness that told him she was lying. "But I needed to tell you. I didn't want any regrets between us, stopping you from what you think you have to do."

He shouldn't have been surprised. "You know?"

"That you have a job to do? And that I'm in the way? A liability? Yes." She held him tighter. "Foster set you up for Jay's murder, didn't he? Those men who came for me, they worked for him. And he had them killed to try to convince you he was still on your side. And to protect himself."

"Don't let anyone ever tell you that you read too many books." He pressed his lips to the top of her head. "You were right. I didn't disobey orders. I'm following them. Foster's been under investigation for weapons trafficking for more than five years. They brought me in to prove their case before they closed the loop and arrested him. I told them they were wrong." He shook his head. "I told generals at the Pentagon they were wrong."

"You're a good friend," Darcy whispered. "Even if Foster and Jay weren't. That's not a bad thing, Riordan."

"He framed me for murder. He nearly killed me. Nearly killed *you*." And that, more than anything, stoked the rage burning inside his belly. "He needs to answer for that. If nothing else, there needs to be justice for him hurting you."

"Your Lancelot sword is showing again." She finally looked up at him. "I'm quite fond of that sword, by the way." Her grin widened. "Especially now."

He glanced at his watch. "We've still got time before dinner."

"Be still my heart. Such a romantic." She laughed as he swung her into his arms to face him. "Promise me something," she said when he set her back down on the bed. She shifted onto her knees, touched gentle fingers to his face. "Whatever it is you have to do—today, tonight, whenever—promise me you'll do everything you can to come back to me."

"I…" He struggled to find the words. "There's a lot you don't know. About me. About my family. I've never…" The emotions tangled together, trapped inside of him.

"You've never what?"

"I've never belonged to anyone before." He couldn't look at her, not now. "I've never been—"

"Loved?" She tilted his chin up. He dreaded the sympathy he knew he'd see in her eyes, but when he looked, truly looked, he only saw acceptance and promise. "What once was doesn't matter, Riordan. The past is just that—the past. And it's gone. You're loved now. More importantly, you always will be." She kissed him. And as the sun set behind them, she drew him back into their bed.

"If I didn't already know Mira hates me, these shoes would have given me a clue." Eyeing one of their two armed captors, who had escorted them to the elevator, Darcy reached down and tugged the strap of the sandal up, then nearly tipped over and crashed into the elevator. Riordan tightened his hold on her and tugged her upright before the stepped into the car.

"Mira doesn't hate you." Riordan said the words in such a placating manner that Darcy wondered if they'd somehow gotten married in the past few hours. As the doors slid closed, one of the suited security officers touched a finger to his ear and murmured something she couldn't hear. "I'll agree they're like torture devices. Fabulous-looking ones but clearly painful."

"At the very least," Darcy agreed. She scrunched up

her toes, and while he still had his eyes on her shoes, she snapped open the sparkling clutch and plucked out the tiny tracking device Eden had given her back at the boat. That, along with a lipstick and her cell were the only things that fit inside.

He turned her into his arms, slid an arm around her waist and leaned down to admire the thigh-high surprise slit in her dress. He leaned close, whispered in her ear, "She might be a woman of dubious actions, but when it comes to fashion choices, she hasn't made a wrong step yet."

"Said the man wearing a thousand-dollar tuxedo and twenty-four-karat gold cufflinks." She reached up and straightened his tie as the elevator continued its descent. It would take a moment given their suite was on the fortieth floor, so she ran her right hand down his side and dropped the tracker into his pocket, then she entwined their fingers and held up his wrist as if to examine it. "Correction. Diamond and gold cufflinks." She didn't want him to know. Didn't want him to tell her it was too dangerous to attempt. "Do you think she's going to let you keep these?"

"I don't care an ounce about the cufflinks." His hand tightened against her hip. Being this close to him made her think of him lying beside her in her bed. Shivers ran along her spine. She loved the idea that he could make her feel this way. "But I'd give just about anything for you to keep that dress."

"Now might be a good time to inform you I get most of my clothes at discount shops." She beamed up at him, doing her best not to cling to the nagging worry that whatever Riordan had planned wasn't going to go over well. Or happen easily. "Cheap and cheerful has more character."

"I don't know." He traced the plunging neckline of her dress with one light finger and skimmed the side of her breast. "I can see quite a bit of character from where I'm standing."

She wanted to laugh, but a good part of her was trapped between fear and dread. "Are we really going to pretend we aren't meeting a pair of potential murderers for dinner?"

"Darcy."

"How do we even do that? I mean, after good evening and thanks for the invite, do I jump right into thanks for drugging me and for framing you for killing your best friend? I'm just not sure of the procedure here."

"I'm going to say something you won't like, but it's something you have to hear." He caught her in his arms, keeping her close. "You don't have anything to do with what happens tonight. He's not going to hurt you. Not only because I won't let him but because we would not be having this meal with Foster and his wife in public if he had some nefarious plot in mind. We're going to go with the flow." He pressed his lips to her forehead. "And you'll let me do what I have to do. Whatever I have to do."

Darcy closed her eyes. How had he become so important to her? How had she gone from having no one in her life to finding a man she couldn't imagine being without? Everything she'd ever wanted was literally in her hands, and yet in a matter of hours, he'd be gone. Maybe forever.

"You need to let this happen, Darcy. It's the only way I'm going to prove what really happened to Jay."

She nodded. "All right. I'll put on a happy face and play along with whatever they have set up for us. Right now, you'd best step away from me before I do something that'll make the guards blush at the other end of that security camera." She moved to the opposite corner of the car. "I looked at the menu for this place online. It's pretty snazzy."

"Snazzy?" He smiled and, when the elevator doors slid open, kept a hand at her back as they stepped out into the marble-tiled lobby. The gold, red, and black accents in their suites were in place here as well, immersed with the touches reminiscent of the lagoon pool. Natural and contemporary design mingled into a pleasing setting that carried the fragrance of jasmine and lotus in the air. "I do love your vocabulary choices."

"My mother always said I had a way with words." She gripped her shoes with her toes almost as hard as she clasped the small evening bag that now contained only her cell, tissues and a solitary lipstick. The floor was so slick she felt like a wobbly toddler learning to walk. If Riordan didn't have a hold on her she had no doubt she'd face-plant or splay like a baby deer on the ice.

If she had any concerns about standing out, she was soon shown to be wrong. She and Riordan weren't the only guests in fancy attire. Visitors clad in formal wear swirled around them, mingling with the walk-through sightseers and slot machine hunters.

Whereas other hotels jammed every inch of space with gambling opportunities, The Medallion had made the obvious choice to designate gateways leading to various venues: gambling, eating, entertainment. Everything was clearly laid out, including the direction for the exclusive dining room that had them crossing the lobby, passing the multilevel waterfall cascading into an expansive koi pond and approaching double frosted glass doors emblazoned with a bright gold Chinese character. Below, in a much smaller font, and in English, the word Change.

"Change. That's an interesting choice for a restaurant name, isn't it?"

"There's no actual word for fusion in Chinese," Riordan said. "Which is the type of restaurant it is. Mira always had unique ideas of what she wanted. She even traveled to Macao and hired Chef Tojo away from a five-star hotel to oversee this place."

"I thought Foster was in security. Why would his wife—?"

Riordan held the door open for Darcy to enter. "She's always been a bit of a dabbler, but what she dabbles in, she tends to have a Midas touch. Foster's business has certainly benefitted from it. She's maintained some important connections in various arenas."

"And here I jump into rivers and lakes for a living."

"You'd best not be lamenting that saving lives and helping people compares remotely to what Mira does." He drew her to the side, where dozens of candles flickered in narrow niches in the walls. "You're smarter than that, Darcy Ford. A lot smarter. What you do matters. You matter."

It was, Darcy thought, one of the nicest compliments she'd ever received.

"Mr. Malloy. Ms. Ford. My name is Ardelle." The hostess behind the front desk, a young Black woman clad in a stunning turquoise-and-gold brocade sheath dress approached them immediately. "Mr. and Mrs. Krinard have just been seated at the Chef's table. Would you like to order something from the bar before you join them?"

"I'm good, thanks. Darcy?"

She plastered a smile on her face and said, "I think I'll wait. I might need a clear head for this."

"Of course." Ardelle smiled warmly and pointed the way. "Your server tonight is Carla and her assistant is Warren. Mr. and Mrs. Krinard requested the Chef's tasting menu for this evening. Are there any food allergies you'd like us to be aware of?"

"Ah, no." Darcy wished she sounded more posh. "I'm game for anything."

"Same," Riordan agreed. "This experience should satisfy your inner foodie," he murmured as Darcy stepped in front of him to follow their hostess.

"How did you know—"

"First morning when I woke up in your bed." The way he said those words—low and so casually—sent a spark of anticipation from one end of her to the other. "You had the TV on the cooking station."

"Food comforts me in a lot of ways." But probably

not tonight. She had to face the harsh reality that was staring back at her now. "Wow...would you look at this place? It's like stepping into paradise."

The dining room consisted of two stories, decorated in the same elegant design as the lobby. Smaller koi pools dotted the lower level with intimate tables arranged around them. Most of the seating was already filled with customers enjoying the menu. So many of the dishes exploding with color and artistry.

Thick columns of orchid-tipped vines wrapped around pillars stretching up to the second level. Tiny soft white lights twinkled like stars caught against the midnight-like arched sky overhead.

At first, Darcy thought they were headed upstairs, but instead, Ardelle led them to a private landing area halfway between floors. The solitary table was both perfectly nestled among the water and floral features but also sat center stage. Darcy realized as Mira and Foster got to their feet that this was likely the couple's personal table and were no doubt quite used to occupying it.

"We're so pleased you could join us this evening," Mira said sweetly with nary an indication of the hostility she'd displayed at the lagoon. She stepped around the table. The rich, black of her silk pantsuit was the perfect frame for the gold medallion hanging around her neck. After barely touching Darcy's arm with her fingers, Mira bussed a kiss to each cheek and did the same to Riordan before retaking her seat. "The dress is simply breathtaking on you, Darcy. Don't you think, Riordan?"

"As I've already told her," Riordan said easily, "Yes. And I appreciate the loan of the tux, Foster."

"You have beautiful taste," Darcy told Mira. "I feel like one of my niece's fashion dolls wearing this."

"Yes, well, every woman deserves a special occasion to dress up. I hope you don't mind." Mira placed her napkin in her lap and reached for her wine glass, acting the perfect hostess. "We asked for the chef's tasting. Rarely does Chef Tojo disappoint. I hope you don't mind raw fish. Sashimi is her specialty."

"Bring it on." Darcy didn't have any qualms about playing up her hometown-girl attitude. She certainly didn't want to disappoint their hosts by proving them wrong in their assumptions about her. "I hope it's as good as that revolving sushi place out near the movie theater," she told Riordan. "Now that's some fine fish."

Riordan ducked his head, but not before she caught the knowing grin on his face. "Foster, I was hoping we could discuss—"

"Business later," Foster said, cutting him off and signaling to their servers to pour two more glasses of wine from the bottle on a nearby service table. "I'd like to spend some time reminiscing with you, my friend. And getting to know this new one."

Darcy kicked Riordan gently under the table. He owed her twenty bucks for her belief Foster wouldn't want to come anywhere close to discussing how he'd set Riordan up for murder.

"What would you like to know?" Darcy lifted her glass in a quick toast. "I'm an open book."

* * *

There were many qualities Riordan had come to admire and love about Darcy over the past few days. Her talent with verbal communication. Her no-nonsense way of calling him out and holding him responsible for his actions, or lack thereof. Her ability to see the humor in almost any situation. But it was her complete adaptability to any predicament that impressed him the most. If she felt the tension from across the table, she didn't appear to notice. In conversation, she gave as good as she got and entertained even more.

Unexpected pride settled inside of him, and he was grateful, once more, for whatever had guided him across the river that first night.

No one turned on the charm better and held it than Darcy Ford. She was a complete surprise, even to his one-time commanding officer.

The man who, Riordan had little doubt, was plotting his demise even now.

The way Foster and Mira sat throughout their seven-course meal, talking and laughing and sharing stories as if nothing horrific had taken place only days before proved one thing. As far as Riordan was concerned, Jay, their friend—however misguided in his actions— had been killed most likely by this man whom they'd both trusted. A man who was calmly sitting across from him, clearly entertained by Darcy.

There it was. The confirmation he hadn't wanted. It had taken Riordan until tonight, until this very moment, to accept that Foster and Mira were both consummate and excellent liars.

And behind everything that had happened to him.

He was more than happy to allow Darcy to take the lead in their charade while he sat back and pondered his potential future. But it was impossible to dwell on the darkness of their situation when her kindness and affability was on full display. An attitude that didn't stop with their hosts but extended to their servers as well as Chef Tojo, who, after coming out to speak with them to introduce their meal, ended up sitting down and engaging in a twenty-minute discussion with Darcy over some of the more exotic ingredients and preparation practices used in and for their meal.

Even Mira hadn't been able to disguise her surprise at the interaction and appeared somewhat impressed by her.

"Let me get this straight, Darcy," Foster said when their last dishes had been taken away and the coffee was being retrieved. "You hate flying, but you've gone on a deep-sea diving expedition in the Pacific."

"Twice. Then a third time as the lead rescue specialist." Darcy shrugged, lifting one shoulder and beaming as elegantly as Mira folded her perfectly manicured hands. "We're each of us born to our own elements. My parents used to tease they wanted to have me tested to see if I was part fish. If there was water around, I was in it. Becoming a rescue specialist was a perfect fit. Plus, I'm always employable. Someone's always going to get into trouble in the water. Take this guy, for example." She motioned to Riordan. "Now, I know he's got his military training and has probably done a lot of dangerous stuff than I can't even imagine, but diving into the American River in winter? That's a bonehead challenge if ever there was one."

"I think it turned out all right," Riordan observed.

"It was lucky you were there," Mira said, and held up a hand to refuse coffee. "I'd have thought yours was a more male-dominated profession, considering the physical strength it might take to haul someone of Riordan's size out of the water."

"Adrenaline and training makes for a powerful combination. It's amazing what another person can do when someone's life is at stake." She dropped a hand to cover Riordan's. He watched as Mira visibly swallowed and narrowed her eyes, as if forcing herself not to look at their now joined hands. "You're a pilot, right?" Darcy asked. "And you served in your country's military. I imagine you've had similar experiences, exceeding expectations where there were supposed limitations. I also imagine there's very little you wouldn't do to protect that which you deem important."

"Truer words were never spoken, so the saying goes." Mira nodded as a cell phone chimed. "Foster, honestly, I thought we agreed no cell phones tonight."

"My apologies." Foster pulled his cell phone out of his inside jacket pocket. "There's always something with a casino." He frowned, scanned his screen then typed in a response. "Well, it seems as if one of my security consultants has important information about Jay's death."

Riordan felt the tension whip through Darcy and immediately turned his hand over, slid his fingers through hers. "Anything you can share?"

"He's not giving me any details. And he won't, except in person." Foster pocketed his cell again and checked his watch. "He's requested an in-person meeting in a little over an hour. We should go."

"What? Now? Where?" Darcy asked as Foster stood and gestured to their main server.

"I'm afraid this meeting isn't a social outing, Darcy. My contact will only speak to me and to Riordan." He looked at Riordan. "You understand."

"Yes," Riordan said slowly. "I do." It was an order, Riordan realized. And one full of meaning. Some things never changed. Except everything had changed. Before Jay's death, Foster could have asked Riordan for anything, and he wouldn't have refused. Now, he didn't have a choice.

"I'll take that as my hint to retire for the evening." Mira rose and offered a pleasant smile to both Darcy and Riordan. "Take care not to cause too much havoc this evening, Riordan."

"I'll do my best. Darcy?" He held out his hand for her. "Why don't you go upstairs and change for another swim. Try to relax." He hesitated before lying. "I'll be back before you know it."

"Sounds great." But she squeezed his hand so tightly the bones almost snapped.

He brought their linked hands to his mouth and brushed his lips across her knuckles. Riordan made a show of buttoning his jacket while Mira and Foster moved away and walked down the stairs toward the exit.

"I guess this is it," she said.

He hated the quiver in her voice. The barely re-strained fear eking out of almost wild eyes. He loathed knowing he was responsible for it. And that chances were he wouldn't have the opportunity to make up for it. "Darcy—"

"I swear, if you let him kill you, I will follow you into the afterlife and drag you back." She grabbed hold of his jacket and pulled him in, kissed him hard enough that he saw stars. "Stay alive. Please. Stay alive."

"I'll do my best," he repeated and touched her face, committing this moment, this feeling, to memory be-fore he shifted his arm around her and they walked out of the restaurant. Together.

"I wouldn't expect them back anytime soon." Mira's warning glided into Darcy's ear from behind.

"Oh?" Darcy turned, but kept her eyes on Rior-dan's back as he and Foster left the hotel. They wound their way through the crowded lobby teeming with new arrivals.

Her stomach clenched. Her heart skipped a beat. She wanted, more than anything, to be with him, but she knew he'd be too worried about her to focus on what was most important. Finding a way to prove himself innocent of Jay's murder.

Pulling her confidence back into place, she refused to believe this was the last time she'd see him. She'd waited too long to find him. Hadn't had nearly enough time with him. A hole opened up in her heart. A hole that could be filled only with the love and strength of Riordan Malloy.

"Those two can get into many hours' worth of trouble together. We'll be lucky to see them before sunrise." That Mira sounded utterly believable triggered Darcy's first hint of doubt. "Would you like to come up to our apartment for a nightcap before I turn in?"

Even with Riordan heading out into the unknown with Foster Krinard, Darcy couldn't think of a worse way to spend the rest of the evening. "Another time, perhaps. Tomorrow, maybe?"

Mira nodded. "Have a good night, Darcy." Mira offered another of her perfect smiles and headed for the elevators while Darcy, grateful for the solitude and unable to wait, hurried to the lobby restroom. With the dress requiring more finagling than expected, a good chunk of time passed before she exited once more. But instead of going up to her room, she detoured over to the restaurant to give their hostess, Ardelle, a tip. She'd spent a good portion of her high school and college years waitressing, serving and hosting not to know what a crummy job it could be and more often than not, how tips made all the difference in whether she could afford food the following week.

As she reached the door to Change, she spotted Mira walking across the far end of the lobby. She'd exchanged her elegant black suit for a pale pink jogger set, tied her hair up in a simple ponytail and, to Darcy's absolute shock, switched into sneakers.

"I would have bet good money she didn't own a pair of anything without heels. Where is she going?" Darcy inclined her head as Mira disappeared down one of the halls that led away from the front entrance of the hotel.

She could only imagine what Riordan might say should she give in and surrender to her curiosity. Turning in clearly didn't mean the same thing to Mira that it did to Darcy. Gripping her clutch firmly, Darcy debated her next move. Mira could be heading into some torrid meeting with a cabana boy. But that was odd timing, wasn't it? Darcy reached down and slipped off one sandal, then the other, hooked the straps over one finger and followed her.

She stopped at the entrance to the hallway, carefully peeked around the corner as Mira turned out of sight. The shift to carpet from marble muffled the sound of her feet as she hustled down one corridor, then another, eventually arriving at a door that was quickly closing behind Mira.

Darcy darted forward, catching the door before it shut, then ducked behind a shrub wall perimeter around a small, square pool. The door clicked behind her. Darcy cringed, as it sounded so final. She was actually doing this. No time to chastise herself, she realized. Mira's intense voice had her tiptoeing forward. She strained to hear.

"You have a little over an hour to beat them there," Mira said before breaking into a language Darcy didn't understand. A murmur of other voices—all male—responded. "Yes, I know. Meet me on the roof by four. I'll get us to the airport in plenty of time to make the handoff."

"You disappearing the same night your husband gets killed is going to raise a lot of questions, Mira."

Darcy almost jumped but carefully stuck her hand

into the shrub and pushed a branch out of the way. Bixton! But he wasn't alone. It was the sight of one of the two men from her apartment—the duo Bixton shot dead in the parking garage—who turned her blood to ice.

She wanted to shout out the truth. Bixton hadn't killed anyone that day. It had all been staged.

"You let me worry about that," Mira snapped. "Malloy's already the perfect scapegoat. It'll take weeks before the police think about another suspect, if even then. You do your jobs, and all of us will be in the clear in a few hours. Go! Now!"

At the sound of retreating footsteps, Darcy ducked down and made her way around the corner closer to where Mira and Bixton remained. The quiet murmurs, the hushed tones and sudden rapid breathing had her popping up and peeking through the shrubs. "Oh, ick."

Seemed a bad time for a romantic rendezvous, but from what she could see, Bixton and Mrs. K had more than murder on their minds tonight. Well, that was depressing. She'd given Bixton more credit than to get involved with his boss's—his former commander's—wife.

Darcy's hand slipped and the branches rustled. In the eerie silence, the sound echoed loudly.

Darcy dropped to the ground. Her clutch and shoes clacked against the cement. Another door burst open at the far end of the pool, and a pair of teenage boys clattered into the area.

"It's not safe here," Mira told Bixton. Darcy tried

to get another look. "Rooftop. Four a.m. If you aren't there, I'll leave without you. Go. Make sure it's done."

Bixton nodded and followed the same path the other two men had taken.

Mira greeted the teenagers with irritated enthusiasm, reminding them that the pool did close at eleven.

Darcy uncurled and stood as Mira made her way around the pool. Suddenly, Mira hesitated, frowned, then looked right in Darcy's direction. Thank goodness for the shrubbery. Darcy tucked herself back but went too far, knocking into a chair as she caught her footing.

"Is someone there?" Mira demanded, her voice coming closer.

Darcy panicked and finally crawled behind a bamboo tree as Mira rounded on her.

"Who's back here?" Mira spat as Darcy squeezed her eyes shut. Darcy drew her hands up to her chest, sucked in her stomach and prayed she couldn't be seen.

Only then did she realize that she'd left a shoe behind.

Mira came closer and stopped, hands on her hips as she looked from one side to the other.

Darcy couldn't breathe. Her mind raced. How could she explain being here? What could she possibly—

"Oh, would you look at that!"

Darcy's eyes went wide. The voice wasn't Mira's. It belonged to someone who shouldn't have been there. It couldn't be... She rose up on her toes and leaned over just a bit as a familiar face appeared behind Mira.

"Hey, there," announced Eden St. Claire, wearing nothing more than a skimpy neon orange bikini. as she bent down and scooped up Darcy's shoe. "Sorry if I spooked you. It's okay, honey!" she yelled and waved both hands toward an upper story. "I got it! Lost my shoe," she added with a goofy giggle and giant smile. "My husband and I got a little carried away on the balcony. Not entirely sure how it happened. One second, we were—"

Darcy let out a relieved breath as Eden launched into what Darcy hoped was a fictional account of how her friend had spent her evening. Her allies had arrived. A day early but curiously right on time. She shifted from her spot behind the tree, leaned over a bit more.

And nearly screamed when a hand locked over her mouth.

Chapter 12

At least he was being transported to his death in style. Not that he had any intention of dying. But it was good to know where, in theory, he was headed.

Timing, Riordan told himself, was probably the only advantage he had left. Darcy's gun was secured in the back of his waistband, but Foster would have to be a fool not to have expected him to be armed. And Foster Krinard, no matter what else he might be, was no fool.

Riordan had waited until the lights of the Strip were far behind them. Waited until Foster poured himself a drink as they were chauffeured into the inky darkness of the night. Waited until they had put enough distance between themselves and Darcy. Waited until he could control the rage when he spoke and finally ended the silence. "How much?"

Foster lifted his glass, twirled the crystal cylinder as if examining the light play in the angles. "You asking or offering?"

"How much did it take for you to betray your country?" Riordan unbuttoned his jacket, felt the gun press against the base of his spine. Thought of Darcy and all he had to lose. "How much to kill one friend and frame another?"

Foster's smile was slow, and if Riordan wasn't mistaking, tinted with admiration. "I knew that amnesia story was a lie."

Riordan wasn't going to argue with him. Why dim the man's need to gloat and give his own ego one serious stroke. "I should have listened to you all those years ago. That first night in Afghanistan, you told me to always remember every man has a price."

"One of my many lessons you neglected to learn," Foster reminded him. "In answer to your question, not as much as you'd imagine. Yet more than I dreamed possible. I don't suppose you're going to share who the anonymous source is who set you on my trail."

"Was." Riordan was happy to correct him. "You mean who the anonymous source *was*." The final puzzle piece fit perfectly. Not because he'd been given the information from his superiors. They hadn't. They'd wanted him to examine the evidence free and clear without any bias or preconceptions. "There was only one person it could be. Not with the tight circle you kept. Jay was your inside guy, and he was the one who turned you in. He had all the access you needed, seeing as his job required him to check in with multiple weapons storage facilities around the country. But he also had the one thing you're missing. A conscience."

"Always were a holier than thou—"

"I'm surprised," Riordan continued as if Foster hadn't spoken. "You kept that circle so tight. How could you not have seen? Fifteen years. In case you were wondering. That was Jay's price." Riordan clarified. "I offered him fifteen years in exchange for testifying against you." Riordan paused because it was something Darcy would have done—making sure she got her point across. He loved that about her. "And the physical evidence, of course."

"What physical—"

"Records. Bank transactions. Texts. Payments. Shipping manifests. All in one giant file on the cloud." The numbers that had been lodged in his mind. The numbers he'd been thinking about, writing down, focusing on for the past few days. When broken apart, they were the website address and password for Jay's online cloud account. "If you sent it to him, he kept it."

Foster downed his drink in one shot, then poured another. "I regret having to kill you, Riordan. You've been a good friend."

"Better than you've ever been to me," Riordan stated.

"Jay deserved to die. You're right. It shouldn't come as a surprise that he's the one who squealed. Don't know why I ever thought I could trust him after he slept with my wife." Foster smirked. "Just like you."

"Me?" Riordan shook his head at Foster's shocked expression.

"No," he said mockingly. "No, she told me—"

"Oh, right, then it must be true." Riordan planted his feet more firmly on the floor of the limo. "The fact you'd believe I would do that to you proves we were never friends. I might be cold-hearted at times, Foster, but I have lines I don't cross. Sleeping with another man's wife is one of them. Selling weapons to foreign operatives would be another. I could go on, now that I'm thinking about it. How are you going to do it? Kill me, I mean." Riordan kept his voice as casual as he could. "Planning on making it quick or messy? We're headed someplace quiet it seems." He turned slightly, looked out the window. "Cliché. The desert. I'd hoped for a little creativity on your part. Not just shovels and hired muscle." He nodded toward the driver and passenger in the front seat.

"Now I'm offended you'd think me so predictable. Let's keep the surprise a secret just a little while longer." Foster finished the second drink and held out his hand. "Your weapon, please."

Riordan reached back, pulled it free and handed it over.

Foster stashed it in the compartment beneath the armrest. "Would you like to continue to reminisce on the drive or enjoy the silence?"

"Silence," Riordan said as he watched the lights flash by. "I'd definitely prefer the silence."

Darcy dropped her purse and shoe as she grabbed at the hand over her mouth. She kicked out her feet as she was dragged farther into the bushes.

"Shhh. Darcy, quiet. It's me." The low male voice in her ear made her hum with recognition. "Eamon."

She sagged in his hold, letting out what sounded like a sob. In the distance, Eden's drunken dalliance of an explanation was in full swing with a clearly irritated Mira humoring her.

"Okay, good talk. Byyyeeee!" Eden squealed. Then the door clicked shut, and seconds later, Darcy's shoe shot across the patio and bounced off the tree she had been hiding behind. "Okay, she's finally gone. Darcy Ford, get out here and start explaining yourself."

Feeling like a high schooler caught after curfew, Darcy waited until Eamon let go of her, and she stepped into the open. "How did you two know where I was?"

"Hotel-wise? Jason's been tracking your cell since you left Sac," Eamon said. "Pool-wise? I saw you heading into the restaurant a few hours ago when I first arrived. I went up to my room, let a few other people in, then came back down and kept watch. I called Eden for reinforcements when I saw what was happening. Who taught you how to follow someone?"

Darcy gnashed her back teeth. "No one."

"Clearly." Eamon touched her shoulder. "You all right?" he asked as she bent down and retrieved her belongings.

"I've had better nights," Darcy told him. "Way to answer my voicemail." She swung around and socked him in the shoulder. "Your cell phone dead or something?"

"Or something." Even in shadow, exhaustion was evident on his handsome face. He'd always been someone she could look up to in every sense of the word, but tonight he seemed particularly imposing when rescuing her from the casino's bushes. His ginger hair, scruffy beard and overly bright eyes spoke of too much stress and too little sleep. "I was working a child abduction case in Denver. I tend to get…tunnel vision."

"Right. Of course. Sorry." It was only one of the reasons he was so good at his job. He took each and every missing child case as seriously as if the child were his. He was a man with experience. Not only as one of the country's leading specialist in this type of investigation but because he knew what it was like to be on the other side of one. To be left feeling helpless, useless and lost. "Did you find them? The child?"

"Elliot. His name was Elliot Chambers, and yeah." He pushed her forward so he could step out of the shrubs. "We found him. Let's get you inside." He took off his jacket and draped it over her shoulders. "You must be freezing."

"*She* must be freezing?" Eden demanded as Darcy stepped out and picked up her other shoe. "This bathing suit didn't come with an external heater, you know." Yet there she stood, one hand on her hip, barefoot, wearing the skimpiest of outfits but more than a little dignity.

"It did the trick," Eamon teased.

Eden walked forward, took Darcy by the shoulders and looked her in the eye. "You good?"

"I'm good." There was so much to tell her, so much to share, but it all seemed to come down to was "Riordan's innocent."

"Yeah, we know," Eamon said. "He's also been on

special assignment. Jason and Eden have been digging deep since you left for Vegas. We have new information for both of you. Information you're going to be glad to hear. Where is he?"

"Riordan? Gone." The word threatened to lodge in her throat.

"He ditched you?" Eden demanded. "Gone where?"

"He didn't ditch me," Darcy snapped. "He's doing his job, and he didn't want me caught in any potential cross fire."

"Okay, bad choice of words." Eden held up both hands in surrender. "Where has he gone?"

"He's with Foster."

"Major Foster Krinard?" Eamon stated in a tone Darcy really didn't like. "Okay, yeah. We really need to get upstairs and talk."

"Here." Darcy began to shrug out of the jacket, but Eden waved it away.

"It's Vegas." She turned and stalked back to retrieve the clothes she'd ditched for her charade. "I've never fit in more."

Eden jumped into her jeans and shirt in record time before the three of them made their way up to the twentieth floor.

No sooner had Eamon opened the door to his room than Darcy was hauled inside and wrapped in a familiar hug.

"Kyla." Darcy hugged her friend back and tried to push away the guilt she felt for worrying her. "I'm okay. It's okay. What are you doing here?"

"You really think I was going to ignore that call of

yours?" Kyla shoved her back, looked at her for a long moment, then pulled her in again. "You scared the life out of me. How am I supposed to get married without my maid of honor?"

Kyla was comfort personified, from her warm curves to the jasmine-scented lotion on her dark skin. "Your what?"

"You heard me. Wow! What are you wearing?"

"You like?" Darcy held out her arms and twirled. "Not bad, right?"

"It's—"

"Continue the fashion show inside, please," Eden called from out in the hall.

"Sorry." Darcy pushed Kyla ahead of her and Eamon, and Eden followed. "Hey, Jason. Thanks for tracking me."

"Hey, yourself. And you're welcome." Seated at the large desk that he'd turned into NASA central with all the monitors and cords, Jason tapped away on his laptop and barely glanced up. "You fill her in?"

"Not yet," Eamon said.

"FYI, my husband is currently with the Las Vegas Police filling them in," Eden squished through people to reach the coffee pot. "And don't think he's happy about it at all. This is pathetic. We'll burn this pot out in two cups. I'm calling room service. Who wants what?"

"Charge it to my and Riordan's suite," Darcy said and recited the number.

Eden and Kyla stared at her. "You have a suite? Why then, are we still cramped into this bubble of a room?" Eden asked with strained patience.

"Because I don't know who or what might be waiting for me up there." Darcy was done keeping secrets from her friends.

"Oh. Good answer." Eden's eyes went wide before she nodded. "Charging half the menu to your room now." She went directly to the telephone.

"Tell me how you know Riordan's innocent of killing Jay Russo," Darcy pleaded to Eamon.

"We know," Jason assured her. "Kyla, hey, hand me that...yeah, that's it." He plugged in a thumb drive Kyla had grabbed for him from a nearby table. "Thanks, babe. Because we're good."

"Long story short," Eamon started as Darcy sat on the edge of the solitary king-sized bed, "Foster Krinard's been under investigation for the past five years for weapons trafficking. They've traced it back to his time in Afghanistan."

"Riordan served with him there." Darcy swallowed a lump of panic.

"Not for very long and not when this started," Jason cut in. "He was already recruited by Army intelligence by then. When the anonymous call came in about Krinard, Riordan was given the choice to take the case. He did."

"To prove his friend innocent, according to a buddy of mine who works in Special Investigations," Eamon said. "But then Riordan identified the anonymous source as Jay Russo. Going to Las Vegas to connect with Krinard and ask for his help was all part of the setup. He and Jay were supposed to lure Krinard to Travis and lock up the case down there. The plan was to fake Jay's death, send him into witness protection, flip Krinard for his connections and sources, and expose whoever he's working for. Although I can't imagine a former major would enjoy taking orders from anyone. Something went seriously wrong somewhere."

Darcy's mind exploded. *Of course!* The answer, the person responsible for all this was standing right in front of them. "There's only one person I can think of who could have that much control over Foster. Mira. His wife."

"His wife?" Kyla sat beside her. "You're joking."

"What did you learn last year, Kyla?" Darcy asked. "Never underestimate how ruthless women can be."

Jason pointed to his laptop. "I did a preliminary check on her before we locked on to Major Krinard, but we backed up when we saw how the case was lining up against him."

"Probably because she planned it that way. Riordan said she's a player. No qualms about sleeping with anyone to get what she wants, and Jay would have been right there," Darcy said. "She tried to seduce Riordan at one point. He turned her down," she added at Kyla's expression. "She's a walking powder keg and she's seriously connected. Full-on military background. A risk-taker. Knows no limits, and not in a good way."

"Not everyone former military is bad news," Eamon commented. "Can't blame her turn on that."

"No," Jason said. "But they also don't have most of their records redacted unless there's something to hide. Don't ask how I know that." He paused and then continued. "She went from being a combat fighter pilot to heading up transportation security for diplomats and dignitaries. She gave it all up when she married Krinard and moved here to the states."

"Riordan said they met when she flew him, Jay and Foster on some kind of mission," Darcy told them.

"Yes, six years ago, according to Foster's military record. Timing works."

"How did you get his…" Eamon trailed off, stalked forward to look at Jason's screen. "Tell me you didn't just hack the Pentagon. Jason, what the—"

"No. I didn't hack the Pentagon," Jason said softly. "I tapped into the pension portion of the VA. Mostly. Over here is where…yeah, okay. Mira became a fully credentialed commercial pilot shortly before she and Foster married. And this is interesting. She has two planes and at least one short transport helicopter registered in the name of a smaller corporation that's also under her name. Hang on. Let me track her flight ID."

"You really think it's Mira pulling all the strings?" Kyla asked Darcy.

"I might not have if I hadn't seen her talking to a supposed dead man out by the pool a little while ago." She quickly summarized what had happened in the parking garage. "Foster's right-hand guy Bixton made a show of killing the pair of them in front of Riordan. Probably to try to convince him they were still on the same side. But, turns out, Bixton didn't kill them. Add to that Bixton's hot and heavy session with Mira—"

"I'll vouch for that," Eamon confirmed.

"Any chance Mira was sleeping with Jay?" Jason asked. "Because I'm cross-referencing Jay's travel itinerary with hers, and they both coincide with the weapons going missing. All seven, no, make that all eight reported thefts. I've got at least three hotel bookings for both of them on the same dates."

"Careless," Eden murmured. "Not exactly the actions of a criminal mastermind."

"Sure it is," Darcy challenged. "It's a backup plan. What if Jay was named as a suspect? She could easily step forward and give him an alibi. She'd be putting her marriage at risk, and what woman would willingly do that if it wasn't true? If they were together, he couldn't have been responsible for the thefts. If it didn't clear him, it would certainly provide some doubt to give them time to get away."

"That is positively diabolical," Kyla said.

"You need to take Mira into custody," Darcy told Eamon.

"I don't think—"

"I overheard her tell Bixton to meet her at the airport at four this morning. They'd only do that if they were making a run for it. Jason, check the airport records. Does she have a plane on standby?"

It seemed to take forever for Jason to access the system. "She does." He looked up at Jason. "Private jet booked for two passengers. Herself and one more."

"Two passengers." Darcy ticked them off on her fingers. "Mira and Bixton. Not her husband. Not Marcus Tate and his creepy doppelganger. Just the two of them."

"That's cold," Eden said with a laugh. "She's leaving Krinard behind to take the rap?"

"No," Darcy breathed as she realized the truth. "No, that's what she was sending Tate and Bixton to take care of. This isn't just about eliminating Riordan. She's going to tie up every loose end and kill her husband as well."

"If I'd known dinner was going to be my last meal, I wouldn't have gone for the sushi."

Foster, head back and eyes closed, smiled. "You never could stand silence for very long."

"Yeah, well, my backside is asleep, and I'm getting antsy." Riordan shifted in his seat and tried yet again to get his bearings. He hadn't spent hardly any time in Vegas. He had no idea where they were. He only knew they'd been driving for more than an hour. "Dragging a dead man's sentence out like this is inhumane, Major. Hey." He moved up behind the driver and passenger and rapped his knuckles on the dividing glass. It lowered. The passenger turned slowly, an arched and amused smile on his face. "Seriously? You again?" The last time he saw this face he'd plowed his elbow into his nose. "Just how many times do you guys have to die before it sticks?"

He had a different view now. A better one. He scanned the road signs, the direction markers. Las Vegas Springs. Thirty-five miles. The name had come up when he'd googled the area back at the hotel. The new wealthy housing development was in various stages of construction but included its own marina used along the edge of one of Nevada's largest water basins. No one was living there yet. But construction projects and dead bodies were pretty much synonymous with the bad company he was currently keeping.

"I suggest you sit back and relax," Foster suggested.

Riordan shifted to the other side of the limo and reached into his pocket for the painkillers that Foster's doctor had prescribed.

"I'd prefer you not make me shoot you in the car," Foster said. "Hands where I can see them, please."

"Stupid me." He pulled out the bottle and held it up. "Guess these won't do me any good after all."

Foster closed his eyes again, and Riordan slipped the bottle back into his pocket and at the same time fished out a tiny metal chip. At first, he wondered if it had somehow come out of his cell phone, but he'd surrendered that to the driver when he'd gotten into the car. There was an infinitesimal white light blinking off and on like a...

Like a locater chip.

"Darcy Ford, you are the love of my very short life."

The front-seat passenger looked over his shoulder and frowned.

"I said Darcy, not you." Clever, clever woman. She must have slipped the tracker into his pocket around dinner time.

He leaned over, grabbed one of the bottles of water from the holder and, after cracking it open, placed the chip in his mouth and swallowed it.

"The number of felonies you're racking up in one night is mind-boggling," Eamon told Jason as they joined Darcy on the elevator ride up to the fortieth floor. "You can't just hack a key card—"

"Sure I can," Jason said. The elevator dinged and the doors opened. "See? Private floor accessed. You're welcome." He followed them out.

"Stay out of sight," Eamon ordered as he checked the safety on his sidearm, chambered a round and slid the weapon back into its holster. "I don't want to be found guilty by association."

"Way ahead of you." Jason walked in the opposite direction and disappeared behind a door marked Housekeeping.

"Thanks for giving me a chance to stop and change first." Darcy hadn't realized how much of a straight-jacket the dress had felt like until she was back in her yoga pants and tank. She tugged the zipper of her sweatshirt higher as they approached the Krinards' door.

"Surprised she doesn't have a guard out here."

"Another person to keep track of," Eamon said. He caught her arm, waited for her to look at him, before he said, "Knock. Identify yourself. Then move out of the way. Understood?"

"Trust me, my risk-taking days are behind me." She flashed him a smile, knocked on the door and shoved her hands in her pockets.

"Darcy?" Mira's voice echoed through the door.

"Yeah, hey, Mira. I wondered if that drink was still an option." She bounced on her toes. "I'm getting really worried about Riordan. If you're busy—"

The lock snapped.

Darcy took two large steps to the right and as the door opened, Eamon stepped forward, FBI shield and ID held open for her to read. "FBI, Mrs. Krinard. Please step back into your apartment."

"What? No, I will not. Darcy?" Mira turned panicked eyes on her, though she had moved behind Eamon. "Darcy, what's going on? What's happening?"

"Cut the act, Mira. We know you're the brains behind the major's operation." Darcy was too exhausted to put up with any of the woman's phoniness. Mira backed all the way into the suite, almost to the giant windows overlooking the Strip. "Are you armed?"

"Am I what?"

Eamon glared at Darcy over his shoulder.

"What?" Darcy demanded. "Like you weren't wondering?" Or maybe he realized there weren't many places she could hide a weapon in her skintight jumpsuit. "Where did Foster take Riordan?"

"I have no—" Mira's eyes went wide as the elevator dinged once more and multiple uniformed officers arrived with at least three plainclothes law enforcement types, including Detective Cole Delaney from the Sacramento Police Department. Darcy hadn't seen Eden's husband on the job, but she had to admit it was an impressive sight. Like a real-life superhero in action. "What's going on?" Mira demanded.

Eamon stepped forward. "Mira Krinard, you're under arrest for weapons trafficking, murder, attempted murder and, well, just about anything else I can think of. Cole." He gestured for a uniform to read

Mira the rest of her rights and to cuff her. "Everything arranged?"

"Took a bit of arm-twisting, but, yeah, the warrant is being processed as we speak. Darcy." Cole walked over to her, laid his hands on her shoulders in much the way Eden often did. "I was sure once I saw you that I'd strangle you." He pulled her forward and into a hug. "Next time you disappear with a wanted murder suspect, please do it when I'm in town."

She hugged him back and laughed a little. "I think on that front, I'm one and done. Welcome to Vegas."

"Thanks. I'm making a lot of friends out here," Cole said. "You got her?" Cole asked Eamon as the agent put a hand on Mira's arm. "Where are they, Mrs. Krinard?"

"Gone." With that one word, Mira's innocent tearstained face turned sunny and downright evil. "You'll never find them. They're over. Vanished. All gone." Her smile was aimed at Darcy.

"All. You're not just talking about Riordan and Foster, are you? Jason!" Darcy turned and shoved her way through the half dozen uniformed officers, ignoring comments and conversation. "Jason, we need you in here," Darcy called out.

Jason poked his head out of the room next door. He spotted the cops, inclined his head. "I don't think you do."

"In here," Darcy snapped. "Now," she told Cole. "One chance, Mira. Tell me where they are." She needed to know. In case it was too late, she needed to know if there was a hope that...

"Coming through. Hey, folks." Jason burst through

the crowd with a strained smile. "Just your good-guy neighborhood hacker and PI fulfilling his duty." He dropped into a chair at the dining room table, hands hovering over the keyboard. "Tell me when, D."

"Again, where are they, Mira? Where are they going?"

Mira remained silent as she plopped down onto a nearby sofa. "I'll tell you," she said finally, "for full immunity."

"If you're responsible for the death of a military investigator doing his sworn duty, that won't be possible."

"I have friends in high places," Mira said. "Friends who won't want me in prison."

"No," Cole said. "I bet they won't. Still, last chance."

Mira took a deep breath, let it out, sat back and crossed her legs.

"The tracker you gave Eden for me, Jason," Darcy said without breaking her gaze from Mira's. "I activated it a few hours ago. Is it still transmitting?"

Mira blinked.

"Hang on." Jason tapped some keys. "It is. It came online here at the hotel and it's currently pinging…" he broke off, looked up at Darcy and Eamon "…Las Vegas Springs."

"That's all new construction out there," one of the plainclothes detectives said. "Private security only."

"It's almost more than eighty miles away," Jason said.

"Detective Shanahan?" Cole spoke to the other Las Vegas officer. "How fast can you mobilize a response team?"

"Mobilize? Five minutes. But it'll take us at least

a half hour to get out there," he said. "We can maybe get a chopper there—"

"Chopper," Darcy whispered. "That's it. She has a chopper. So does Foster. That's how he brought me and Riordan here." Darcy swung toward Mira. "You were going to chopper out to the airport. I heard you tell Bixton." For the first time, Mira looked worried.

"Darcy—" Eamon began.

"No. We need to get out there. We need to get out there now." She stepped forward, loomed over Mira and glared down at her. "Where are the keys?"

"Would you like me to tell you how many regulations I'm breaking by commandeering a private citizen's aircraft?" Eamon shouted at Darcy as they raced up the staircase to the rooftop landing pad.

"Not really, no. Jason? What's that tracker doing?" she yelled. They'd just reached the five-seater chopper.

"It's still active," Jason informed her. "That doesn't necessarily mean—"

"That Riordan's alive." Darcy nodded. "I know." But he was. She believed that with all her heart. She had to. "Wait, Eden? What are you—"

"Like I'm letting you three have all the adventure." Eden leaped up the final two stairs. "What are we standing around for? Let's go get him!" She plucked the keys out of Darcy's hand and tossed them to Eamon, who shook his head and followed.

"Darcy?" Jason asked. "You sure you want to do this?"

"No." She couldn't feel her legs. Or her stomach. In

fact, the only thing she could feel at the moment was her heart, and that was because it seemed to be hopping all over the place. There wasn't time to process the fear coursing through her. This lightweight air vehicle was nothing compared to the luxury chopper she'd forced herself into before. The white and gold paint job made it look even more delicate; as if a brisk wind would cause it to disintegrate. "No, I'm not sure. But I have to." Climbing into the front seat, she focused on anything inside the cab of the chopper.

"Headphones on!" Eamon shouted and started the engine. He pointed to the various headsets. "Eden? You and Jason keep an eye on that tracker. Darcy, you keep your dinner in your stomach."

Oh, how she wanted to laugh. She dragged on the earphones, copied Eamon when he clicked a switch. Static burst in her ears before his voice came through loud and clear. "This is going to be a fast ride, Darcy. It has to be if we're going to get there in time. I know, Darcy," he added when she looked at him. "I know this is the last place you want to be. Is he worth it?" The blades began to whir and spin.

Worth facing her greatest fear? Worth catapulting herself across the Las Vegas night sky in a glass-and-metal bottle? She adjusted her microphone, reached up and grabbed hold of the bar over the door. With her other hand, she gripped the edge of her seat. Eamon clicked on the exterior lights and spotlight. He pulled back on the throttle. Darcy lost the ability to speak.

"Darcy? You can still stay, if you want." But the chopper was already lifting off the roof. "Is he worth it?"

"He's worth everything," she choked out. "Now fly, Eamon," she told her friend, as she flinched at the building below dropping away. "Fly."

Chapter 13

"Someone supposed to meet us here, or are you going to kill me yourself?"

"Darcy's rubbed off on you," Foster said as he attempted to right himself in his seat. "I don't recall you being this mouthy before."

"I certainly hope she has." Darcy. She was the only good thought in his mind at the moment. She was the only thing he was clinging to even as hope dwindled.

Limos weren't meant for dirt roads. They definitely weren't made for no roads at all. He felt every bump, every pebble, every speck of dirt as they drove onward into the darkness. With the dividing glass still down, he could at least see the path illuminated by the headlights.

He saw mounds of dirt and construction equipment. Trailer offices and fence that had yet to be erected. And in the distance, he saw water. Endless dark, murky water.

"One of Nevada's deepest basins," Foster said as if reading his mind. "We thought it a fitting place for you to disappear. Although the irony won't make it all the way back to Darcy, I'll take great care in telling her how you met your end."

"You won't get anywhere near her again," Riordan told him. "You weren't the only one with a plan, and while I might not have many friends, she has more than you can imagine. Including Special Agent Eamon Quinn of the FBI. She's already called him by now." He smiled at the way Foster's eyes darkened. "Killing me won't make anything go away. It'll only drag you deeper into the depths of what you've made of yourself."

"Sir?" The passenger turned in his seat. "We've received a message from Bixton. He's suggesting we drive—"

A shot rang out. Riordan watched as the passenger's head bounced forward before he slumped. The windshield spider-webbed as the driver slammed his foot on the gas.

"What's happening?" Foster demanded as the car lurched forward and took off. "Who's firing at us?" Another shot, this one slamming through the back window and catching Foster in the shoulder.

Riordan dropped to the floor of the limo, but the second he did, another shot must have taken out the driver. The car veered recklessly but didn't slow down. Instead, the driver's foot hit the gas even harder. The engine roared. The limo caught something solid beneath its right front tire, and the vehicle launched into the air. For an instant, Riordan felt weightless as he floated, the car spinning around him as it flipped once, twice, a third time, tumbling them forward and straight into the water. He bounced, tried to latch onto something, but he couldn't hold on.

The car halted, almost hovering it seemed, for a brief silent, peaceful moment.

Water streamed in through the bullet holes and busted windshield.

"Riordan!" Foster's shout was muffled by the sound of racing water.

Riordan fought his way back through the water as the car began to sink. In seconds, the level was up to his chest. In another two, his chin. In the distance, he heard an odd mechanical rhythmic sound he assumed was his heart beating its last. He grabbed for the door handle, but he knew from previous training he couldn't open it until the pressure equalized inside the vehicle.

Foster cried out, his head disappearing beneath the surface as Riordan turned his attention to the passenger window. He clawed his hands into the roof of the limo, tried to lift himself up and kick his feet against the already broken glass. Once. Twice.

He gasped in air. The water was nearly to his nose. They were still sinking. The water was still coming in.

Riordan looked up and out the window, saw a light streaming down, but it was too late.

He took a huge breath as the water closed over his head.

He was out of time.

* * *

"No!" Darcy's scream pierced her own ears as she clung to the handle above her door and watched the limo take flight and soar, spinning straight into the murky depths of the basin. "No, no, no, no."

"Darcy!" Eden grabbed at her from the back seat as she scrambled to unhook her belt. "Darcy, there's nothing you can do!"

But she refused to believe. She hadn't spent the last ten minutes in this monstrosity of a creation to give up now. She would not be too late! She was not going to give up.

"Shine the light. Shine the light there!" She ordered. "Eamon, turn this bird around and shine it…there. Jason? Is he in there?"

"Uncertain," Jason said. "But the transmission's fading. Best guess?"

"That's all we have!"

"Yes," Jason said softly. "He's in there."

Not for long he wasn't. "Take us down!"

"What? Darcy, you can't be—"

"Eamon?" She looked at her friend and hoped, prayed, he'd understand. "Take us down."

"The wind is picking up, Darcy. Not sure how long I can hold this thing steady." He was already struggling to keep the throttle in check.

"Do as well as you can. And turn on the rest of the lights." In the far distance, she saw spinning red and blue lights headed their way. But they were too far off. "Eden, call for the emergency vehicles. Tell them we have…" she wasn't going to say it. "Tell them we have water rescue on-site and to prepare for potential drowning victims." She ripped off her headphones, tossed them to the floor and shoved open her door.

"Darcy!" Eamon's voice held all the fear she couldn't let herself feel.

She unzipped her sweatshirt, discarded it and vaulted from the helicopter.

"Wait!" Eden screamed and jabbed something at her. "Here! Waterproof flashlight. You take longer than ten minutes in that water, and I'm coming in after you. You hear me?"

Darcy nodded and wrapped the flashlight cord around her wrist. She flicked it on, got a solid grasp on it and looked back one more time at Eamon. "Keep the lights on us as long as you can."

Turning off her mind, her fear, her terror, she took one giant breath, looked down into the pitch-black water and jumped.

Drowning, Riordan thought as his lungs began to burn, had never been on the top of his list of ways to die. He wasn't afraid of dying. Serving in a war, where uncertainty was the only constant one could count on, removed that from the equation. He wasn't ready, though. Not now. Not when there was something—someone—to live for.

The light he thought he'd seen blinked off, then on again. Grew brighter as he pushed himself down toward the shattered corner of the window.

Major Foster Krinard's body floated beside him, bobbing against the roof of the limo. That wasn't going to be him. Not him, Riordan told himself as he called on his training and tried to calm his racing pulse. The air in his lungs thinned.

He drew his elbow back, turned away from the window and hit it hard against the glass. Again. Again.

More cracks. He could feel the car settling into the bottom of the basin, but his energy was all but gone. The light that streamed from above arced away, circled back.

His arms felt heavy. He had one good punch left in him. Only one. He had to make it count. He had to make every effort to get back to Darcy.

Cloudy light shone through the tinted windows. Shadow light, he told himself. His mind was playing tricks on him as it became starved for oxygen. He opened his mouth, and a giant bubble of air escaped. He couldn't...

He banged a fist before feeling the darkness close in.

The window shattered, exploding in on him, and he jerked, his eyes opening against the beam of light streaming in. Beyond it, he saw a swirling mass of red and gold caught in the shadows of the water.

Darcy!

No. That was impossible. His mind was dying. Playing tricks on him.

A hand reached into the car, flailed before grabbing hold of his arm and yanking him forward. He knocked his head against the door before finding his way free. He wanted to help. Wanted to swim, to push himself up to the surface, but there was nothing left to his body except weight.

The light arced down as an arm locked around his chest. Behind him, he felt a body, a familiar body, pressing against him. He was slowly, oh so slowly, being dragged up through the water.

Breaking the surface, he felt the air on his face first. Heard the concussive whopping in the air second.

"Breathe!" Darcy's voice roared in his ear as she continued to hold on to him with one arm and swim with the other. "You'd better start breathing, Riordan Malloy. I climbed into a helicopter just to save your butt, so you start breathing! Right…" she began to pant "…now!"

He choked, whether on her determination or his own desperation. But once he started, he couldn't stop. Coughing, spewing, he sucked in air and nearly puked it out when his back hit solid ground. She dropped her hold, stood over him, knee deep in the water and waved her arms in the air beneath the flashing spotlight of the chopper overhead. "Here!" She yelled. "Over here!"

"They're up there?" Riordan could barely hear his own voice, but she heard him. And she dropped down beside him to grab hold of his shoulders and keep his face and head out of the water. "I think they see you. Who…" Even as he began the question, he knew. "Eamon?"

"Among others," Darcy confirmed. She bent down and pressed her mouth to his, half breathing life into him as she kissed him. "That's twice I've had to pull you out of the water."

He lifted a hand and touched her hair. "My mermaid. How did you—" He tried to sit up, did with her help, but there were no cars around. "Did you... Darcy," he couldn't believe what he was thinking. "Did you jump out of that helicopter? For me?"

"For you? No. Of course not." She half laughed, but there was no mistaking the love shining in her eyes in the dim edges of the spotlight. "I did it for me."

He reached up, caught her face in one hand and smiled at her. "That's my girl."

The chopper circled them once. He could see the people inside as it veered off and, as a line of police cars and spinning lights approached, it landed in the near distance. Moments later, three people made their way over.

"He's okay!" Darcy yelled. "He needs to go to the ER, but he's okay."

"I don't need the ER." He tightened his arm around her waist, felt his legs wobble, but he stood. "Special Agent Eamon Quinn, I assume?" He nodded. "I'm Special Investigator Riordan Malloy. Good to meet you."

"Likewise." Eamon ducked under his other arm, and together, they walked him a safe distance from the basin. "I expect there'll be a commendation or two for you when this all shakes out. Major Krinard?"

"Dead. Shot first. Driver and passenger, too."

"Bixton," Darcy said, and they lowered Riordan to the ground. "And Marcus Tate."

"Shots came from over there." Riordan gestured to the sand dunes. "Might want to steer some cops over that way."

"We've already got an all-points bulletin out for both of them."

"It was Mira," Darcy explained at his confused look. "It was all her."

Riordan couldn't believe it. But, yeah, he actually could. "Of course it was. Hey, Eden. Jason." He blinked into the darkness. "Good to see you again." He swallowed hard, held up a hand. "Darcy, don't freak out, okay?"

"Why?" She grabbed for him. "Riordan? What's wrong?"

"I'm just going to…" His head spun like a whirling dervish. "I'll see you later."

The darkness swallowed him whole.

"Your country is grateful for your service, Captain Malloy."

"Sir." From his hospital bed, which he'd been occupying for the better part of a week, Riordan saluted General Matthew Powers with barely a wince of pain. Riordan's stay had been a precaution for the most part. Between the dual head injuries and almost drowning, the ER doctors wanted him watched and monitored. He had little doubt Darcy had some say in that decision, but he wasn't going to argue with her. She'd earned some peace of mind where his health and well-being were concerned. "I appreciate you coming here to speak with me in person."

"It seems the least I could do, considering the job you did." With his hat tucked under one arm, the general stood at the foot of Riordan's bed. "Thanks to you, we've closed down at least four different illegal weapons distribution pipelines, and now that Mira Krinard is talking, we should be able to close the case completely. We'll be rebuilding our security structure at all military bases both here and abroad."

"What kind of deal did she get?"

"Not the one she wanted." General Powers walked over to the bed and stood next to him. "She was right about one thing. There are a lot of people out there who don't want her in prison. They want her dead. With the new identity she's requested, she'll be serving what's left of a life sentence. Case closed thanks to you and the evidence you retrieved from Jay Russo's dog."

From his self-appointed spot on the floor, Watson, all sixty-two pounds of him, shot to his feet and sat at attention. Riordan reached out and rested his hand on the dog's head. "I'm glad Darcy thought to have someone retrieve him from animal control." He sank his hand into the dog's fur. "When I told her about how important he was to Jay, she thought that giving him a new home would be both redemptive but also a clue as to where Jay had hidden the evidence against the Krinards." Only Darcy would have thought to check Watson's microchip.

"Ms. Ford does seem to have a talent for thinking things through to their rightful conclusion," General Powers agreed. "She also only gave me a few minutes to speak with you, so I'll get to the point."

"Sorry about that, sir." He sat up straighter in bed. "She's gotten a bit overprotective."

"I can't imagine why," General Powers said with a low chuckle. "Word is you're considering retirement."

"Not considering," Riordan said. "I've decided. I've given the Army twenty years." He looked to the open door, where, out in the hall, Darcy, along with a good number of her friends, stood by the nurse's station. Watching her laughing and joking, he couldn't imagine a more beautiful sight. "I'm ready for a different kind of life."

"I understand. I suggest you hold off on that paperwork for a few weeks so there's time for your promotion to come through… Major." General Powers faced him once more.

"Major?" Riordan frowned. "Sir, that's not necessary."

"Oh, I think it is. The secretary of the Army certainly does, and I've learned not to disagree with my superiors."

"Yes, sir."

"Until those orders come through, you've got plenty of vacation and sick leave stored up. Consider that training for civilian life. Riordan…" Major Powers gave him a curt nod "…you ever need anything—and I mean anything—you call me. You've earned whatever life you decide to have. We appreciate everything you've done."

Watson tilted his head and watched the general leave. Watson whimpered and looked back to Riordan, who smiled and patted the bed. "Okay. Settle in before she can tell you no."

Watson was up and on the bed in a flash just as Darcy walked into the room.

"I can see I have my hands full with the both of you." She sighed, but instead of telling Watson to jump down, she circled around and sat next to him. "Everything okay?"

"Everything is great. I got a promotion."

"Well, I should hope so." She caught his hand. "Eamon sends his regrets. He had to get back to work. Another case, this time in South Carolina. He'll be back in Sacramento soon, though."

"Don't know how he keeps at it." Riordan couldn't fathom the emotional toll working missing and exploited children cases took. "I assume Eden and the rest are ready to head to the airport. You get our things from the hotel? Ready for the drive back tomorrow?"

"Oh, yeah. About that." She stroked a thumb against his wrist. "I had a visit from the operations manager at the Medallion last night."

"Don't tell me. They're billing us for our stay."

"No, actually. The opposite. Turns out they're exceedingly grateful to us for helping to expose Foster's criminal activities. They've given us exclusive guest status at any of their hotels around the world and extended our stay here for as long as we'd like. Damage control," she added with a quick smile.

"I thought you were anxious to get home."

"I was. I am. But I think I'd like to be here a few more days. There's something I want to do before we leave."

"Name it."

"Okay." She took a deep breath and met his eyes. "Okay, you've opened the door, so I'm just going to walk through it, and if you say okay, great. And even if you don't, it'll be fine, so I don't want you to—"

"Darcy."

"Marry me. I know!" She waved her other hand in

the air. "It's crazy, right? We've known each other for like, a week, but all I kept thinking when I was in that helicopter, other than the obvious, was that you were it for me. There is no one else. I love you, Riordan. And I know, I know you probably aren't in a place where you can say it back, and I totally—"

He tugged her close and kissed her. Kissed her into silence and surrender.

"No more doubts, Darcy Ford," he murmured against her lips and touched her cheek. "Not about me loving you. How can I not?" He pressed his forehead against hers. "I belong to you. I love you, my redheaded mermaid. I have from the second you pulled me out of the river."

"So…that's a yes?" Darcy's eyes lit up like the Las Vegas Strip. Watson stuck his nose under their linked hands and whined. "From both of you?"

"It's a yes. Just one question," Riordan added when she nearly jumped off the bed. "What should I do about my clown costume collection?"

She yanked a pillow from behind him and smacked him with it, her laughter lightening his full heart. "Just for that, you're stuck with me." Darcy leaned over and kissed him again. "Forever."

* * * * *

For more exciting adventure romances
from acclaimed author Anna J. Stewart,
visit www.Harlequin.com today for stories
in the Honor Bound miniseries!

#2251 COLTON'S MONTANA HIDEAWAY
The Coltons of New York • by Justine Davis

FBI tech expert Ashlynn Colton's investigation into one serial killer has made her the target of another one. Only the suspect's brother—handsome Montana cowboy Kyle Slater—will help. But as the duo grows closer, their deadly investigation isn't the only thing heating up...

#2252 LAST CHANCE INVESTIGATION
Sierra's Web • by Tara Taylor Quinn

Decorated detective Levi Greggs just closed a high-profile murder case and took a bullet in the process. But when his ex-fiancée, psychiatrist Kelly Chase, returns to town with another mystery, saying no isn't an option. Searching the wilderness for a missing child reignites long-buried desire...and more danger than they bargained for.

#2253 HER SECRET PROTECTOR
SOS Agency • by Bonnie Vanak

Marine biologist Peyton Bradley will do anything to regain her memory and finish her important work. Even trust former navy SEAL Gray Wallace, her ex-bodyguard. Gray vows to protect Peyton, even as he falls for the vulnerable beauty. But will the final showdown be with Peyton's stalker, her family, her missing memory or Gray's shadowy past?

#2254 BODYGUARD MOST WANTED
Price Security • by Katherine Garbera

When his look-alike bodyguard is murdered, CEO Nicholas DeVere knows he'll be next. Enter security expert Luna Urban. She's not Nick's doppelgänger, but she's determined to solve the crime and keep the sexy billionaire safe. If only they can keep their arrangement all business...

YOU CAN FIND MORE INFORMATION ON UPCOMING HARLEQUIN TITLES, FREE EXCERPTS AND MORE AT HARLEQUIN.COM.

HRSCNM0923

Get 3 FREE REWARDS!

We'll send you 2 FREE Books plus a FREE Mystery Gift.

FREE Value Over **$20**

Both the **Harlequin Intrigue®** and **Harlequin® Romantic Suspense** series feature compelling novels filled with heart-racing action-packed romance that will keep you on the edge of your seat.

YES! Please send me 2 FREE novels from the Harlequin Intrigue or Harlequin Romantic Suspense series and my FREE gift (gift is worth about $10 retail). After receiving them, if I don't wish to receive any more books, I can return the shipping statement marked "cancel." If I don't cancel, I will receive 6 brand-new Harlequin Intrigue Larger-Print books every month and be billed just $6.49 each in the U.S. or $6.99 each in Canada, a savings of at least 13% off the cover price, or 4 brand-new Harlequin Romantic Suspense books every month and be billed just $5.49 each in the U.S. or $6.24 each in Canada, a savings of at least 12% off the cover price. It's quite a bargain! Shipping and handling is just 50¢ per book in the U.S. and $1.25 per book in Canada.* I understand that accepting the 2 free books and gift places me under no obligation to buy anything. I can always return a shipment and cancel at any time by calling the number below. The free books and gift are mine to keep no matter what I decide.

Choose one: ☐ **Harlequin Intrigue Larger-Print** (199/399 BPA GRMX)   ☐ **Harlequin Romantic Suspense** (240/340 BPA GRMX)   ☐ **Or Try Both!** (199/399 & 240/340 BPA GRQD)

Name (please print)

Address   Apt. #

City   State/Province   Zip/Postal Code

Email: Please check this box ☐ if you would like to receive newsletters and promotional emails from Harlequin Enterprises ULC and its affiliates. You can unsubscribe anytime.

Mail to the Harlequin Reader Service:
IN U.S.A.: P.O. Box 1341, Buffalo, NY 14240-8531
IN CANADA: P.O. Box 603, Fort Erie, Ontario L2A 5X3

Want to try 2 free books from another series? Call 1-800-873-8635 or visit www.ReaderService.com.

*Terms and prices subject to change without notice. Prices do not include sales taxes, which will be charged (if applicable) based on your state or country of residence. Canadian residents will be charged applicable taxes. Offer not valid in Quebec. This offer is limited to one order per household. Books received may not be as shown. Not valid for current subscribers to the Harlequin Intrigue or Harlequin Romantic Suspense series. All orders subject to approval. Credit or debit balances in a customer's account(s) may be offset by any other outstanding balance owed by or to the customer. Please allow 4 to 6 weeks for delivery. Offer available while quantities last.

Your Privacy—Your information is being collected by Harlequin Enterprises ULC, operating as Harlequin Reader Service. For a complete summary of the information we collect, how we use this information and to whom it is disclosed, please visit our privacy notice located at corporate.harlequin.com/privacy-notice. From time to time we may also exchange your personal information with reputable third parties. If you wish to opt out of this sharing of your personal information, please visit readerservice.com/consumerchoice or call 1-800-873-8635. **Notice to California Residents**—Under California law, you have specific rights to control and access your data. For more information on these rights and how to exercise them, visit corporate.harlequin.com/california-privacy.

HIHRS23

HARLEQUIN
PLUS

Try the best multimedia
subscription service for romance
readers like you!

Read, Watch and Play.

Experience the easiest way to get
the romance content you crave.

Start your **FREE TRIAL** at
<u>www.harlequinplus.com/freetrial</u>.